BEFORE EVERYTHING

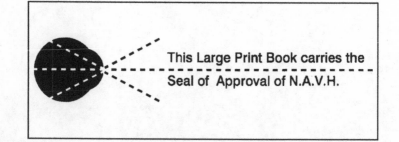

BEFORE EVERYTHING

VICTORIA REDEL

THORNDIKE PRESS
A part of Gale, a Cengage Company

Farmington Hills, Mich • San Francisco • New York • Waterville, Maine
Meriden, Conn • Mason, Ohio • Chicago

GALE
A Cengage Company

LIBRARY OF CONGRESS CATALOGING-IN-PUBLICATION DATA

Names: Redel, Victoria, author.
Title: Before everything / by Victoria Redel.
Description: Waterville, Maine : Thorndike Press, a part of Gale, a Cengage Company, 2017. | Series: Thorndike Press large print core
Identifiers: LCCN 2017028672| ISBN 9781432841447 (hardcover) | ISBN 1432841440 (hardcover)
Subjects: LCSH: Large type books. | BISAC: FICTION / Contemporary Women. | FICTION / Family Life. | FICTION / Literary.
Classification: LCC PS3568.E3443 B44 2017b | DDC 813/.54—dc23
LC record available at https://lccn.loc.gov/2017028672

Published in 2017 by arrangement with Viking, an imprint of Penguin Publishing Group, a division of Penguin Random House LLC

Printed in Mexico
1 2 3 4 5 6 7 21 20 19 18 17

ACKNOWLEDGMENTS

For Nancy and the girls

Praise to them, how they loved it, when
they could.

— Adrienne Rich

■ ■ ■ ■

LATE MARCH 2013

■ ■ ■ ■

1

Simply Said

On a late March day when you could taste spring's muddy tang, Anna was given results from the new scans. Anna, who had done it well — actually managed a couple get-well miracles — simply said, "No more."

Starfish

Anna didn't remember having come out to the living room, but here she was on the couch, and they are here — Helen, Ming, Caroline, Molly — her oldest friends. When had they arrived? Who'd told them? She'd let Helen's daily calls go to voice mail. But no, of course, she'd picked up thinking it was one of her kids. Instead it was Ming. She'd told Ming the whole shebang — from new recurrence to hospice. Didn't give any room for questions. "You'll tell the others for me."

"Don't." She'd shuddered when Ming

said, "I'm coming. Of course, all of us are coming."

Now they were here, her gang since childhood, and it felt good to have them gathered in her vaulted living room. Caroline, telling a story about her older sister, Elise, who always has all the trouble. Caroline, describing another of Elise's episodes, but in her usual way, funny, a bit resigned but not sarcastic, never ironic with Caroline, instead always reserved hilarity.

How had they done all this getting here? Anna knew they'd driven — Great Barrington, Manhattan, Arlington, Larchmont — but all that moving seemed impossible. Leaving the house felt impossible. And then the skein of highways, tolls, turnoffs for gas, fishing out wallets from pocketbooks gaped open on the passenger seat. More than even the effort, it seemed the world with its unstoppable movement was an undoable tangle or an extinct language she'd once understood.

"Speak louder," Ming called. Ming was in the kitchen making soup. "I don't want to miss anything."

Anna followed the story. Or mostly she did. She laughed along. Helen laughing her big, optimistic whoop. Molly's eyes tearing up the way they do and her silent, gulpy

14

laugh. And there was Caroline's hilarious way of gesticulating with flexible eyebrows as much as with hands that swooped and sliced the air.

They have done so much laughing, these five, they'd managed to laugh their way through even the unlaughable.

Funny, how even now it was the girl, not the woman, Anna saw, hearing Ming's three-trilled laugh in the kitchen — seeing Ming's compact teenage body, not the rounder, squat shape of middle age. And she still pictured Ming's hair as a gleaming, waist-length, dark curtain, not the professional salt-and-pepper layers trimmed every six weeks.

"Is this too much, Anna?" Helen asked, massaging her feet and legs.

She looked down the length of her body to Helen's thick fingers on her calf. Not a muscle left on her athletic legs. She'd always teased that Helen had the hands of a dockworker, not a painter. Georgia O'Keeffe's elegantly tapered fingers, those were a painter's hands. Still, Helen's hands felt good. It felt good to be touched. She wouldn't have guessed that she'd want to be touched but she did, and when Helen slowed, she stretched the other leg into Helen's lap, nudging it under Helen's hands.

I'm going to take care of you, Helen mouthed. Helen, who needed always to make things better. Helen, who'd promised more than forty years ago to be Anna's best friend and had never faltered. She stretched to touch Helen's hand.

Molly tensed forward, rested her elbows on her knees. This was how Molly listened. Muscularly. Her whole body attentive. And, just as Anna knew she would, Molly cocked her head and lifted her dimpled chin toward Caroline's voice.

Anna hadn't been out here in the living room for days. There was almost too much to look at. Every wall covered with art she'd bought or been given. There, on the table, in a blue glass bowl, hundreds of tiny starfish collected at Point Reyes. There, mounted on the wall, the scrap-metal sculpture she'd bought in Provincetown. Clustered on a shelf, mason jars of cardinal feathers. Hours she'd spent selecting and arranging. All the tableaux of pretty — how had she ever done all that? All that going and doing. All that caring for beauty.

Anna closed her eyes. Listened. So entirely familiar the dips and lilts of her friends' voices. Even Caroline's pauses to find a more exact word were familiar. She couldn't explain it, the ease she felt. She wouldn't

16

have imagined this. Part of the easiness was that she no longer had to try.

The Old Friends
End of sixth grade, they made it their official name. It was a joke one afternoon, but they liked the way it sounded. Permanent. *The Old Friends.* A declaration that anyone who came into their lives, maybe next year in seventh grade or later in high school, anyone else might be new and exciting, even counted as a friend for life, but not part of *The Old Friends.* Not like they're running to stencil T-shirts or roll out an official announcement and cheer. But they love the way it sounds. Like a rock band. Or a mystery series. This way, the five girls agree, it's just a fact. And ours forever.

Secret
Days earlier the eldest boy was alone in the room with her.

"Momma." He held her hand.

She nodded her head to show she was awake.

"Mom, I have a secret to tell you."

She smiled. He was her first child. Now a grown man. Oh, those years she'd spent unnecessarily worrying about Julian. Shy boy, the one to play at the corner of the school

17

yard where the pavement yielded to weedy scrub, a boy poking sticks into dirt, serious and happy and unworried about kids whizzing past him. "Got you!" they screamed, tagging a shoulder, not his. At pickup she'd ached watching him happy alone. She'd wanted him to be in the center of the playing field calling teams, the one named captain.

Now here he was, a gentle man, still quiet, with a boy's stuttery laugh, still happiest in the woods foraging for black morels and ramps.

"Mom," Julian said again, "I have a secret."

She nodded.

"Can you open your eyes?"

She'd do anything for him. Her eyes were so heavy, nickel-lidded, heavier even than the given doses, heavy with some thickness she could feel weighted in her bones, in her blood.

She opened her eyes.

Beautiful. It was his father's face he wore, that halo of curly dark hair. The light was behind him. She saw the lace of the curtains and, through the curtains, the trees of the yard. Her lace, her window with her crystal hanging on filament and the yard where her three children had played. So slightly hers, any of it, anymore.

"Yes, baby."

He said, "We're having a baby."

There was a rush. Happiness left for the having. Even in these last days, she'd felt happiness, momentary, sometimes sharp almost like pain. Here, though, was the apex.

"We don't want anyone to know. Not yet. But we want you to know."

The baby of her first baby. She had loved the shape of him unborn inside of her so much that when she came to full term, she hoped for a long birth, wanting, she said, for each moment to be exceptional, hers to savor, and then the joke for years with friends was that after hours into her labor, curled into some jagged harbor of agony, she had begged for drugs. But at the end there was this child, perfect lips, hands, feet, and she was forever changed.

She sat up in the bed and kissed her son. "You'll be a wonderful father," she whispered. She kept a hand at his shoulder and looked at him, working to make her face clear and direct. She wanted him to have this. His mother beholding the father he was becoming.

There was wind through the window, spring air, a last, best secret.

She smiled. "I won't tell a soul."

Forever

"I'd be lying if I didn't say you've looked better." Helen thumbed into Anna's arch. "But we'll find our way through this one, too." She pressed her paint-stained fingers up the long, ropy thread of Anna's shin. No muscle left to squeeze. Her stubby hands pawed wide, overlapping Anna's leg.

"There's only one way through this time, Heli," Anna said.

"That's not true," Helen said quickly. "But we have all day to figure this out." Anna had been down to bone before, slow walks around the squared antiseptic hallways of hospital units, Anna pitched on a walker saying, "Really, Helen, this is some serious shit." Helen always had a comeback. "Toots, you should have seen your sorry ass a month ago." The Truth — capital T — they'd promised it to each other as children. Easy in the best-friend flush at seven or the high romance of twelve. A challenge as they got older and truth felt more wobbly, when encouragement was sometimes more essential. Helen thought of the buzz and whir of ICUs, mornings she'd pleat open the curtain, stand by Anna, intubated, sleeping. "Hey, beautiful," Helen would say. "You're

20

missing a lot of cool stuff. So get better already."

But forget truth or encouragement, vigilance mattered. And Helen had messed up. Big-time. For years they'd called each other every day. Even phone messages deemed contact. These last couple years, with Helen's painting shows in Dubai, Hong Kong, Miami, Paris — she'd called from crazy time zones.

"I'm talking to you from tomorrow," Helen marveled when she was in Sydney.

"So you're still the art world's it girl!" Anna allowed Helen no modesty.

When Helen asked what was new, Anna breathed into the phone, "I'm not inducted into the Rock and Roll Hall of Fame yet, if that's what you're wondering."

"Well, hurry up, sweetheart. We're not going to live forever." And they laughed to ward off disaster.

But this time Helen had slacked off and the situation was going to be hard to un-mess. She'd called every day, but traveling made it rough to keep up, and it had been two weeks before she realized Anna wasn't returning any messages. "Hey, love ain't a one-way street." Helen crooned a new message country style while looking out a hotel window in Prague.

Then, a week ago, at a dinner in Rome, she picked up and heard Ming's dredged voice. "You've got to come now, Helen."

Dog

Zeus growled. Zeus, the teacup poodle, tangle-haired, bur-stuck — like a tossed-off slipper on the floor below Anna — Zeus out of nowhere, as Helen sat on the blue love seat with Anna, Zeus baring his tiny teeth.

Done

1. Done with IVs. Not ever even one more IV.
2. Done having another round of those thank-God-I'm-alive days — crust-breaking snowshoe walks up the backyard trail to the cliff view or weekend nights swaying close to the microphone, pulsing in rhythms while her band swung up into the last verse of "The Harder They Come" — before a shortness in her chest begins again.
3. Done secretly managing, till she's stopping on the walk from the car to the front door to catch her breath, thinking, This is a just a cold. Everyone in the Valley has this

late-winter cold — until the cold spins into pneumonia and Reuben finds her bundled under blankets and the doctor's ordering a full PET scan.

4. Done with scans.
5. Done asking Bobby, the lanky, pony-tailed technician, what he sees and him saying, "I'm a technician, Anna. You know I don't read these," and Anna saying, "Cut the shit, Bobby. We've been at this for too many years, so please just tell me what you see."
6. Done with remission.
7. Done with recurrence.
8. Done with the medical team encouraging a new protocol.
9. Done with the truckloads of medicine.
10. Done with that fourth remission, hauling herself back to full gear so that, yes, hello world! here she was — back in the glorious thick of life, everything a peak experience — again back at school running the math center, again out meeting up with friends, again out gigging on Saturday night with her cover band, again her grown kids calling breathy

with good possibilities — a job, a romance, all the regular stuff they called to tell Anna when they weren't starting with a hesitant "How are you feeling today, Mom?"

All the Hungers

"I can eat a little." Anna was, surprisingly, a little hungry. She immediately regretted that she'd said it. Too much eagerness on her friends' faces. All that commotion to bring her more food. Impossibly active. And hopeful. Helen propped the beige velvet pillows behind Anna so that she was upright.

"Too much," she said when Ming put the bowl on the cobbler's table. Molly followed, placing a wood board with bread and salmon next to the soup. They looked all too ready to feed her like a child.

"Just eat what you want," Ming bubbled triumphant, when Anna sipped from the spoon.

It made Ming so happy to watch her spoon the cream of spinach and mushroom soup into her mouth. Her full cheeks blushing in anticipation. Anna forced the spoon to her lips again. So that, too — Anna wasn't entirely beyond wanting to make someone happy. Especially Ming. Anna knew she couldn't have managed what

24

Ming had managed — her daughter Lily's seizures. The everyday terror of the grand mal, ambulances, and deadening medications. Then that cutting-edge brain operation. A success, but still a lifetime of children's taunts and all the constant special accommodations — no, Anna thought, it would have broken her to have a child so compromised.

The creamy, warm spread of soup tasted good. There was this, too. Food had been a pleasure. Another kind of beauty. She'd never understood the desire for eating in company. Food was pleasure for the mouth. Talking was also pleasure. But together, less.

The conversation veered newsy. That was a screen. They were always watching, measuring how much she ate.

She cut a small piece of salmon and let it melt against her palate.

Molly worried to the others about a baggie of weed she'd found in Tessa's desk drawer. How much was her daughter smoking? She was so uncommunicative most days. There have been terrible fights. Molly raked her fingers through her cropped hair. "She's not a girl you'd at all recognize."

Anna thought it would help to remind Molly how when they were in eleventh grade they'd snuck out every afternoon that spring to smoke pot behind the woods near school. There'd been no shortage of baggies and film canisters of pot. There'd been no shortage of battles with parents.

But it took such effort to bring the spoon to her mouth, to swallow the soup.

It was enough to think, Molly, it will be fine.

Molly and Serena. Their two children. Once, all of that had been radical — a woman, a mixed-race couple, children — these had been the battles Molly had fought. Eighteen years later they'd all danced at the wedding. Molly had a house in the Boston suburbs just miles from where they'd all grown up. A thriving therapy practice. Now Molly's golden mane of hair was silver, cut in her mother's short, blunt cut. Serena was talking about retiring from her surgery team.

We were children. Give it enough time, Anna thought, and The Old Friends actually become old.

Then she remembered what her son had told her. His beautiful secret. The beginning of his fatherhood. Was it just yesterday he'd come to her room to tell her the secret? These were her dear friends. She could boast to them. They had been children together, and then they were mothers together. They would know what this meant to her. But she would not tell. Not even Helen, her ultimate secret sharer. She could barely look at Helen. Still, she would say nothing. She had nothing left to give her son except her word.

When

Ming first, then Anna the same year, then Caroline, then Helen, and last, Molly, with two daughters from the sperm bank's same anonymous donor. Between them, twelve. It shouldn't, but it still surprised them. "Mom," one of the kids called out, and any of them might, without stopping what she was doing, call back, "Yes."

And Other Good News

She'll have long hair at the end. Her own. There had been that first wig, hand-tied, expensive, from a store on Newbury Street in Boston. But the stiff bangs made Anna look like a young Orthodox wife. The next time she'd gone synthetic and cheap with multiple wigs, brunette and pink, a shag, a bob. One, her homage to Stevie Nicks. The third time — come on, who was she kidding? — a floppy cotton hat some days, on others a knitted beanie.

Lather

Once they'd gotten Anna out of the leggings and T-shirt she'd been wearing God knows how long, Molly shot Helen a this-feels-precarious look as they maneuvered Anna through the bathroom door. The towel they'd wrapped around her slipped undone. Why hadn't they left this to the nurse? Molly stood inside the shower with Anna, Helen, just outside, holding under Anna's other arm. They kept small talk going. As if this were something they've always done together, as when, at the end of a playdate, before starting dinner, they'd thrown batches of their kids into the tub. Helen and Molly worked together. Each lathered up one hand, trading secured holds of Anna. The skin was pebbly and dry, mottled blue and purple. If even lightly touched, would it abrade, slough off in pieces? They checked for splits, broken patches. There were no grazed-open bits. Molly lifted an arm, and Helen circled the hollow. Helen lifted the other arm, and Molly made circles with her hand. They will not describe her limbs to anyone; there was no word for what a leg becomes. Instead Helen had gossip. One of the guys they'd known in high school was in jail. Another — remember Eddie? — marriage gone south, a wife who'd run off with her yoga instructor. Still, the wife got beaucoup bucks. He apparently was worth a barrel of millions. Who could have guessed that one? Back in high school, they agreed, Eddie had been pretty cute but otherwise pretty useless.

"Wasn't he someone you did something with?" Molly asked Anna.

Anna's lips were blue, a tremor moving through her body. Molly motioned to Helen to shut the faucet.

"You definitely did something with Eddie." Helen held a towel open while Molly lifted Anna's foot over the tiled shower lip.

"I did something with a lot of them," Anna said.

"Lucky them," Molly said, steadying Anna while Helen swaddled her in the towel.

Art History 1

Helen's fingers sketch against the wale of her jeans. Involuntary. This is what she does. Look and take measure. The distance between bodies. The thin shape Anna makes on the velvet love seat. The way the others group, gesturing, leaning toward her, their faces wrenched and taut, echoing centuries of deathbed paintings. The room. The suffused light. Who hasn't painted this? Rembrandt, Picasso, Munch. Paintings of men

29

gathered around Christ. Alonzo Chappel's canvas of Lincoln's room crowded with men paying homage. She draws the shapes. The hard line of the sofa back. The women stack close to Anna. Anna's pale face, a blue tint to it, already distant, not quite of them anymore but offering some last glowing courage. This, too, is part of the iconography. Always someone in the painting looks away. And someone turns to face the viewer as if to plead for hope.

Train

"I actually feel pretty good. Is that strange?" Anna was bright-eyed, pink in her cheeks. She sat upright and tossed away the velvet pillow Helen had wedged behind her.

"You look great," Helen encouraged.

Anna rocked into a Bee Gees chorus: *stayin' alive, stayin' alive.* The others chimed in, arms pumping: *Ah, ha, ha, ha, stayin' alive.* Anna's voice was strong. Caroline took up the harmony. They had years and years of singing together — Aretha, Poco, Cat Stevens — even their goofing around sounded pretty good. At least to them.

"It's the soup." Ming glowed. "I'm taking all the credit."

"I didn't want you to come today," Anna admitted. "It seemed pitiful and dramatic.

But it feels good. Almost weird. Like I'm getting better."

"Then go back on medication," Helen spit out. "You've done so well before." She tried to adjust her voice. Less harangue. More bolster. "Better than well, you've kind of been a miracle."

"I'm just glad you feel good," Caroline said.

"Forget *feeling* good," Helen snapped. "Anna can come through again. It's another bout. That's all. This whole hospice is ridiculous."

Helen shot a please-back-me-up at Ming. Ming welled up and glanced away.

Really? This sudden, teary quiet. They'd already wasted two hours talking nonsense. They'd all witnessed the other unexpected recoveries. There was reason to hope. More than hope, it was even pretty logical.

Helen levered herself up from her place behind Anna. She climbed over the back of the couch till she was standing. She needed to stand. To be able to see each of their faces. Pitiful. Hadn't Anna just full-throated belted out "Stayin' Alive"? Hadn't Anna admitted she felt well?

Looking across at Anna, sparkly, actually sparkly. "Basic question," Helen challenged. "Who thinks hospice, right now, right here, is an excellent choice? Raise your hand."

She fidgeted through the room, skulked close to each of them like she was ready to tag them for Duck, Duck, Goose.

"Come on, Ming, tell me. You think this seems right?" When Helen touched her, Ming flinched.

"It's Anna's decision." Ming's voice was dry and wiry.

"Since when have we ever stopped from chiming in on any of each other's decisions? That's what we do."

Did Helen need to remind them that Anna had been ready to toss in the towel during the last recurrence? Did she need to remind Ming of that brutal day, Anna's mouth and throat so thickly blistered from medicine that when she'd whispered, "I'm done. I'm stopping," they'd both said, "We understand." It had taken Anna's brothers barging in for her to grudgingly agree to adjust medications. One more month, they'd negotiated, and then make a choice. Did Helen really need to remind everyone how, less than a year later, at the Thai place in Great Barrington where they'd met for dinner before the Red Molly concert, Anna admitted she was ashamed to have considered giving up treatment? She'd thanked them for their steadiness. There'd already been so many peak nights — "peak nights" was Anna's exact phrase. "Like tonight." Anna smiled. "And we haven't even gotten to the concert." "Believing for you, that's our job," Helen rushed in. "That's what friends are for." Without missing a beat, they'd burst into song, giddy and crooning, *That's what friends are for,* which led to Caroline and Anna harmonizing on Carole King's "You've Got a Friend."

Now Helen pleaded. "What about more peak moments?" She was pacing. She didn't care if it sounded like pleading. "You say you feel good now. Please."

"I've told the kids, Heli. I've gotten them on board."

"That's idiotic, Anna."

"Helen, stop," Molly cut in.

"Just try for a while." If she was going to have to push this all on her own, she'd better go tough. "What's the big problem? Hospice is going to have a conniption? They'll kill Anna for changing her mind?"

"Helen." Anna patted the cushion next to her.

"No, Anna." No way was Anna going to try her usual bossy routine.

"It's all I can do." Anna was clear-voiced, nothing tired and quavery. None of her usual stubbornness. She sounded so open, so loving. It hurt. "You're going to have to live with my decision."

Then Helen was yanking open the sliding glass door to the porch. "I'm going to have to live with your decision? That's the whole problem."

1965, Bunnies, Too

First day of second grade. Anna stands at recess in a circle with the other girls. Her hair, plaited in tight, thick braids, is so shiny. And her delicate ears, pierced! A tiny garnet pinned on each lobe. Where has she come from? Newness makes her exotic. She tells the other girls she has two younger brothers, a dog called Kissy, a cat named Sweets, and a wounded crow she'd found with her father. The bird has her name. Anna. The other girls shout, "A crow with your name?" Yes, she and her father have saved lots of birds. Bunnies, too. They set them free after nursing them to health. She's held mauled bunnies, run-over bunnies. She's splinted the broken legs of birds found in marsh grass. She's given every one of them her name, Anna.

Years later, at Anna and Reuben's wedding, Helen held up her wineglass and told the story. "Imagine all those bunnies. Just to be clear, she'd actually name every one of us here today Anna if she thought she could get away with it."

"Right there, on that second-grade playground," Helen said when the laughter quieted, "I determined I wasn't going to let this oddball out of my sight. That our friendship would be the adventure of a lifetime."

When the last of the wedding party hung at two pushed-together tables, everyone wielding a fork and having another go at the whipped-cream tiered wedding cake, Anna's father sat down next to Helen.

"Good toast, kiddo." He looked gleefully exhausted.

"Thanks, Mr. Spark. If you don't get it right for your oldest friend, who *are* you gonna get it right for?"

"That's funny." Anna's father took a drink from a glass Helen didn't remember him holding when he'd sat down. "I came over to tell you we never saved anything. No wounded anythings. Not a rabbit or a bird."

The Matter, Exactly
All heart. Heartsick. A heart-to-heart. Heart on your sleeve.

The heart of the matter?

It was in her heart. Cross your heart and hope to die.

NK/T, rarest of lymphoma cell types, and this, hers, the rarest of the five strains of NK/T. An NK/T-cell mass in the left atrium. The heart pump, with its continuous flushing system, was not a place where anything easily roots. A lifetime in the field, and it's still a remote statistic. The first time, the first occurrence, it was so rootled that when they opened her chest, cracking ribs to see if it could be dislodged, they found the matter branching deeply into the ventricle wall and they just sewed up. Began CHOP chemo, the four-part cocktail. But can it be shrunk without tearing open the heart? Doctors who are not her doctors swipe open the curtain, shake their heads staring at Anna's chart.

Even now, this final time, who didn't flinch when they heard that it had returned to Anna's heart?

To Be More Exact
There should be no medical jargon. What does NK stand for?

Oh, Natural Killer.

1975, What Are You?
The two girls look down the steep ravine to the railroad tracks. The spring foliage is not fully in, the leaves a vivid, electric green.

Wind gusts up the embankment. Everything vibrates. Helen feels too high. Even the rocky escarpment is a glittery vibration.

Anna says go with it; the vibration is excellent. Anna wants to smoke the second joint.

"You go on," Helen says.

Anna can take more. She wants more. Always more than Helen. Always been that way. Now it seems Anna wants to blaze all the time. Party with Molly and Ming. Helen wishes that she had it in her. Even when Anna is wildly wasted, she's sweet and lovable and pretty. Helen's unwildness feels clunky.

A train passes. Heading into the city.

"Lean back." Anna stretches flat to feel the motion of the train rumble up the hill.

Knees pulled in, Helen's wrapped tight to stop the shiver in her legs. Tries to keep her gaze steady. Helen can't take any motion. Needs something solid to ground her.

Anna slips the roach flat between two matches. "Let's at least smoke this doobie down." Anna hands the matches to Helen.

Last Saturday night, at another party that Helen didn't want to be at, a boy tapped the back of her head to say Anna needed her. She found Anna in the backyard, a group of girls clustered close. "Helen's here," and the circle instantly opened to let

Helen kneel close to Anna. Anna was a mess. A drunk, stoned, crying mess. Anna reached for Helen, her arms moving through something thick and viscous.

"I knew you'd come," she repeated like a revelation.

Helen took off her flannel shirt and used it to wipe Anna's mouth and arms where she'd puked on herself.

"I need you to tell me I haven't made the biggest ass of myself. He hates me."

There was puke in Anna's hair. Helen didn't know who this "he" was, but there wasn't a "he" worth a nanosecond of Anna's time. Definitely not worth getting fucked up over.

It had taken a bit of annoying drunk-convincing, but Helen got Anna out of the yard. They found Ming and Molly in front of the house, and the three girls led Anna through their suburban streets. They were taking the long way home, walking her sober. Cool spring night. They stayed outdoors. Anna seemed in okay shape. They did cartwheels in line on the empty streets. The girls wandered through the estate section, massive Tudors and Colonials, every house with a winding driveway, landscaped yards, a swimming pool in back.

"Let's pool-hop." Anna was so enthusiastic.

"It's only April," Ming said.

"Who cares. I'm ready to jump."

"You would, Anna," Helen said dryly. "But it's better to jump when the swimming pools are filled."

Now, with the wind and her shaking fingers, lighting the roach seems an insurmountable task for Helen.

"You're hopeless," Anna says.

"I'm high." And like that, that's all Helen is — high — not shivery or jittery but happy to be stoned with her best friend out in the woods.

"I'm really high," Helen announces, her voice singsong. "Extremely high."

"What are you, *high*?" Anna lifts a lilting question inflected in her voice. The girls break out in uncontrollable, snorting laughter.

"What are you, *high*?" This time British.

Then French.

They're hysterical; it's hysterical. Just as they pull back, almost back in control, one of them says in a clipped German accent, "What are you, *high*?"

Half Husband

Caroline took Reuben's groceries as he struggled through the back door, and then the women, one by one, hugged tight to him so it looked to Anna like a country line dance. Years earlier she would have implored him to give her time alone with her friends. These last years, since their separation, if Reuben showed up at the house without first calling, she glared, told him flatly to get out and leave them alone. Helen argued with her about the hard line she, Anna, had taken, saying, "Admit it, this is really the way you want the marriage, Anna. A half husband. Separation works for you. If you weren't so stubborn, you'd see that."

Now, despite a faint rash of old angers — what were they? — Anna was pleased that Reuben was here. No need to rally for him. No need to pretend for Reuben.

But where was Helen?

Stormed out in a huff. Not in the room.

Reuben switched out an empty roll of paper towels on the wooden holder. Then started in unpacking groceries. Always so pleased with what he accomplished. Endless lists of what still needed to be done. All that exhausting energy, that infuriating energy, that demanding bubbly energy Anna wanted to quell in her husband.

"I made a mistake," she told him the day he set up the mechanical bed and took out her four-poster bed. Her bed that had been their bed in the bedroom that had been their bedroom. Now it was her room. Reuben rented another house in a town the next town away. She'd refused to set foot in that house. But still, he was here, helping set up the motorized bed that had been brought in. "I thought I could do anything and you'd stay." Anna spoke from the corner chair as Reuben stretched the fitted sheet over the crunchy, plastic-covered mattress. "I thought no matter what, I was really the one in charge."

Anna watched as Ming set down a bowl of soup for Reuben and Molly followed with her plate of salmon. Reuben curled over the soup.

They feed him like they feed me, Anna thought. Like he is wounded. She'd insisted in the last years that her friends show loyalty. If he wouldn't return to her life in the way she wanted, then they were not allowed to speak to Reuben.

Now her friends circled and fed him. Poor Reuben. Hunched over like it hurt to eat. And she had thought him a man who would always look boyish. He still had a full head of curly hair. But now there was a thinning patch at the crown of his head.

Had their son told Reuben? Watching him talk with Ming as he ate, Anna knew for certain that Reuben did not hold that kernel of the future inside him. It was hers. The only flame left within her. Momma, I have a secret to tell you.

They had made mistakes. Still, their boy had come into her room. It was hers. And she would not tell him. Reuben would have everything later.

Now he could barely hold the weight of the spoon. He was exhausted. An exhausted man dutifully helping her die.

1978, Trust Me

Here, on what had seemed a not-unusual Thursday night at the pub, was the man she'd have babies with. It was weird, but on the second date Anna already knew. His green eyes, his dark curls. They'd have beautiful babies. They'd marry. Their babies would be pretty.

She knew she shouldn't be thinking about the pretty babies they'd make. They were nineteen. They were in college. Anna couldn't admit to anyone how happy she'd be to have babies right now. Helen would cringe. Call her retro. Scold her as anti-feminist. Ming was off in the mountains of

Guatemala with that anthropologist. She insisted that all she wanted to do was to travel, the more remote the better. The anthropologist was great, but not even necessary. Caroline had dropped out of college and as far as Anna could tell was barely leaving her parents' house, let alone dating. Molly was off men, extolling the joys and complications of women. Lately she'd used the word "breeders." Even Anna's own mom intoned, Career first, career first.

Anna looked around the pub, wanting to gather it in. She wanted to see the room in some special cast of light. To tell her friends. Of course she'll phone Helen tomorrow, tell her all of it. Even if it meant being called retro.

But more than for Helen, she wanted to collect every detail so that years later it would be part of the story they'd tell the children: "I knew I'd marry your dad on our second date at the Whisker Pub." It wouldn't sound crazy then. It would be what it was. Inevitable.

The pub was the same dingy pub it had been every night. Same stoners grouped around pinball machines debating flipper techniques. Same grungy wood-stained walls and green globe lights. Now even its sameness seemed exceptional. That was how it was, Anna thought, the jukebox playing Loggins and Messina's "Vahevala" when it should be playing something more romantic. Jesse Colin Young's "Sunlight." *Yeah, that's the way she feels about you.* But Anna knew that the exceptional happens quietly inside the mundane. Unadorned, often unnoticed. She would wish it otherwise. Still, it was enough watching Reuben, his enthusiasm and sincerity. His playful, crooked smile. She could see he was into her. It would unfold. For now this was perfect, knowing quietly what could not be said, that Reuben would be the father of her children, that her life would unfold in the special way she'd known it would since she was a little girl.

"I've been trying to talk to you since the beginning of the semester," Reuben admitted.

"I'm glad to have been noticed," Anna said.

"Noticed?" Reuben grinned. "You're hands down the most radiant woman on campus." Radiant? When had Reuben ever described a girl that way? He was just getting used to the imperative to say woman, not girl. But Reuben wasn't just talking pretty to try to get Anna to sleep with him. He was already flipped, smitten — fuck it

— head over heels in love. He couldn't admit that on a second date. It would be certifiably nuts to admit that he was in love with Anna. Her long dark ringlets. Those incredible green eyes. And not just because she was beautiful. Yes, radiantly beautiful. Not just because she had the most exciting laugh and she laughed a lot. Not just because she also got really serious and pouted her lips when she asked those penetratingly intense questions that he didn't think he could answer but then was answering, and all the while she was looking at him with complete concentration. No, he was in love with Anna because they were meant for each other. She was meant to have his babies. Now, that was certifiable. Reuben knew he'd better shut up. Not say anything close to that. Thinking it was weird enough. It was enough to be cool and focused on the conversation. Saying something ridiculous, like, "I'm already in love with you, Anna Spark," would get him nowhere fast.

Anna didn't ask where they were going until Reuben turned in to the trails behind the library.

"Trust me," he said, and took Anna's hand. He kept her small hand in his even when the trail narrowed and was not wide enough for them to walk side by side. She nudged close behind him.

"Sorry, it's dark," she said when she stepped on a root and they both tripped.

But it wasn't all that dark. The moon had risen almost full. It spilled through the trees, surprisingly bright. She'd never thought to go into the campus woods at night. She'd taken runs or walks with friends on the trails, but always in the daytime.

"Watch your head," Reuben said.

Anna didn't really see what she was ducking under, but she ducked. Now it seemed they were off trail, moving through rows of pine. More underfoot to trip over. How far was he taking her?

"This is a little Hansel and Gretel," Anna said.

"Well, I thank God we're not brother and sister," Reuben said. "Anyway, we're here."

He held back a branch and swept his hand for her to step ahead of him. The gesture was formal.

"Go on," Reuben whispered.

Anna hesitated. Go where? Why was he whispering?

"Oh!" she said, stepping forward. "Oh," she said again. Her own voice had dropped to a whisper, too.

"I know," Reuben said. "Amazing, right?"

But it was more than amazing. Or maybe this was the actual definition of amazing. It was unbelievable, otherworldly. A clearing, a large circle, lit up; everything was silver. The bark on the trees ringing the circle was sheathed in silver, the tree trunks looking like encrusted silver columns or like a huge silver candelabra that they were standing inside. And the ground — thick moss, or was it miniature ferns? — every tiny blade dipped in silver light. The earth was a soft glitter cushion, and Anna's shoes sank into it, almost disappearing. Even the air was feathered silver. Anna held out her hands as if the air, the particles of light, were something she could hold.

She turned to look at Reuben.

"I love this place," he said. He was smiling, a big excited smile. He looked exuberant. Like a kid. "It's my secret. It's the most beautiful thing. And now you in this place, that's double beautiful, that's stupid beautiful."

Dog

Where was Zeus? Had someone let Zeus out?

Zeus, here Zeus.

Hey

"Hey, sweetpea." Anna clears her throat. It's immediately obvious to Caroline and Molly that it's one of Anna's three kids on the phone.

"It is good. Nothing like best friends." Anna's voice is all theater. No rattle. No slur or slick of the morphine. Even her shoulders, winged back, suddenly stronger than all day.

Caroline and Molly don't even pretend they're not listening. They both figure it's one of the twins — but Andy or Harper? — that they can't tell.

"A conference?" Anna nods. "When's that happening?" Questions to steer the conversation.

"What kind of meeting? Today. Sounds promising, right?" She deflects all questions with new questions.

"Was it what you'd hoped?" That's Anna's job. What parent wasn't an expert at pulling information?

"Yes, yes. You're kidding, right? That's crazy!" Delight and laughter. Deep from the belly.

Molly and Caroline know she actually is delighted. More than anything has delighted her all day, hearing her kid's bubbling enthusiasm — and Anna's right there, inside

48

her child's happiness.

"No, please. I know, sweetheart. I'm so sorry." Anna winces, a shuddering no. They watch her face like watching a spectrometer, the slightest shifts registered.

"I've got the girls here. Stay put. Just call if you get a second to tell me how the meeting went. That's your only job. I'll be waiting. Love you, monkey."

Anna works to keep her voice spunked up until the last "Love you, monkey." She clicks off the TALK button, and Molly and Caroline see her body deflate, withering back onto the striped cushions.

"This better be fast." She scans their faces for a promise.

Actually, for What It's Worth

Between them there were twelve delivered babies. Three six- to eight-week abortions. Three miscarriages. One post-amniocentesis selective abortion. That's just for the record.

Faith

Ming asked, "How are you managing? How's Harper? And the boys?"

"How do we manage? We're managing." Reuben sounded like an old Jewish man. He scrubbed the stove. He leaned in and scrubbed.

49

"Reuben, are you really?"

Reuben raised his hand, the yellow sponge caked with cleanser in his grip. Stop. Stop. Stop. He looked older and Jewisher with every minute.

At All Times

The refrigerator looked as if preparations for a party were under way. How many quiches could be stacked on one shelf? The back door had opened all week long with local friends carrying more food, labeled and stored in the freezer. A pan heating in the oven at all times. Word must have traveled through the Valley that two days ago Anna had drunk a mango smoothie. Now there was a shelf jammed with every kind of organic mango smoothie available, from Stop & Shop to Trader Joe's.

Made Reuben wonder if anyone understood what "hospice" meant.

Food was a nervous reaction. He knew that. The demolished tray of brownies on the counter attested to this. People had gone at the squares like there was no tomorrow.

And to watch the childhood gang go giddy each time Anna lifted a spoon, as though they'd performed healing magic with soup.

"Reuben? How are you holding up today?" It was Kate, the hospice nurse.

He nodded but kept low, arranging food on shelves. He appreciated her insistence that hospice was also about the caregivers, but answering Kate's daily concerns felt like yet another thing he was making sure he'd done right.

She crouched next to him. "Does everyone think hospice is a potluck? I hate to be a party pooper, but all these friends showing up every hour of the day seems a little extreme."

Reuben snorted, "That's life with Anna." He knew he should say more. Give Kate a picture of the person she was caring for. How crazy loved Anna was by everyone. But Kate's wisecrack hit a satisfying dark edge.

"Has anyone considered this might take some peace and quiet?"

"Oh, you better get ready. There are busloads coming." Reuben couldn't remember the last time he'd joked around.

"Maybe I'll borrow a few for my patients who have no one."

"Forget borrow. We can rent. Start a business." He was having fun. Good wrong fun.

Kate touched Reuben lightly on his shoulder. "Anna told me yesterday she wants to stop eating."

He pulled out a casserole, spinach and thick slabs of cheese. "Was she nauseous?"

Reuben stretched a crimp in the Saran Wrap.

"She's asking how to move this along."

Reuben kept pulling things from the fridge while Kate explained that stopping intake could speed up the process. He balanced a stack of Tupperware. "She's announced this? Stopping?" He sat back on the tile floor in front of the open fridge. Reuben should post a sign: NO MORE FOOD. PLEASE. But people will say he has lost the right to declare what Anna wants.

"She's considering what's available."

Reuben stood up, leaving the casserole and Tupperware in a jumble on the floor. He yanked open the odds-and-ends drawer, rummaging for paper and a pen. What right did he have posting anything on a refrigerator in a house where he did not live anymore? He grabbed a green marker. NO MORE FOOD. Shoved it under a pizza-slice magnet on the fridge.

Fuck them all. He had all the right.

2008, Wreckage

Ming blamed the Valley. Blamed Reuben and Anna's local friends. Said the only reason Reuben and Anna came up with their separation on the verge of their kids being out of the house was that it had become a kind of local fashion. Now instead of potlucks the Valley friends were off on mindfulness chakra retreats and sweat lodges. And with mindfulness, it seemed, came radical awakening. Mostly genital. With the obvious yoga instructors or colleagues. Even a monk. Half of their Valley friends suddenly needed space. Didn't believe in the old paradigm, the constraint of marriage.

"Believe?" Ming argued with Anna and Reuben. They'd driven over to Great Barrington for their monthly dinner at Ming and Sebastian's.

"Adulthood is a constraint," Ming said, and topped off her glass of wine. Breaking up was frivolous. Two homes, two heating bills, two phone bills — who had that kind of extra cash? Ming was practical. Who wouldn't want a love affair? But who had the time?

Reuben and Anna insisted there was no one else. Just their old story. Twenty years. Now wreckage.

"What are you guys doing?" Ming knocked back her wine. "You have a way better marriage than us."

"Hey!" Sebastian snorted. He wielded cooking tongs. The whole house fragrant with herbs and garlic.

Ming inclined old-school. Believed the vow she and Sebastian had made. The whole point of which was to bind during the ebb, not the flow. Chinese and Ecuadorean — she supposed that also made them Old World.

"Who else will feed me like this?" Ming beamed as Sebastian carried out the platter of roasted fish and vegetables.

He waited for everyone to be seated before he put down the platter. Food was formal pleasure.

"With good food we are not permitted to speak bitterly or with regret." Sebastian bowed.

But after the meal and the wine, Ming started to cry. "You're our best friends. We have these dinners. We took vacations. What about all our kids?"

"Ming, we're trying this. It's not for forever," Anna said. "We want to look at who we are now and see what makes sense."

What could survive that kind of scrutiny?

Reuben started clearing dishes. He looked too excited. So did Anna. Like they were both already off at music festivals or heli-skiing without parental supervision.

Ming, suddenly stony and pissed. "You're both idiots. Have at it."

The Real

"Well, well," chimed Kate, setting her nursing bag and knapsack down. "A whole new Anna."

Anna, in clean leggings and her daughter's college sweatshirt, her wet hair combed into a side braid, lounged in the living room sipping a mango drink in a tall glass.

"That's insane." Anna laughed in response to something Caroline said. Radiant smile. The regal angles of her jaw.

"This is actually Anna." Molly's voice was defiant, like an annoyed teen's. "This is the real Anna." She ta-dahed her arms. The morphine, the drifty sway, the shallow smudged breath, the eyes unopened, the not more than a wrinkle under the sheet — that was not Anna.

Kate took out the blood-pressure cuff and started to unwind it. "Well, Anna, let's see how the real you is doing."

1976, Against the Elm

Molly was still pretty sure that the only one who ever knew about their kissing was the caretaker at the Farm. When Molly and Anna saw him holding pruning shears by the ragged hedges, they didn't stop.

"Give him a life thrill," Molly whispered,

and drew her tongue across Anna's upper lip.

Kissing had been Molly's idea. "Why not?" she'd said. "It will be fun." She reasoned that they'd both let boys they hardly knew do way more than kiss them. They each kept a list and liked that some boys appeared on both lists. Robbie Branford kissed like a fish. Clumsy Frank snuck his stubby finger inside them. Jose was so excellent they named him "King Make-Out."

It might have been Molly's idea, but it was Anna who stood Molly against the elm tree. "You're so pretty," she'd said, and leaned in with a tentative kiss. Then she kissed Molly again, their tongues flashing and fast. It made Molly ache. Molly turned Anna so that now she had her back to the tree, and Molly pressed against her, their bodies thickening together in a grinding sway. Unlike with the boys, they kept their eyes open until, so lost in the heat and drift, their eyes could not stay open.

"Let's never tell anyone," Anna said after they'd snuck out through the break in the fence.

"You mean Helen." Molly hated the petulance she couldn't shake.

"I mean I like having this secret with you."

Anna circled her mouth against the dimple on Molly's chin.

"Just me and the caretaker," Molly joked, because it was always better to feel in control.

Mud

Helen leaned against the porch railing. Wobbly. The deck seemed wobbly. The house, too. Not exactly in full-on disrepair, but untended. Warped boards, nails sticking up. The railing ready to give way. The buckled deck was in dire need of maintenance. Then a power wash and a stain. Who could keep up with all the repairs? Even under normal circumstances, a home was a constant drain. And here, these last years, ridiculous — Reuben living in another house. Anna more of the time sick than well. Stop. Just stop it. She hadn't come outside to discover more problems. Get a full breath. Catch your breath.

Helen let go of the top rail, swiped the chipping paint off her palms. She should bundle Anna up, bring her outdoors. Anna will say no. Or she'll just narrow an eye at Helen, give that imperious shake of her head. Insisting it's all impossible. Impossible to manage the outdoors anymore. But it was possible. Helen would make it possible. She'd wrap Anna in wool blankets and carry her outside. Settle her in the Adirondack chair. Once out here, Anna would like breathing in the rough thaw. She'd notice the slight sweetness in the air. Helen needed to believe Anna could still like that. Though she wasn't sure how much *liking* Anna had left in her.

Something flashed near. A wing, blue. A jay? But she couldn't spot a bird in the bare trees. She waited for it to fly out. Maybe she hadn't seen anything. She looked back into the house. It looked normal to see them inside talking and eating. Hanging around as they've always done. Ming threw back her head in response to something. Molly had moved over to the couch, taken over massaging Anna's legs. Her friends were inside laughing. They were themselves. Caroline nervously flicking her ringed fingers as she spoke. Ming's head tossing every which way as she laughed. All the tiny, specific, defining gestures of a self that Helen recognized in each of them. Except Anna. It wasn't that Anna was unrecognizable. That she wasn't herself. Actually, Anna looked better than the last time Helen had seen her. Her face was full. Color in her cheeks.

Yet nothing inside the house was normal.

Each day Anna drifted in and out of being Anna. The hospice nurse reported "a matter of weeks." Or less. Just like that. What Helen watched inside was a sad theater of normal.

Why was she the only one who felt betrayed?

Helen looked at a smattering of age spots, ginger splotches that have appeared on her hands. She was used to the scaly dryness and paint caked under her nails, but when did these hands become old-lady hands? It was all so off kilter. Anna was dying, and she, Helen, had fallen in love. And now, marrying. Inside the house her best friend was dying, and she was a middle-age woman undertaking a new life. Old or not, there was giddiness in her, happiness, an uncontrollable flitter just thinking about Asa. Alive and eager, that was what her body was. Jesus, the body in love was ridiculous and hopeful. Anna will be dead, and Helen will be saying I do.

She wanted to call him. Touch base with Asa. But she wasn't sure her phone had reception in these dense woods.

Talk about betrayal. Was she just guilty about her own happiness? What about any of this was right?

Helen wished Anna's brothers were here.

She still thought of them as Mikey and Bobby, Anna's baby brothers, even if they were men in their forties. She'd heard they came up last weekend to plead with her to try again. Supposedly it had all gone wonky. But together, like the last time, they could turn Anna around. Michael was an internist and Robert an ENT guy; they believed in medicine. Forget Ming and Molly and Caroline — they were proving useless. Deferring to Anna as if they didn't remember how much over the years she'd needed them to resist any negative thinking. Already four times, each unpredictable. Not unpredictable — rare — weird cells, a tumor massed in the heart. Wasn't that Anna's punch line? *Why bother beating normal when I could beat special?* And now, just like that, Anna could decide to give up?

A jeering squawk and a flash of cobalt between the dull boughs of a pine. There was the bird. And then a second. It lifted her to see them. An inexplicable hopefulness to hear their chatter. Not metaphorical hopefulness. Just dumb happiness that the air had a cool tang of dirt and leaf. That the season was changing. That if Bobby and Mikey would back her, stand their ground, Anna could be swayed. That she and Asa will have their life together.

I miss you. It is beyond sad here, she texted Asa. Pressed SEND and watched the line stall. It might not complete. She was desperate for it to go through. She'd walk up the driveway. Drive to town to find a signal.

She hasn't told her friends yet. She wanted first to tell Anna. That Asa, out of nowhere, had asked her to marry him. Asa who claimed he'd never marry again. Anna said from the start, "Helen, Asa is obviously the one. He's the light out of that moldy cave you've been in." She thought of an afternoon at her apartment. Third remission. Anna had finally taken off that stupid wig. She looked like a French model, gamine with her short hair. Only Anna could look gorgeous with a practically shaved head. Asa downright silly with Anna and Anna teasing him right back. That afternoon, watching her best friend and this man she'd fallen for, teasing and joking with each other, Helen had felt so proud of Anna, who'd jumped back into life with such abandon. All that infinite hope. She looked at Asa and promised herself, I'm going to let myself have all of whatever this is.

But there it was. Delivered. And bubbles showed Asa writing back. Don't waste time missing me. More important be funny fun it up for her. She read Asa's text. Read it again.

Wished it gave her a clue to how she might find the funny. Or that there were more bubbles. How many times could she read it to stall going inside?

"Helen." Molly slid open the door.

Molly regarded her with such kindness, such tenderness, that Helen needed to look away.

"Anna's asking for you," Molly beckoned. "She doesn't know where you are."

Anna's looking for her? That was almost funny. It's Anna who was leaving her. Helen didn't want to go into the house. Not in this state, this nasty, breathless confusion. She wanted at least to see the bird's royal plumage again.

"I'm all messed up," Helen said. "I'm useless."

Molly laughed. "Come on, honey. There's no useful left."

2009, Whir

Asa was Anna's fault.

Helen said, "Who comes to a hospital and falls in love?"

Anna took a careful pull on the plastic straw. Swallowing was a struggle. "I had a relapse to save your pitiful life. And all I got from you was this vanilla milk shake."

Helen went along with Anna's matchmaking because she was ready to go along with anything while Anna was stuck in treatment. Anyway, talking about boys had been a pastime of theirs since they first both loved Timmy Cannon in the fourth grade.

"I've told him that you're the smartest person I know," Anna said. "But, Heli, get ready, he's a lot smarter than you." Anna hadn't enjoyed this much leverage over Helen in a long time. "Once you meet him, I'll have proved, hands down, I'm the way better best friend." She clearly had every intention of getting a lot of play out of her dominance.

Helen climbed in next to Anna on the hospital bed. She'd found that was easier than facing the bank of beeping monitors. All the dips, the sudden jagged chartings, freaked her out. A lot of afternoons, they napped like that together.

Helen reminded Anna that she'd already tried matchmaking. Spring of tenth grade, Anna and Molly stood on the front porch of Colin O'Reilly's house. He was a senior in Helen's art class, a swimmer who only senior year had figured out he could draw like nobody's business. "Do you think you would date Helen?" Anna beamed up at Colin, certain he just needed to be told. "Helen's incredible," Anna said. "But she's

63

a little shy." The only saving grace of this humiliation was that Anna and Molly waited a full year before they told Helen. "He was really nice," Anna said. "He said you were great. He just wasn't looking for anything serious before college."

Anna set the unfinished milk shake down on the crowded bedside tray. "Face it, Helen, you've never done very well picking on your own."

Helen closed her eyes while Anna told her why this man, Asa, was the right one. It wasn't just the wisecracking with his sick mom in the room across the hall from Anna or his refusal to capitulate to doling out deathbed pity or the way he'd begun stopping by Anna's bed, handing off a banana and peanut-butter smoothie. "Screw the killer chemo. Girl, it's calories you need." And it wasn't his sneaky smile and the serious crazy pale color of his eyes. Or it was all this, Anna said to Helen. And that Asa was solid. Funny, smart. And solid. And best of all, unpredictable.

"A grown-up." Anna untangled a wire that crimped under Helen's leg. "And he just might be weird enough to keep you interested."

"What kind of weird name is Asa?" Helen said.

"That's exactly what I'm saying."

The first time Helen met Asa, she heard him before she saw him. He was yelling in the corridor.

"For what return precisely, Doctor? What do you pretend to be promising my mother in those fabulous extra months, except for nausea and an excruciating recovery from surgery?"

Anna mouthed, *That's him.*

From where she sat on Anna's side of the curtain, Helen saw a man's hands karate-chopping the air. She couldn't see his face. Helen thought he could be a radio announcer with that confident and smooth voice.

He actually seemed a little scary.

The doctor couldn't get a word in. Asa was high-speed-drilling the doctor a couple of new orifices. Helen nervously rooted for the doctor to shut this guy down with absolute facts and proof.

The doctor phumphered. Tried a couple of tacks that Asa blew apart, smoothly eviscerating the doctor's reasoning each time by asking, "How will this help the quality of her life?"

Anna looked delighted. Like with each undoing, she proved to Helen how inevitable a match she'd made.

"Asa," Anna called when the doctor limpingly excused himself. "Now that you've killed off your own mom, you bastard, get in here."

Before he walked in, Helen decided that she actually hated Asa, who encouraged gallows humor in Anna. But the Asa who sat down by Anna's bed was soft-spoken and kind. He asked about Anna's daughter's swim meet. He knew all her kids' names.

Then he nodded to Helen. "I know too much about you to pretend I'm not really curious to finally meet you."

"Just be aware, she's a complete liar," Helen said, busy thinking Anna was right about his eyes. Then Asa smiled, and Helen thought Anna was right about the sneaky-smile thing, too.

Inside

Molly stayed outside on the back porch. There's no useful left. That's what she'd said to Helen. But last night Serena told Molly she'd spoken to colleagues and done her own bit of research. There was reason to have a good feeling about this new drug. Anna's doctor was making remarkable discoveries about the immune system. Serena suggested she come along to help

66

clarify the protocol, since Anna always claimed that Serena made medical mumbo jumbo less inscrutable. "Forget remission," Serena instructed Molly. The new model was chronicity. Think relapse. "By Anna's next flare, they'll be miles past this novel drug." But Molly argued it was fair to say no to more medicine. Wasn't it fair to say enough is enough? "Fair? I'm really surprised at your response." Serena had been curt; she didn't have to spell out what she meant. In the late eighties, Molly's first clinical therapy job was at Fenway Community Health Center. So many young men sick. So many nights Molly practically limped in from work and crawled right into bed. It was all she could do. So many dying that terrible new death. And no medicine for AIDS. No real research. Every week for two years, it seemed there was another funeral she and Serena attended. Or they stood buttoned up against the Boston cold, shouting, "Silence equals death!" It wasn't until '94 that the real drug trials for HIV were initiated. At Fenway Community Health Center, Molly witnessed how medicine had changed everything.

Molly refused Serena's offer to come with her on the visit.

"But she has to understand this is a new

frontier. It's all moving fast. Supersonic," Serena said.

"New medicine isn't always the answer."

"That's stunning, Molly. Of everyone, you really saw what medicine could do."

Was Serena insinuating that Molly owed it to all those men she'd worked with who had HIV? That it was a betrayal of all their dear dead friends not to fight with Anna? That it was a betrayal of Anna?

Did she, Molly, hearing her friends laughing inside, truly believe there was no useful left?

February 2012, Medicine

Helen buzzed in Robert and Michael. They bounded up the stairwell, two stairs at a time, neither slowing his gait on the four flights, popped Helen a kiss, and moved purposefully into the apartment. It was always astonishing how much they looked like their sister. Like Anna before years of treatment.

"She's not feeling well." Ming nodded toward Anna, who was curled, burrowed down into the white pillows on Helen's couch. "She can't speak." Ming gestured to her own throat.

Helen rummaged at pillows till she found a bit of Anna's face to kiss. "Hey, sweetheart," Helen said, "Bobby and Mikey are here."

"Anna." Robert pushed past Helen and sat down practically on top of her. "I need you to sit up." He pulled off the pillows. Like he might force her to sit up.

"She feels terrible," Helen said, and looked at Ming. Maybe it had been a mistake when Anna's brothers insisted they come over. Anna had asked Helen to relay her decision. "She doesn't want this much pain anymore," Helen said when she'd reached Michael. "The medicine's killing her, Mikey. She's made a choice." Helen tried to convey neutrally Anna's position. "This is her body." Rushed, Michael scoffed, "Don't be ridiculous. Stopping's not an option."

Robert worked Anna upright. He enveloped her in a big, protective bear hug.

"They'll adjust your medicine, Anna," Robert explained. "There's also pain medicine."

Anna kept her eyes shut. Slowly shook her head. No. No.

Michael dropped down on her other side. "You're scheduled to see Dr. Lee. I've spoken with him. There's a plan."

No. No. No. To each thing her brothers said.

Anna pursed her lips for Ming and Helen to intervene, but her brothers silenced any effort. They were fierce, relentless in their argument. Plus, it started making sense. Anna could control the blistering she might have this time if she'd start the rinses as soon as she felt the slightest tingle. Anna admitted she'd been so defeated from the mouth pain that she hadn't bothered to use the other medicine.

"I'm not saying you don't have a choice. Of course this is your body." Michael's voice softened slightly without losing any purposefulness. Then he went mushy, full-on baby talk. "But come on, my big sister, I need you. Pretty please. Even one more month."

Helen carried in spoons and bowls of yogurt. Anna worked to swallow. In solidarity they all ate slowly.

Anna agreed. A month. A month and then reevaluate. It was easier to agree.

"But it's my choice," she whispered, struggling to enunciate. "You each need to hear. From now on. It's my choice."

The Percent

When Kate left the room, Anna said, "She's perfect for Reuben."

It was funny, except Anna wasn't trying to

be funny.

"I'm serious. I thought it the first time she came to the house to discuss my care. She's rambling on about hospice, and I'm thinking, 'You can marry Reuben.' She's pretty. Really pretty and kind. And doesn't she look a little like me?"

"She's cute," Ming agreed. "And she's got green eyes like you." Ming was ready to go along with anything, delighted to see that Anna wasn't done being her quick, outrageous self.

"I told Reuben that he has my ninety-nine-percent approval."

"Is he ready to be married off to your nurse?" Ming just wanted to keep joking around with her.

"Oh, poor Reuben. He tries so hard not to do what I say. But kicking and fighting, Reuben winds up seeing I'm right."

Twitch
Anna moved her head, scanning the room to find Helen. Everything took effort. She was looking for Helen. There she was. With Reuben. The two of them seated at the table. Helen's head tilted, her cheek smashed against Reuben's shoulder. Reuben talking and Helen crying.

Come back to me, Anna thought, surprised to find the muscle of possessiveness still twitching.

But whom did she want back more? Anna wasn't sure.

A Catch

Reuben had tried a little to date in the years after he and Anna separated. But it always went the same way. Maybe there would be a good first date. And then, on the second date, perhaps after a dusk cross-country ski, at a promisingly low-lit restaurant, he'd hear the dull tenor of his own voice as he explained his circumstance. It was *his* medical insurance for starters. Who could blame a woman for hurrying through the meal, for saying that she admired him, his loyalty, but that it couldn't work for her? Check, please. He wouldn't date himself.

Lifeline

Caroline recognized the exhaustion carved on Reuben's face as Helen hunched close to him. She should go help. Give him the we're-both-long-suffering-caregivers clandestine handshake. But staying clear of Reuben was the nicest thing Caroline could do. Less talk. She knew he couldn't afford to lower his guard. So let him tuck down and polish the kitchen like some kind of neat-freak psycho. He couldn't admit he might actually even be glad this was going to come to an end. Sure, "chronic" might sound hopeful to Helen. But Caroline knew what "chronic" really meant. She knew, firsthand, what it took. What it had taken from Reuben. However scared she'd been anytime Elise had an episode or went missing, didn't she half wish for that worst call? Shit, she had to admit this at least to herself: she admired Anna's determination to have an end. And to call the shots.

Reuben was putting up with Helen, but Caroline saw he just wanted to scour the sink or do anything that had a result. Cleaning, joking, shopping, knitting — there wasn't a caregiver Caroline had met who didn't have some fallback, to get through the slog of it, find a way to cope. If any of it could be called coping.

It wasn't that Caroline found any of her sister's breaks actually funny. But what was the choice? Had there ever been a choice, an official sign-on for being her big sister's caregiver? It had happened. Slowly. It had taken years for her to realize that it wasn't isolated episodes, that her vibrant, wonderful sister wasn't having a temporary life glitch but an illness. And just when Caroline thought she could rest back into whatever she called regular life, Elise would blow off meds and be found wandering barefoot — more likely naked — in Toronto. Toronto if Caroline was lucky. Elise had a penchant for faraway places. You had to give it to her for exotic and expensive. Funny — not really. Not funny the steady erosion of Caroline's beautiful sister, her childhood idol. Lost teeth, drug bloat, group homes, loops of paranoid thought, loops of grandiose thought, caseworkers, unpaid-for apartments, collect calls, weeks with no calls. But it made for good stories. Caroline knew her friends let her have that. Because what was the other option? Whining? Sounding like one of those long-suffering, insufferable family members who spent days online, creating chat-room friendships with family members of what was these days called a "person with emotional challenges?" Or a "neurodiverse" person. When exactly while Caroline was taking care of Elise did good old "nutcase" or "certifiable" become verboten?

"Helen." Caroline might as well throw Reuben a momentary lifeline.

Helen didn't look up. She was deep into her rant.

"Helen." Caroline pressed in, practically wedging herself inside the grip Helen had on Reuben's arm. "Anna's asked if you'd bring her a glass of ice water."

The Vow

Cut it out, Helen, Reuben felt like calling over as he watched Helen slide onto the love seat and lift Anna's legs onto her lap. Helen touched and talked, no doubt making her selfish plea for medicine. She'd gone at him, and now he could only guess what she was saying to Anna. Helen could not be counted on. Anna predicted it, and now, Reuben understood, she was right. Always good at picking her allies. Maybe not the battles, but definitely the allies.

What did Helen think? That Reuben was having a jolly time with hospice? Till death do us part. He was the one who'd taken that vow. And whatever had happened in between, including all these years living apart in this unmarried-married, uncertain state, he could be counted on. Anna knew this. He thought back to their wedding. Anna's face upturned to him. Pretty, pretty face. The flower garland crowning her long wavy hair. Twenty-five years old. They'd held hands and made promises. For a marriage. What a hopeful word "marriage" is. They were just children. What could a child know, promising, as they promised, adventure and joy. Who could imagine the uncertainty that became a marriage? There was his girl, Anna, on a couch. Always his girl. He'd led her into the woods one night into a circle of silver branches. He'd offered her the secret of those woods. Only her.

Marriage

Once, just after the separation, Anna said that if she couldn't make it work with Reuben, if they couldn't reconcile, maybe she'd go lesbian. "I obviously like being around women a lot more than men."

"I'll marry him if you don't want him anymore," Helen countered when Anna complained.

"You've just forgotten how annoying a husband can be."

Anna then was in the first flush of separation. Happy not to have fights. Happy to stay up late and not have Reuben ask when was she coming to bed. She'd been gigging and recording with the band. Every suggested caution bounced off her.

"But only a waist-up lesbian," she announced.

"Oh, you'll be real popular," Molly said. "Belle of the dyke ball."

Tic-Tac-Toe

Molly heard laughter even through the closed sliding glass door. She looked into the room, but first there was her own reflection and through her reflection the friends gathered inside, Helen scooting close to Anna with a glass of water.

More and more these days, accidentally catching her own reflection, it was her mother's angled face Molly saw, and with a flush of anger she'd quickly duck away. This mother Molly had worked hard never to become. Years ago, after school, she'd walk through the kitchen door uncertain which mother she'd even find. Mother of sprinkle cookies still warm or mother slumped off the ladder-back chair, drunk, asleep in piss on the linoleum floor. Or, worse, she'd find her mother awake, a hurl of vicious, slurry questions. She'd been accused and accused. "You slut!" her mother screamed before Molly had ever even kissed or been kissed. "You'll lose all that pretty!" Her mother filled the juice glass with sherry. "I should know." Then her mother wrinkled her nose and drained the tumbler as if its contents were bitter medicine.

Now Molly watched her friends inside. These friends who knew her so well didn't know. Never knew. Or never knew the extent. Caroline stopped sleeping over. But Caroline never really knew. Not about the bottles tucked behind ironed pillowcases in the linen closet. Not about the force of her mother's fist or the day her mother came at her with a paring knife. She had washed puke from her mother's face, changed her mother out of another soiled dress. This was the storm inside. Outside the house, her mother barely existed. Outside the house, boys talked softly and wanted to touch Molly's long hair. And once Anna had kissed her. "I wish I were you. Everyone wants to be you," Anna had said, her mouth moving again to Molly's. Later that afternoon Molly had driven alone through town. The light on the trees glowed pink. The roads were blue. Finally she forced herself to go home.

"You're late." Her mother was at the kitchen table. The overhead lights off. Even in shadow Molly could see her mother. Churlish, furious. And drunk.

"For what?" Usually she didn't say a word, since every word was the wrong one. But that evening her mother's sour breath couldn't hurt her. She brushed past her mother. Kept from actually pushing her. Tonight she wouldn't be afraid to see her mother stumble. Maybe hit her head. But even more, she'd wanted to get upstairs.

Wanted to call Anna. "Caretaker," she'd coo conspiratorially. Everyone wanted to be Molly, Anna had said. Molly was the wild girl, and everyone wanted a taste of her. But Molly had seen her mother's lined face, the wreck her mother slurred that she was doomed to become. If no one knew about her mother, she'd never become her mother.

I just want this to be our secret, Anna had said that day, and Molly felt ashamed. Sometimes Molly was certain her own daughters felt her old damage, her mother's hand smacking her skull against the floor. That she carried the rancid odor of her mother's vomit. Her mother now a withered, sober, old woman she couldn't forgive. Over my dead body.

She looked through herself at her friends. Inside, Helen was whispering to Anna. All the things they'd all confided, pinkie-sworn to secrecy. They were all a tic-tac-toe of secrets. All the beautiful confidences of friends who promised to tell one another everything. Then there were their shames. All that they could never tell.

Serena was wrong. Molly's silence with Anna's choice was not an insult to the men who died for lack of medicine. This was a choice beyond medicine. A measure of what Anna could accept as a life.

Serena could push. So could Helen. But Molly's acceptance, her silence with Anna, was her love.

I Remember

Here was Helen's moment. "I need you, Anna, at my wedding."

Instead Helen said, "Do you remember that hopeless summer when I wanted to follow Lucien back to Toronto? You kept me from going."

She needed to believe that Anna knew where the conversation was going, because *her* Anna would look up and say, What is it, Heli? Get to the point. Don't bore me with building your case.

Or her Anna would say, Lucien the addict from Toronto. Yes, that beautiful muscled back made up for his pathetic personality. Not to mention the coke.

Or her Anna would say, Lucien was another serious waste of your life. And, thank God, you learned nothing from that mistake.

Or her Anna would say, I knew as soon as I saw you today. Asa wants to marry you.

Instead Anna murmured, "I remember."

"You've saved me from so many mistakes," Helen began.

That was the understatement of the century. But Anna knew what she meant. The spindle of Anna's leg under Helen's hands, so breakably delicate that Helen almost couldn't speak as she concentrated her fingertips along where the tendons knit against the bone.

"Anna," she tried again. She was ready to tell her, to bargain for Anna to stay alive.

But Anna had slipped into sleep.

Hospital 101

Late in the evenings, when the unit quieted to hums and beeps, the stuck wheel of the blood-pressure cart, Anna had walked the hallways. From his mother's room, Asa watched. Then one evening he joined her.

"Do you mind?" he asked. They walked slowly together.

"You probably shouldn't walk with me. I might be the Grim Reaper," Asa said. His wife four years before. Now his mother.

They were staring at the vending machine as if some new option might have been added since they'd studied it on the prior lap.

"I'm over all of this." He pushed two buttons, and a granola bar dropped. He was over how quickly he slipped right back into mapping the hospital unit, figuring out which resident to step around. Or how he

81

made sure to befriend the cleaning staff, who, amazed to be acknowledged, let alone saluted with Asa's "Morning, Captain," slipped in extra bags of lemon swabs when his mother suffered from mouth blisters. The good nurse. The idiot nurse. All the effort. Still, the multitudes of incompetence. He'd learned to press hard on Thursday. The Friday-noon dread that now nothing important happened until Monday.

They'd circled again to the vending machine.

"Want to know how much time is too much time in hospitals?" With his eyes shut, Asa incanted line by line the exact order and names of the snacks and candy bars.

"That's quite the party trick. No one should ever know this about you," Anna said, and started walking another lap. "Given my life expectancy, your secret's still pretty safe."

Well, She Was

"I can't get anything here." Caroline wandered the periphery of the living room, holding out her phone as if it were a Geiger counter. A moment before, in some surge of connectivity, there were eight texts from one of her kids. Not completely decipherable, but something was up. Caroline needed to get hold of Danny and learn exactly what was what. Hopefully, it was crisis averted. Danny could handle kid shenanigans. Though why exactly were they still managing any shenanigans when the very last college bill had already been paid? Wasn't there a clause in the parent job description that said *basta, finito,* finished, task accomplished? That at some point Caroline might actually stop feeling that she's steering. Still, there'd been a kid texting and retexting: MOM. CALL.

There was also a text indicating that a new Serious Situation loomed on a short horizon with Elise.

It seemed she was always in one situation while managing another. Not this or that, but this and this. Always calibrating what needed the most attention.

Still, she had to admit — even a little — that a Home Crisis or a new Sister Situation was momentary relief from the way the skin on Anna's arm sagged and folded on itself with no muscle left. Who wouldn't want to avert her gaze? At least Caroline was skilled in caring for her kids and her sister. Here, with Anna, there was nothing she could do. Just be present. That was almost funny — wanting to be entirely present for unbearable sorrow. It seemed pretty lame.

"I can't get anything." Caroline held up her phone but stopped — mid-room, mid-sentence — at the sight of Molly curled close to Anna, the two of them tucked into a conversation that seemed private. So private they didn't even look up, and now Caroline was stuck foolishly in the middle of the room waving her cell phone. She felt a flush of childish uncertainty — uncertain if the normal thing to do would be to plop down next to them and fold into their conversation. Or would she be intruding, breaking up their intimacy? There it was. All the old awkwardness. The odd girl out. Even now, after so many years, Caroline couldn't switch off the itchy worry. Where she fit in the group. Really? She checked herself. How petty it turned out — over and over again — she was.

She looked down at her phone and angled purposefully toward the back of the room. *The Old Friends.* Whatever they called themselves, there was always a pecking order. Pretty pathetic considering the circumstance. If she felt a little displaced, maybe she was to blame. All those years she'd basically checked out. Still, always, even now, when she knew it was she who had moved to the periphery, it was that feeling of having been replaced. Early on, she'd had Molly. They'd pledged the whole best-friend thing. They'd walked to school together as soon as they were allowed to walk alone to school. Then there were matching orange Sting-Ray bikes with sparkly banana seats. Afternoons they practiced popping wheelies. Caroline pulled off a half spin. Then, after the summer between seventh and eighth grades, Molly came back from camp and everything was different. It wasn't just those startling breasts. "I know, it's like hello, Inflate-a-Boobs!" Molly said when Caroline looked kind of gaga. Breasts were old news; Caroline had started wearing her bra in seventh. But with Molly it was different. She looked dangerous. And not just her body. Molly's pretty strawberry curls had tangled into a sun-streaked mane. And everywhere Caroline and Molly went, boys showed up. Whatever Molly wore — it could be her baggy overalls — she looked like Ginger from *Gilligan's Island* in a tight evening gown. And Caroline was that side-kick, Mary Ann. But less cheery. It wasn't just the stupid boys from their grade. What scared Caroline was high-school boys. They had cars. They took Molly out on dates. God, even Caroline's dad said something about Molly growing into quite a beauty, and Caroline's mother laughed and told him, "You keep those wolfish eyes to yourself." It was disgusting. Caroline invented reasons to permanently shift their regular Friday sleepover to Molly's house. Then, by ninth grade — certainly tenth grade — those sleepovers pretty much stopped. Molly stopped inviting her over. Which was terrible but also kind of okay, because she found Molly's house and Molly's mom a little scary. If Caroline shrugged off trailing behind Molly and the flocks of stunned and drooling boys, Anna and Ming seemed thrilled to be close to all of Molly's heat. Though they never excluded Caroline or Helen. Helen seemed actually okay on the sidelines, showing up to get Anna out of trouble. But Caroline wasn't okay. She felt anxious around Molly. Forget the show-off boys swerving in their fathers' cars, Led Zeppelin's "Stairway to Heaven" cranked, just watching Molly dump out a film canister to clean seeds and sticks from pot made Caroline anxious. "It's all cool," Molly said, looking up through the perfect fringe of her lioness hair. None of it was cool for Caroline. Not the way Molly tossed that hair at the end of every sentence. Not when Molly lifted her Minnie Mouse T-shirt to show off the twenty hickeys that Jeff Thomas had given her, ten to a breast, and Anna squealed, "That's amazing!" Amazing? It looked gross. Gross like a disease Molly might not recover from. Then Caroline learned that Molly and Anna were bringing boys to the Farm. Anna and Molly described a Saturday evening they'd partied at the Farm. Somebody shook red capsules out of a tennis-ball can, and Anna woke to a boy touching her, and she described the effort it took, the slow taffy drift up to make her mouth and tongue work together, "Please stop." Caroline said, "That's horrible," but Anna and Molly shrugged it off, saying, "Caroline, we're fine." But Caroline wasn't sure anything was fine. She wanted to declare they couldn't bring other people to the Farm. The Farm was Caroline's special place, one she'd shared with her closest friends. She'd shown them the break in the fence, the pine forest, the rose garden. The Farm was sacred. Their sacred place. She wanted to say they weren't allowed to smoke pot or do stupid things and practically get raped. But she knew it was ridiculous. It wasn't Caroline's anything. They were all trespassing. Really, she just wanted her friends back. She wanted Molly back. Caroline missed Friday nights playing

Parcheesi and Monopoly. Eating ice cream directly from the pint containers. Forget board games, Molly, Anna, and Ming had concocted dumb-ass fake IDs and extolled the virtues of vodka-and-Kahlúa drinks. Why wasn't Helen worried when she heard about the night the three of them got wasted on Singapore Slings? She dismissed it. "Yeah, they're idiots, but they sure make it sound fun." Wasn't Helen even a little jealous that Anna was always off with Molly, basking in Molly's golden heat? Helen argued that friendship wasn't monogamous, it wasn't predicated on or affirmed by who you hang out with most. But Caroline thought that sounded like a tagline from a consciousness-raising pamphlet. Or Ram Dass's *Be Here Now*. Wasn't actually the whole point of a best friend — of wearing those stupid necklaces Helen and Anna had given each other with their names engraved on either side of the silver disk — that it was exclusive, that a best friend came first? Finally Caroline screwed up the courage and told Molly she seemed like a wobbly roller coaster about to derail. That she, Caroline, was scared just watching Molly. How many boys had she already done it with? And now she's sixteen and dating a college guy? What about that sounded like a good idea? Wasn't this part of being best friends? Not just treating Molly like she was some new Marilyn Monroe. Molly smiled her assured smile and snuggled into Caroline's neck. Even her voice was a purr. "You're my nervous Nellie. That's why I love you. But relax. I'm just having a little fun before we turn into our parents." Caroline never made a big declaration. She didn't have to. She just started staying home.

Years later at the Bengal Tiger, over Helen's spring break, she told Caroline that Molly had a girlfriend.

Caroline held a forkful of saag paneer midway to her stunned, open mouth. "As in lesbian?"

"Yup, as in totally, completely lesbo." Helen sounded so easy with what Caroline was having trouble wrapping her mind around.

"But wait?" Caroline said. "She didn't cut off all that beautiful hair?"

Helen's abrupt laugh blew out the votive candle on their cloth-covered table.

"I'm tempted to tell you she's gone all butch with a crew cut, a biker jacket, and a trucker wallet. But Molly's still her long-haired self. She's still her same gorgeous, irresistible Molly. She just likes women."

How long had it been since Caroline had seen Molly? More than three years. What else had changed in her friend? Things had certainly changed in Caroline's life. Molly didn't even know about Elise's psychotic break. Or Caroline's subsequent panic attacks. Caroline dropped out of school, waking anxious and hiding out in her parents' home. As if Elise's break were contagious. She spent three years helping Elise and waiting for her own crack-up. She'd just begun driving again. She'd even driven Helen to dinner.

"Would Molly think it was weird if I called?"

"Oh, my God, call her. Please."

She missed Molly. She wouldn't have been embarrassed in front of Molly. Molly might have called her a nervous Nellie, but she'd have said it with love. She could see how Molly would wrinkle her nose and say, Don't worry, you've never been at all like Elise. You're really normal. This is just a temporary bout of weirdness. She missed Molly, and she missed being a part of the larger group, which she learned from Helen still hung out together, even traveling to get to know one another's college friends. She'd given up the solidity of this. For what? Even if Molly's changes had scared Caroline back in high school, now Caroline understood that they were all changing all the time. That was a given. The beauty of these friends was just that — they actually wanted to stay with one another through all the changes.

"Are you sure Molly won't think my call's too late?"

"We'd all be thrilled, because Molly would finally shut up about how hurt she is that you abandoned her for being a raging teenage slut."

"Well, she was." Caroline gave her best shoulder shimmy.

"Oh, she still is. But now she's a madly-in-love lesbian slut."

Caroline looked at her phone, the icon circling as it tried to connect. The screen said ICE. Danny was her "In Case of Emergency." Not even his name on the screen, just ICE. She wanted to hear his voice. Needed it. She'd been able to stay steady because Danny was so solid. She wasn't that same panicked girl she'd been, partly because Danny was a rock. He called her his wild thing, and compared to him she *was* a little wild. Her friends called Danny the good man. Good man sounded boring. Her life still sounded boring compared to the others'. But it was Molly who said that Caroline had to stop caring what things sounded like.

"It keeps failing," she said to no one now. Caroline pressed REDIAL. She felt a thickening and constriction in her throat.

"Try the porch." Helen came close, rubbing her own phone like a rabbit's foot. "I got bars."

The Old Friends

Nothing went unnoticed.

What are you doing?

You don't even wear lipstick!

That's the exact shag haircut you had in tenth grade.

Only now gray streaks instead of that Sun In bleach catastrophe.

You couldn't get away with anything. Which was, of course, horrible and the very best thing about having been friends forever.

1976, Acid

"Save us," Anna says, climbing barefoot into Helen's car. "We're in a full-blown nightmare." The whole drive back to Helen's house, Anna and Ming alternating in breathless thanking Helen for saving them, for being a really good person and actually a perfect friend, and really, "Thank you, you saved us," until Helen says shut up or she'd kick their barefoot tripping asses onto Hastings Road.

They'd taken the hits with plans to wander to the Farm and be there by the time the acid kicked in. The girls all call it the Farm, but it was really an estate, not exactly abandoned but the stone mansion unlived in for years, a few pieces of furniture sheet-draped and a caretaker left to manage the grounds. The Farm was behind Caroline's house. She'd shown them the break in a back fence. It was a magical place in the middle of their town of tidy lawns. A pond, a rose garden gone wild, and a maze of rocks and flowering shrubs. But beyond the derelict formal gardens, the land went wilder, high grasses unmowed, blackberry tangles, and a pine forest with a soft, needled floor. The girls make a show of hiding from the caretaker, but they know he watches them. He seems not to care that they act like the place is theirs.

For Ming and Anna, tripping at the Farm on a gorgeous day had seemed like a perfect plan. Pretty much perfectly thought out, pretty much a guarantee for a magical experience. But after they'd dropped, Ming's father had had one of his Chinese conniptions, claiming Ming had no sense of family priorities. He yelled that she behaved like every foolish American girl. No honor for parents. No respect. All the yelling meant that Ming was to stay in and clean her room and take a verbal practice section of the college exam. And then, because she'd not obeyed with instant politeness, she needed to continue with additional house chores. Mostly Anna stayed put, hiding in Ming's room tripping her brains out until Ming had done the final obeisance, which involved kneeling before her father and asking forgiveness.

"Forgive me, Papa." Ming demonstrates, kneeling on Helen's kitchen floor and kissing Helen's fingers. "I am not a worthy daughter."

Helen practically wets her pants as Ming describes vacuuming her bedroom with Anna curled on the bed terrified of getting sucked into the hose like a piece of lint.

"It wasn't funny," Anna says. "None of it's funny." But it *is* funny Helen insists, especially when Ming admits she scored her highest on the practice test, particularly on the analogy section, which, despite swearing she'll never ever trip again, makes it something to consider.

Helen spreads blankets out in the backyard. "It's not the Farm, but hey." Helen's parents are away for the weekend, so, as she declares, everything's copacetic. The girls sprawl on blankets watching wind tousle the high crown of trees in the yard. Except for the trails Ming and Anna describe tracing their hands in the air, Helen's pretty much keeping pace with their descriptions of shadow and light playing through the trees.

"You're like a natural high!" Anna shouts when Helen instructs them to squint and see how the tree arbor shimmers like a glittery web. And it's Helen who finds three ladybugs in the grass, their mystical insect doubles.

"Promise me." Anna rises up on her elbows to stare hard at Helen. "You don't need to do this. I don't want you to ever trip."

Helen gives Anna her fiercest glare. Followed by the finger. Because — fuck you, she has no interest in taking acid. Fuck you — Anna knows that. Fuck you — right now, right here — even with Ming and Anna in their simpering state pledging to never do a drug again, it looks like fun, and — a final major fuck-you — why should Helen always be the one who does the saving?

Press

She'd known all day. One look at Helen and Anna knew. Anna saw her friend in the cream-colored dress, the lily of the valley tied with rough twine to hold in her paint-stained hands. Helen looking at Asa, who looked back at Helen. I do. I do. This would happen. In early-evening light, the achingly crisp summer light. Anna knew all this, and she knew, too, that Helen wanted to tell Anna, here, right now. Anna, I need to tell you something before I tell the others, she might begin. Or, Anna, I have a secret you'll like. Instead, pressing thumbs along the arch of Anna's left foot, Helen stalled, waiting for some exact moment that might have pivot. Was it that she imagined that it would be enough to stir Anna, that Anna couldn't resist wanting to be there with Helen when she had been with Helen for practically everything new that had ever mattered in their lives? Or Helen waited because she was scared it wouldn't matter. Not the light. Not the slight pooling fabric at the back hem. Smell these, Anna, lily of the valley, our favorites! But there was something more. Oh, there it was. Helen wants forgiveness. This unfolding newness, this hopeful wanting when Anna has stopped wanting. Helen wants forgiveness for wanting a

96

future. Helen's fingers circled tentatively along the tendons and bones of Anna's foot. Oh, it was true they had both loved lily of the valley, the tiny white bell and the wide green leaves like a girl's spring dress. Go have your new, Anna thought, and closed her eyes. There was only one secret that mattered, and she turned again to the child of her child that she had begun seeing in her mind.

Lesson
They were talking, but mostly just watching Anna sleep. Ming started to shake. Molly linked her arm under Ming's and guided her out of the room before the deep, guttural racking began.

Hospital 101
Asa found it beyond annoying that Anna's room was always packed with visitors, and beyond beyond annoying was how hard the visitors worked to keep everything upbeat, then huddled somberly outside her room hanging on every word of the on-call doctor. As if he actually knew anything.

Asa came in at night to read the newspaper and share a Kit Kat bar.

"I've had an idea for you," Anna said.

"You've got way too much time on your

hands. You clearly have to do something with your life."

He was glad for her delighted yelp. Any dose of dark humor was better than all the treacly concern he heard from her visitors.

"You need to meet my Helen."

"That's the geeky tall one who naps with you?" Asa's chair was pulled bedside, his boots wedged up against the metal rungs.

"Wow, and you think *I* have too much time? Yeah, she's my oldest best friend and your future wife."

Asa couldn't understand why it was so hard for people to understand he wasn't looking for a new wife, let alone a girlfriend. His friends, out-of-nowhere high-school classmates, the parents of his children's friends — all had suggestions. Yesterday his mother's surgeon actually handed him her niece's phone number. Young, old, American, Argentinean, with offspring or dusty-egged — everyone had *the* great lady for him.

And now Anna.

"Thanks, but I hang around oncology to prey on the terminally ill. Excellent for one-night stands."

"That's grief talking. Wait till you meet my Helen."

"You're wrong, Anna. You don't know

me." He tore open the wrapper, bit into the center of the candy bar.

"Actually, I really do, Asa. Which is why I'm allowing you to have a chance with my best friend."

What

Something else in the fridge had gone bad. Hopefully the taped-up NO MORE FOOD sign meant this was Reuben's final, full-on excavation to figure out what needed tossing. It falls on him. This and the mortgage, every electric bill and house repair. Note to self: need a quote on the porch decking. He was the go-to guy. Conversations with Kate from hospice. Every two seconds family, friends checking in, "What's the plan?"

And their children. It didn't matter that the children were not children. They were *their* children. Anna and Reuben told the three of them together. First all those years ago. And then two weekends ago — has it been only two? — Reuben looked right through the etch of panic on each of their faces and said, "We all need to agree. This is Mom's choice."

Now ten times a day, "What's happening now, Dad?"

"Okay, enough. Each of you tell me something," Anna insisted that Saturday after they'd all had a massive family cry. "Some-thing good about your lives, your work. Let's just have no more big feelings for a little bit," she'd said.

Reuben was amazed how the kids com-plied, perched on their chairs like school-children eagerly reporting on projects. Ju-lian, their first, blushed as he quoted the famous food critic who'd written not only that Julian's restaurant was stellar but that he was Vermont's Alice Waters. The twins waited till Julian finished describing the new plans he had for the restaurant. Then Andy was overflowing, excitedly describing the commission he'd landed. "It's huge, Mom." A couple's house on the Oregon coast. Their Boston town house. "Mom, these people, they're crazy rich. Rich and with taste. I'm not just building all the furniture for the two residences — I've been hired to do all the interior wood design and restoration for both houses. I'm busy with this project for four years at the least."

"I'm good, too, Mom," Harper started, then crumpled like she'd suddenly been gut-punched. But when Reuben put his arm around her, Harper straightened up and pushed him away.

"I'm good," she tried again. She gripped her fists in her lap. She was a nurse, first year on the NICU. Harper described a baby born at twenty-six weeks who'd finally gone home with his parents. After three months. "We threw him a good-bye party," she said. "His name's Nino, but we all call him Hercules."

"Hercules." Anna laughed. "That's quite a wonderful name. What about you?" And she turned to Reuben.

His first sound was more a grunt of air than words. He'd been holding his breath while the kids spoke. He mumbled something about starting his indoor seedlings — peas, onions, and tomatoes.

"Every year you love getting the garden started." Anna smiled, keeping him steady and bolstered for the children.

Now Reuben opened the freezer door. More food. Packed in. Wrapped, labeled. Eggplant parm. Broccoli and mushroom quiche. It's there to soothe everyone else. Today, tomorrow, even after, it will get eaten.

Then, out of nowhere the other day, Anna told him he should marry Kate. "You've definitely noticed her," Anna teased. "I know your taste."

"Wow, now here's an excellent line," he shot back. " 'My dying wife thinks I should date you.' " He was taking apart the four-poster bed. She'd refused the hospital bed until she could no longer refuse. "I'm a real catch, Anna," he said.

"You *are* a catch, Reuben. You're my only regret," Anna said. "I should never have let us separate."

"Please, we both screwed up."

Still, it felt good to hear Anna say, "I abandoned you first."

How sorry and petty a thing was vindication. The ice trays needed filling.

2

Assessment
"You've done well, Anna."

The doctor's broad fingers were light on her wrist. Her eyes took in the rail on the mechanical bed. The gray plastic commode in the corner.

"I wish I'd done better."

Prayer
Someone had ringed the house in prayer flags.

Jesus.

"This kind of nonsense makes Anna want to puke," Helen said.

"Forget puke," Molly said. "It's made her want to die."

"And now I understand why," said Helen.

All the women laughed so hard they could barely catch a breath. Bundled close to one another, they moved in a pod toward where sunlight quilted on the ground.

"Who's done this?" Molly demanded. They stood halfway up the long drive, looking back at the dark-stained house. Colorful handmade flags were strung along the A-frame roofline. Embroidered and painted words of encouragement. A Rumi poem stitched across two joined flags.

"It's these local women." Helen spun in a circle as if she'd catch an intruder. "The hospice, these flags. It's basically all their fault."

"Helen, you've certifiably flipped." Ming was laughing so hard she could barely speak.

Caroline managed, "No, Ming, now we understand. Helen's right. They're killing her, New Age style. Alert the authorities."

"Officer, Officer!" Molly waved her arms.

"I'm going to pee my pants," Helen squealed. "You've got to stop."

"Kegel, woman, Kegel," Molly commanded. They couldn't stop. The quips and puns. Laughing, leaning on each other for support. They couldn't bear to stop. Halfway up the hill, the four women looked back at the decorated house where Anna had asked to be alone with Reuben and the doctor.

More

"Of course," the doctor said. "We can try that, Anna."

The doctor, John, biked with Reuben on weekends when the weather was warm. His wife, Connie, was one of Anna's closest local friends. They lived two roads over. Through the years John had been called for any number of middle-of-the-night emergencies. He'd risen from bed, Connie calling after him, "Tell her I'll be by in the morning to get the kids for school."

But when he was in the room with Anna, John always stayed the doctor she needed him to be.

Now, this afternoon, she'd asked him to try to turn off her device.

"What if the pacemaker keeps shocking me back as my heart slows?" Anna said.

Reuben stayed at the bottom of the mattress, his knee doing its bouncy thing, steadying himself. It steadied her.

"Defibrillator," John corrected her, and explained again that Anna had an implanted combination defib and pacemaker. The pacemaker, he explained, should stay on. It would keep her comfortable. But the defibrillator could be deactivated. Yes, it might shock the heart as it slowed. John wanted her to know that not all doctors agreed on the necessity of turning off a defib. Or if it even actually slowed things down.

"I want it off." Again she said that she was afraid not of the end but of getting to the end.

"I'm not sure I can today." He didn't have the correct communicating device for an ICD. He held up a ceramic device that housed a magnet. "This might work," he explained. "Or I'll get the right one from a cardiac friend."

Floorboards creaked out in the living room. Hadn't Reuben asked everyone else to leave the house? Take a walk. Yesterday when he opened the bedroom door, two local women squinted at him, guarding Anna's old marital complaints. "She wants you in there?" But there was no one out there today.

Still, when Reuben sat back on the bed, he said, "Man, they went to Taser me," just to hear Anna laugh.

"Let's try." She shoved herself up in the bed. Took measure of what she knew.

John held a ceramic device to her chest. She couldn't breathe. Pushed his hand away. Her mouth grabbing for air. Panic then. She waved her hands. "No, no. I can't."

When she quieted, she said, "I think I just got scared."

"The whole point of hospice is to keep you comfortable. I'm not sure this needs to be done at all."

"I should try again."

"No rush, Anna. It's not a contest." He knew that Connie would be glad to hear it hadn't worked. His wife kept reminding him that Anna was impatient. "She doesn't want time," Connie said to him this morning. "But I need time."

"You're wrong about the rush," Anna insisted now.

"Turning it off isn't going to really speed this up."

"I have children. Their lives need to move forward. It's not right, this dragging on and on." She asked for more. More drip. Morphine under the tongue. More of whatever made it all faster.

"There'll be more of everything as you need it. I'll get the defib part turned off in a few days if that's what you want. But I want to keep your arrhythmia smoothed by leaving the pacemaker on. It can get uncomfortable. And that's not what we want, Anna."

He wouldn't tell Connie that he could

have made it work. Could have turned it off today. Taping the magnet over the implanted device would have done the trick, at least temporarily. It was used in emergency situations. But he couldn't bear the look he'd have seen on Connie's face when he went home. He'd do it, eventually, like he promised Anna. He was a doctor. But he was also Connie's husband.

Anna held John's hand, which still cupped the magnet. "You know what I want, John. It's not really about comfort. I need your help."

Done
And she was done with fear.

a) All that nattering, constant interior conversation she couldn't banish — gone.
b) All the effort not to let on to others that fear was always there, a gauze between her and the vivid rest of her life.
c) That the fear was way more present than the rest of her life.
d) Done with the terrible shame that her body had betrayed her, had harbored rogue cells, allowed killers to hide out in her heart.
e) Might right at this moment be begin-

ning a new round of unfaithfulness.

Oregon

"I'm going to need more help," Anna said as soon as she'd sent Reuben out for a glass of water. "You need to help me." She fixed on John, widening her green eyes. Tilt of her shoulder. Using all her tricks. Flirting her way right to the end. Had to give her that.

"I can't do it, Anna." He could pretend he didn't know what she was talking about. But he did.

"John, you know you can't resist me," Anna vamped. Always been a looker. She'd used it well, openly and without consequence. Tragic now, this twist of gaunt and swollen, her blinking eyes popped more bulgy than she'd ever care to know.

"Not allowed. Not in Massachusetts."

"Do you feel that's right, John?"

"It doesn't matter what I feel. It's the law, Anna."

"Can we pretend this is Oregon?"

"Sure." John played right back. Had to give it to her, she was quick, always an original. But he'd been through enough of these conversations to believe she wasn't as certain as she sounded.

"We won't tell anybody." Anna grinned,

satisfied. "Not Reuben, not Connie."

"You'll have to ask me again in fifteen days."

"No." She swiveled, her face reset from coy to resolute. "I'm ready now. Or after the weekend. When the kids leave."

"But we're playing Oregon, right?" John pulled his case up onto his lap. It was an old-fashioned doctor's bag. Most of his colleagues had long ago switched out to more casual instrument-rigged backpacks. But John found it comforting, calming his hands along the worn leather skin.

"In Oregon there's a first oral request, then a fifteen-day hold till the patient can make a second oral request. Then comes the written request."

Anna flipped John the bird. Waggled her finger for emphasis.

"What did I miss?" Reuben backed through the door. "What's going on?" He stood by the bed balancing three glasses of water in his hands, looking between Anna and John to figure out what weird vibe was ricocheting through the room.

"Just your lovely Anna trying to seduce me and break my sacred vows yet again," John said, blowing her a kiss.

Reuben handed John a glass and clinked an imaginary toast, "Does this mean it's a full-on swap and I can move on my twenty-year infatuation with Connie?" Reuben said, winking at Anna.

The Secret

"Stay," Anna said after John took up his leather bag and left the bedroom.

Reuben flopped into the armchair across from her.

"I just want to be quiet. For a bit. I love my friends, but they're —"

"Exhausting, annoying, morose," Reuben interrupted. "Take your pick."

They could finish each other's sentences. Since they were nineteen. They loved that. The private language of the marriage. Even if often they used it against each other.

"What happened with John?"

"Forget it. That was useless."

Then Anna smiled. That lopsided smile. He knew that look. Her secret smile. Sly and smug. He knew all her expressions.

"What?"

"Someone told me something." She wiggled her lips. "And it's pretty much the greatest thing. Ever."

"What? What do you know?" When she did that lip wiggle, it meant she was on the edge of telling, that she was dying to tell him.

"That it's wonderful. It's a beautiful surprise."

"At least tell me who it has to do with."

"For me to know and you to find out."

"You're a major asshole." He could tease any secret out of her. "You'll die an asshole."

"Yes I will. You'll know that terrible and brutal truth. But everyone else will claim that I was perfect."

1978, All You Girls

"This better not be what's happening," Anna says without looking up from the clipboard. Helen watches her flip a page; she's writing furiously, as if she has so much she needs to fit in the small spaces. The waiting room couldn't be bleaker. Orange plastic bucket chairs, mustard walls, green carpet — each color choice, Helen decides, is uniquely bad, the mix beyond terrible. On the walls are metal-framed prints of paintings, the colors soft, the light diffuse. Impressionism. A Degas dancer. A Mary Cassatt. All meant, no doubt, to create a calming effect. Psych 101 meets art history 101. Notably, she thinks, not one of Cassatt's mother-and-child paintings.

"At least it will be both of us." Then Helen quick-checks "No" to a long list of medical

111

problems she never wants to have.

"That's not a good outcome." Anna scowls as if Helen hasn't really understood where they are. As if Helen thinks this is like when they wore matching dresses in middle school. Obviously Anna's right. Both of them are late with their periods. Obviously it's better if neither tests positive. But second best, Helen thinks, is that they're both pregnant. That way what they face, they face together.

Other than the two of them, the office is empty of clients. There's only the dour woman behind the glass partition who snaps up both clipboards when Helen slides them under the gap. She tries to keep unbroken eye contact with the woman. Helen hopes in a glance to convey that she has a steady boyfriend, that she uses birth control. That she's not embarrassed to be in this office. Truth is, it makes her feel grown up. Like at the end of her junior year of college, she's finally, almost, caught up with Anna.

"I know I am," Anna says after the bloods are drawn and they're both fidgeting, back in the scooped plastic chairs. "I really feel different." She starts to cry. Anna's coiled down in her seat, so that Helen has to force her own hand between Anna's squinched legs to hold her hand.

"Me, too," Helen says. But sitting there, she's afraid she feels too much like herself. She presses her palms to her breasts, testing for telltale soreness. Are her breasts more sore than any month's soreness? Isn't her period regularly irregular?

Helen gestures to a Seurat print of bustled women strolling in the park. "They've got the preggers bump backward in the picture."

"It's all fine, Reuben," Anna announces later when she calls to tell him. "I mean, it's fine for me. We were lucky. It's Helen. She's scheduled for Friday." Anna's voice drops as if signaling to Reuben she doesn't have the privacy she needs. "No, they'd broken up. He's an idiot. . . . Of course. . . . Obviously. I'll take her. I've gotta get off, Heli's a mess. . . . Sure, I'll tell her."

Anna hangs up the phone and falls back on Helen's bed. "Reuben says he's really sorry."

"You're sure about this?"

"Of course I am. You don't understand. We've got this all worked out. We graduate, work for a year, maybe two, he goes back to school, and after that we start our family. Our first at twenty-seven. Twenty-eight the latest. It's ridiculous how much time we

113

spend talking about our babies. I can't bear us both being heartbroken."

Anna sounds so confident. Not at all teary. And Helen hears in her tone that mix of determination and denial that allows her to convince anyone of practically anything. Even herself.

"But telling him it's me?"

"Well, I needed a reason he couldn't come down."

"Come on, Anna, it gets so complicated. It's a lot of lies. Shouldn't Reuben know?"

"You don't get this. He can't. It would wreck everything. Forever. Either way."

Anna rolls away, yanking the comforter over her head. She's crying now. There's some relief hearing waves of sobs come up from the blanket. But when Helen puts her hand on Anna's back, she squiggles away from Helen's touch, her body in a clutch at the edge of the twin bed. Helen wishes it actually had been her. To spare Anna. But also because it's always Anna to whom things happen first. And as wrong as it is, Helen thinks it would feel weirdly good to be the focus of the drama. To be hysterically crying. Or stoic. But it's not her, and Helen isn't sure what to do. Push Anna to come clean? The whole festering-lie thing can't be good. Should she even open up the larger question?

But with Anna it's best to stay quiet. But stay. That's what works for them. Let Anna know that above all else Helen's right there for her. Anna will unravel whatever knot she's twisted inside. She always does. Then she'll be ready for talk.

But when the phone rings and it's Reuben telling Helen how sorry he is but that he's glad she has Anna, she lowers her voice to sound quietly devastated. "You know I'd do the same for her."

This is how it will be. She will lie for Anna. She will do whatever Anna needs her to do.

Anna takes the phone, then sits with her back to Helen, her feet dangling off the bed.

"Yes, I've been crying." Anna's tone is terse. Almost contemptuous. "Helen's a wreck. What do you expect? We both are. . . . No. No. You can't come down. There's nothing you can do. It would make everything harder. I need to be there for Helen."

Helen knows that Reuben will also do exactly what Anna says, because part of loving Anna is being bossed around by her.

Helen listens while Anna unwinds a plan to Reuben. The appointment is scheduled for Friday. That part's true, but from there the confabulation begins. And it's elaborate.

When did Anna come up with this plan? Without even a momentary hesitation. Helen learns that after her procedure she and Anna are leaving for Nantucket. To find summer jobs. Something they'd apparently been talking for months about wanting to do. And Ming's offered to drive them to the ferry. They don't have jobs, but they have a friend waitressing at some fancy hotel, the White Elephant, where the staff are given rooms. She's said it's cool for them to sleep on her floor while they figure it all out. They'll probably wind up working right there at the hotel. There's a lot of turnover. When they're settled with jobs and a place to stay, then Reuben can come. For a weekend.

"Come on," Anna says to Reuben, "how sexy will that be? Me changing sheets and scrubbing shower stalls? It will be great.

"That's ridiculous," Anna dismisses, already an expert. Helen understands that Reuben is suggesting that traveling on the same day sounds a little dangerous.

"There's nothing risky. God, this isn't like a back-alley thing. I've got to go deal with Helen."

On Friday, Helen sits with Anna in the pre-procedure meeting. "I'm the family-planning counselor," the woman says, speaking so slowly that Helen wonders if she believes English is not their first language. Helen thinks there should be two counselors — the family-planning and family-unplanning counselor.

The counselor works a kind and neutral expression as she asks questions. "Yes," Anna says, her voice opaque and distant. This is necessary. What she needs to do. Yes, she's considered alternatives. Yes, she has a boyfriend and she's spoken with him. Yes, they use birth control. Yes, she knows how to insert the diaphragm. Yes, she knows to reapply the jelly each time.

The counselor leans toward Anna in what wants to be an empathic gesture but seems oddly threatening as she describes how the morning will unfold.

"But I need her with me," Anna says, grabbing Helen's arm.

"She isn't allowed in the room," the counselor repeats. "I'm sorry." Her eyes narrow in a firm but compassionate way. It reeks of practice. Reeks of training sessions with role-playing — women crying, hanging on to boyfriends and mothers, and counselors learning to show firm friendliness.

"Please," Anna pleads while the woman continues the description of the aspiration and termination.

"There will be a nurse with you the whole time. Your friend will be right outside in the waiting room. She'll join you in recovery. We just have to take care of the fee, and then we shall move forward. I know you're anxious."

Anna starts to argue, then looks up helpless, digs into her leather bag, and takes out her checkbook.

The counselor taps a line with her finger on the paper Anna has in front of her. "Only cash."

"I don't have cash." Anna's voice cracks. "I have checks."

The counselor remains quiet, just her finger moving to underline the bold type.

"It's okay, Anna," Helen says. "I'll go to the bank while you're inside."

Helen's struck by how familiar the world is outside the clinic. It should somehow be different. The light dramatic. Or dark even in daytime. But the world is the same world. And she's driving, the way she always drives. Cars have not stopped because her best friend is back in a room with a nurse holding her hand. Out here the clinic doesn't exist. The lights go red. Then green. Helen presses smoothly on the gas pedal.

She drives effortlessly. Turn signal. Speed limit. Everything lawful. Her hands spin the wheel for a right onto Woodward Avenue. There's the school and then the public golf course. Just where they always are. In the distance white golf carts and men bent over clubs on the green expanse. A normal day in early July. Men hitting tiny white balls into holes. How is it that the ordinary continues? Even this thought, this small revelation, is not a new one for Helen. She's always been astonished at how the exceptional barely announces itself. In art history she learned that even this revelation is not exceptional. That was Brueghel's observation as Icarus falls. Then she is passing Sacred Heart, where as a little girl she accompanied Rosie, her Irish babysitter. What was the story she learned about Rosie? That when her mother sought help from the parish priest, he frowned bitterly, practically spit, "Those girls come over and right away they're pregnant." What happened to Rosie? Where did she go? Did she have the baby? Helen wishes she could ask her mother. All this braiding through her mind while driving toward the bank and all the time trying, too, to stay in tune with Anna, as if she's really sitting in that clinic waiting room ready to be called into the recovery room.

She imagines Anna on a table. The electrical thrum of the vacuum aspirator that the counselor described.

Helen angles her car into a parking space. Bolts into the bank. This will take two seconds, to withdraw two hundred dollars. It's going fine. It's all going to be fine.

Except then it isn't fine. And the whole normal-day charade crumples when Helen sees Anna's father, Mr. Spark, on the bank line. Three in front of her. It's impossible. She's never run into Mr. Spark. Not ever. Not once. But here he is. She's not sure what to do. Should she leave and hide in her car until he's out of the bank?

"Well, hello, Helen." A lifted question of surprise in Mr. Spark's voice.

"Helen? Where's Anna?" he says. "Didn't you girls leave for Nantucket?"

Now the world is not ordinary. Not at all. And the utter recklessness presses down on Helen. *Where's Anna?* The question echoes through her body. It feels like she's being offered an opportunity to fess up. *Where's Anna?* I've left your daughter. *Where's Anna?* She's having an abortion while I stand on a bank line talking with you. *Where's Anna?* I wasn't pregnant, and she was, and I was going to take care of her, and I didn't even have the wherewithal to

120

read that we needed cash, not a check. Is this the moment to confess? Didn't she do that once with Rosie, go into the wooden box at Sacred Heart. "I'm not Catholic," she whispered when the priest asked if she had sinned.

"Anna's with Ming." Helen marvels at how coolly she's tossed off the lie. The lie feels so good it almost doesn't feel like a lie. "I had to cash a check so I'd have money for our trip."

"All you girls, everything last-minute." Mr. Spark shakes his head. "And I think of you, Helen, as the responsible one of you kids. Jesus. Just don't miss the ferry."

And

It was Mikey — thank God, finally — Anna's younger brother, on the house phone.

"Oh, Michael." Helen took the phone into the bathroom and leaned against the shut wooden door. "It's me, Helen. I need you here. Everyone's drunk the hospice Kool-Aid. But you're sane. She can't resist you. Or Bobby." She said it all in one great rush. Just having Michael on the phone made her feel hopeful.

"She's not budging, Helen."

"We made her budge before." Helen

waited. Her breath huffed loud against Michael's silence. His too-long silence.

"Michael," she pushed. "We did it before. Really, it was you and Bobby last time. She'd do anything for you."

"Stop it, Helen." His voice cut sharp, almost shouting.

But when Helen backed down — "I'm sorry" — there was an even heavier silence before Michael spoke, and then as if each word dragged a lead weight behind it.

"I tried. I pulled out all the stops. I told her I was in the middle of training for the Boston Marathon. That I had a super-demanding life. Balancing my job, training, and the family schedule. But I'd put everything on the back burner if she'd give it a go. That medicine still worked. That there were new ones."

"And?"

"But if she said no, then I was finished. Done. I told her I wasn't coming back."

"And?" Helen edged around the small bathroom. Folded each bath towel in three and rehung them on the bar. She fiddled the toothbrushes so they were slotted straight. There was nothing left to tidy.

"She said neither was she. Coming back. Maybe we were both done and both of us had to make choices that were right for ourselves. She said we could say good-bye now."

"And?"

"I'm coming this weekend, Helen. Bringing the kids. I'll save my long runs for the dirt roads between Leverett and Montague."

"And?" Helen leaned on the sink. Her scowl in the mirror looked unintimidating. She tried winching her brows toward menacing.

"Finally, it's her life. I don't have to like it. I give up. Or at least I'm trying to."

"You give up? She just gets to choose this? What about us?"

"You tell me, Helen. What about us?"

"I don't know, Mikey. Exactly why did you even call?"

The New Frontier

Forget remission. The new model was chronicity. The doctor said, "We are the cutting edge." The doctor said, "By the next flare, we'll be miles past even this novel drug. There's always a panel of new possibilities. There's so much we have yet to deploy. The medicines are artisanal. The horizon is far beyond trials." The doctor said, "It's a new frontier. It's all moving fast. Supersonic."

1969, Honorary Girls

Helen paints flowers in Day-Glo orange, hot pink, and lime à la Peter Max when Anna's parents give the girls the okay to transform their attic into a clubhouse. The five girls take turns posing against walls until they each have an outline to fill with colorful swirls, peace signs. Quotes from *The Giving Tree* and Beatle lyrics float in puffy painted clouds. When Anna's brothers, Bobby and Mikey, clump-clump up the narrow staircase, the girls can't bring themselves to shout, "Keep out!" The boys flatten against an unpainted swatch of wall. "Paint us." Who can resist Mikey's chocolate-chip eyes? Or the way Bobby begs, "Me, too, me, too"?

"You'll be in our girl club. But only honorary," Anna announces after the girls huddle for their first vote.

In the House

There was only the house. Anything past the porch or, at the farthest stretch, beyond the driveway, gone. Like something half remembered. A once-upon-a-time. Gone the new pope. Gone the president's second term. The Higgs boson, gone. Even a six-car pileup on the highway twenty miles south in Springfield. "Oh, that's terrible," they would have said if it had occurred to anyone in the house to turn on the news. But there was no news. The world steeply fell away. The morning news, the headline lost. No big world. Even their lives at home tapered to a few images. Just Anna.

<h1 style="text-align:center">3</h1>

Leverett, Fruit Tree

Connie stood calf-deep in the dug dirt of her side yard. This was a two-person job. She was flat-out idiotic to take it on alone. But John was at the hospital. Then he was checking in on Anna. He'd asked Connie to wait with the tree; they'd do it over the weekend. If she was worried about keeping the bare roots in the bucket, he suggested digging a shallow trench to temporarily heel in the tree. Anyway, he reminded her, there was a good chance of rain tonight, freezing rain.

But it was going in today. Had to be. She had the time. She'd been all but banished from Anna's by Helen last night on the phone. "We're coming up to spend the night," Helen said. "We'd love to be alone with her."

So Connie had nothing but time. No trench. No heeling-in. She wasn't taking a chance of killing the tree. She needed this second pear tree for the trees to cross-pollinate and begin bearing fruit. She was getting this pear properly in the ground. And that was going to be the real trick. Not digging this serious hole. But hefting the tree, keeping it upright and not listing to one side while she filled the hole back in.

There was an impressive hill of sod loosely mounded around the hole. Her fingers were numb. She'd ditched the work gloves. Useless. They were John's and kept slipping off. Blisters or not, she needed a grip on the spade's T-handle. The hole needed to double in size. At the very least. The width also had to double for the root ball to fit. And really, to be realistic, wider for tree roots to establish.

The good part was that digging curbed her mind. Narrowed the straggly, ugly thoughts. She was like a one-woman chain gang of repetitive phrases that mimicked the shovel. She was pissed. She wasn't really used to being pissed off. Not part of her emotional arsenal — hurt, guilt, insecurity, yeah, plenty of those three. She'd pretty much terraced and landscaped their yard — lilacs, dogwoods, a rose trellis, the perennial and herb gardens, and her meditation rock garden with its spiral stone paths — just managing that trio of negativity. But this morning she'd woken trembling. She actually thought she had a fever until she realized it was pissed-off fury.

She jammed the shovel. Fuck. Tossed a scatter of dirt. Fuck. Jammed again. She never cursed. Pried out a rock. Lobbed it. Fuck. Fuck. Fuck. Connie was a cursing fool. It worked for digging, that's for sure. Anna was always a mad curser. The crassest things came out of Anna's mouth. Shocking as it was for Connie in the first years getting to know Anna, over the years it became something she treasured. She could just see Anna's satisfied smirk: I knew I'd drag you over to the naughty side. But how would Anna like knowing Connie was shoveling dirt to the rhythm of *Fuck The Old Friends, fuck The Old Friends*? God, Connie hated that smug title. And what about that smug tone in Helen's voice last night: "Connie, can you also let the others know? The Old Friends are coming up. We'd love our time with Anna." Then, as if that bullshit weren't enough, there was the condescending, "I hope you know, Connie, we really appreciate everything the new friends have been doing."

"Sure, Helen," she'd said. "It will be good for Anna to have you with her."

Now knee-deep in a hole, Connie had no shortage of other responses. From an emphatic phone slamming — Fuck you, Helen — to a cooler-toned jab: Actually, Helen, here's the deal. Whatever you love and appreciate doesn't mean anything. Anna isn't interested in time alone with anyone, not even her own kids or brothers. So get off your high best-friend horse that says showing up here with your old-friend gang is going to brighten her day.

The blade struck, a metal vibration twingeing through her arm. It jolted up her neck. She leaned over and wedged out a small boulder. Heaved it. Struck rock again. Gardening in this valley, you really had to respect the old farmers and their stone walls.

Maybe she should simply have said, That's twenty years of new friend, Helen. That would be twenty years of soccer carpool, riding-practice carpool, Wednesday- and Friday-morning speed walks and showing up anytime at each other's back door when we needed a break from kids or husbands or just needed to show each other the new suede boots we'd splurged on, and then, when our kids were all off at college and we'd go out to dinners midweek, first because we were free and didn't have to cook and then because it was actually sad not to have kids to cook for, and oh, there was weekly driving to Springfield for chemo infusions or sitting on a chair while she was in the tube for MRIs or her seeing me through foot surgery and my breast scare or any of the other every-single-day things that Anna and I did together for the last twenty years of being new fucking friends.

The sky loomed low, bruised. Weather was coming in sooner than later. Her hands were beyond numb. Stinging needles. Connie could smell the storm. A half-dug hole filled with rainwater would be useless. Great. So fuck John, too, for being right. And for that other thing he'd said while eating his morning oatmeal, raisins, and nuts. He'd looked up at Connie and said, "It's a pear tree. Not your dear Anna. You can't make this better."

Connie knew too much. Always had. She was the doctor's wife; she was Anna's friend. Anna hadn't been a good patient. Skipped appointments, checkups, ignored months of post-stem-cell quarantine. Infection be damned, Connie knew that Anna couldn't abide the way friends looked wearing surgical masks. The double loyalties put Connie in an awful position. She knew that even with a high fever Anna had played two gigs. Had gone back to teaching when doctors had insisted she had no immune system. Connie forced John to make house calls and pretend he was just coming over to play Scrabble. When other friends asked her how Anna was doing, Connie had to sort through two camps of privileged information.

Connie threw down the spade. She wiped sweat from her face and felt the grime from her hands stick to her skin. Her lips had a sandy coating.

"Make it better." That was the other thing Helen said. "Connie, I'm worried you all have too easily accepted the choice for hospice. Anna needs resistance."

Maybe that was the thing that pissed Connie off most. As if Helen could possibly know what she, Connie, felt or accepted.

She crouched, trying to fit herself in the hole. "Fuck!" She screamed it out loud. Breathed in dirt. She closed her eyes and screamed again. She heard a car door slam, the scuffle of leaves. Probably John between patients scrambling home to help. She didn't want his help. She squinted up to the bulked shape of a woman's down parka. Even backlit, she knew it was Layla.

"What's going on?" Layla worked to sound unfazed by the mud-caked sight of her. Thank God for Layla.

"Gardening." Connie stood. She climbed, one big step, then another, out of the hole.

"Need help?"

Connie stormed past Layla and jammed the spade against the shed door. She tugged John's gloves out of her back pocket and clapped them till there was no more dirt. Pinned them between the spade and the shed side. She dragged the bucket with the pear tree and tilted it in through the shed door.

"Need help?"

"I've got to wash off. Then I need help. We're going over to Anna's. I made her rice pudding. I want to see her today. I don't care who's visiting and wants time alone when Anna doesn't give a flying fuck about being alone with any of us anymore."

The New Friends

They watched a car turn down the driveway. What the hell? Then a second car. Twenty-four hours alone with Anna, that's all Helen had asked. Again and again, over the phone, Helen had said how appreciative she was of Connie, of all Anna's new friends.

"You called them new friends?" Caroline sneered. Had Helen actually used that phrase? Caroline looked like her old judgmental self.

"I don't know. Probably." Backing away from the window so they couldn't be seen, Molly, Caroline, Ming, and Helen watched Marsha get out of a Jeep parked by the trash shed. Layla and Connie emerged from the other car.

"New compared to us," Ming defended. "It's a fact. It's not Helen's fault."

They watched as the Valley women took bowls and more bags from cars. Then clustered by Layla's van deep in animated conversation.

"I'll tell them to leave." Helen knew she wouldn't tell them to leave. Caroline was right. Nothing *new* about the Valley friends. They'd been Anna's everyday friends for twenty years. More than that, they were Anna's front line. Now, *that* was a terrible phrase, "front line." The whole illness-as-battle imagery — pathetic, trite. Worse, like tick medicine you'd put on a dog's nape. Call it whatever you want, Helen had noticed the sign-up chart tacked on the wall in the kitchen. It was Layla, Connie, Marsha, A.G., Pamela. Other names Helen didn't even recognize, who were scheduled for sleepovers midweek, when Anna's children and brothers went home to their families and jobs. These women were here every day.

Helen would be here these twenty-four hours. Then she would drive home to Asa and the life they were beginning.

Helen opened the kitchen door and waved. "Anna's up and festive." Then she shouted, "It's a party! Come join!"

Caroline slid behind Helen, resting her chin on Helen's shoulder. "You're a terrible bodyguard, tiger."

Local

"Hey, beautiful." Layla twirled a lock of Anna's dark hair. "I see you're happy to have your girls visiting."

"They've made me feel pretty good." Anna squinted, apologetic.

The Valley

Reuben and Anna had lived in the Valley almost twenty years. The Pioneer Valley, that seam of Massachusetts farmland that stretches along the Connecticut River, with long tobacco sheds on floodplains, then the steep uplift into wooded ravines, traprock ridges, basalt and iron, and winding, narrow roads carving through forests until opening onto hill towns with craft-goods shops and farmers' markets. The schools were great. Friday potlucks with music.

Kids catching frogs. Everyone belonged to a co-op. Everyone had gatherings. Reuben grew vegetables in raised beds, kale in hoop tunnels all year long. Anna was invited to play in a cover band. She sang in local pubs with another woman also named Anna. A bumper sticker on every car. Everyone was anti-something.

"We've found just the right community for us," Anna announced to Helen after the first full year.

"Isn't it all a little self-righteously alternative and precious?" Helen countered, though when Anna said, "Well, hello, Miss Mainstream USA," she quickly confessed she was plain old jealous. Every woman Anna met sounded ridiculously cool. Every mom in the Valley was a weaver or an herbalist or a children's-book writer.

"You have a different walking partner every morning." Helen couldn't believe just how poutish she sounded. "I feel eclipsed."

"But I show off to them by bragging about you," Anna said. "It's not everyone whose best friend has a painting in every major museum in the world."

Old and New

Look, look, how the room was practically a party! Now it's a party, Anna thinks. Draped

134

on the arms of chairs and sofas, women in clusters, sparks of conversations. Ming and Layla. Molly and Connie, a do-si-do of her women friends. Not only her dearest Layla and Connie. There's Marsha, Pamela, and A.G. Here's Betsy, who, with Anna, started the middle-school math center. She's dropped by with a card made by the art teacher and signed by all the middle-school teachers. And there's a manila envelope stuffed with cards that students have made. Here's Jeanie, the eighth-grade social-studies teacher, kneeling before Anna. "It's ancient Chinese medicine," she says, holding out a potted pink orchid. Anna watches Helen drag in the painted dining-room chairs. Connie and Caroline pass bowls of rice pudding. Extra holiday folding chairs stored in the hall closet unfold. Everyone claims she's only staying a minute. A.G.'s positioned behind Anna on the couch, fingers tapping along Anna's temple.

Was this actually some tribal chant issuing from A.G.?

Then Susie, the up-the-hill neighbor, arrives with a platter of warm sugar cookies. "I've brought your name to my church circle," Susie says, leaning in and placing her palm on Anna's forehead. "There's energy in silent communal prayer."

During the sick-and-well-and-sick-again yo-yo, Anna tolerated prayers and chants, any nonsense that her Valley friends insisted helped with healing. She didn't want to hurt anyone's feelings, but she never believed in any of it. Not smudge sticks or mantras. Not focused meditations. Not prayer circles. But she'd believed in her friends. She loved A.G.'s support even if it included dragging in Native chants she had no business singing. And Anna knew she was better for the hours spent on the porch with her closest friends, Connie and Layla. Always so much to talk about with them. Wednesdays and Fridays she speed-walked with Connie, Tuesdays with Layla. It was well known that Anna didn't answer the phone, so the Valley women took to dropping by. When she couldn't walk, they'd show up at her door in sneakers. The Friday Craft and Wine formed in Anna's living room. They gossiped, drank, and glued shell boxes. Belly laughing — there was medical proof it made you well. Sometimes they sang. How many afternoons, a blanket bundling her and two pillows wedged to cushion all her bony jutting, had she closed her eyes and listened to the good sound of friends talking?

She had collected all these women. Like all the beautiful things in her living room.

Friends and beauty, Anna had wanted more than more. More friendship. More talk. She was like that silly song about the new and the old. Sometimes she'd felt herself insatiable. But now, as the room buzzes, everyone trying to press close, everyone trying so hard, all the meaningful long looks, there's nothing she needs. She doesn't need the dear friends. She doesn't need the room with its cathedral ceilings and thick wooden beams. Or the beautiful antique chandelier she'd found in a shop that sold mostly lace dresses. "Not for sale," the shopkeeper declared. "It will cost you an arm and a leg." Anna carried home the chandelier, telling Reuben a softer price tag. "Come on, Reuben, that's what makes it beautiful," she scolded when he asked how she planned to clean the murky and scratched lead crystals.

The chandelier, the dear friends — she has so little need of any of that now. All that loving, what had it accrued? And that bowl of starfish from Point Reyes — there'd been hundreds she and Reuben had come upon on the beach, collecting them in a baseball hat. She had moved those starfish from house to house, carefully unwrapping them so that not an arm broke. Now she can't understand why they hadn't left them on the sand.

She sees how everyone tries to keep the room bright and festive. The lustrous silver and gold of them. She sees fear on all the faces. But she's not frightened. She's finally free of the looping dread. Now she will stop eating. When she was alone with the nurse, she begged the woman to help her die. "I can't," the nurse said. "It's not legal. But you can stop eating. It will move things along. That's a choice you can make." Yes, she will stop. Now, here is the party. She will keep this a party. After tonight she knows she won't make it out to this living room again.

Dog
Ming stood in the doorway. "Are you out there, Zeus?"

The Other World
A car bomb that rocked Mogadishu. A bailout. A tumbling market. The traded accusations of Syrian government and rebel. The president spoke. Officials scrambled. The wounded. The killed. The mountain slipped down. Mud slid over sleeping families late Saturday morning, fifty miles north of Seattle. Violence flared in Myanmar. Refugees attacked in a Pakistani camp.

The news, the only news, was whether

Anna had eaten, was she speaking, what had the hospice nurse said.

That March, for the Record
President Chávez of Venezuela died. Amanda Knox's acquittal was overturned. Malala Yousafzai went back to school. Poachers killed eighty-six elephants in Chad. A Virginia marine base shooting resulted in three dead.

Friday Craft and Wine
Last Friday when the group convened, Marsha asked Anna in what way they could be most useful. Connie was knitting the second sleeve of a sweater Anna had begun in January. Anna lay on the love seat wrapped in one of her kids' old Scout sleeping bags. She wasn't napping, but her eyes were closed. It was time, Anna said, for them to take away the bead box, the collage papers, and all the other craft tools. "I'm done making new things," she said.

"That's not what I meant," Marsha said.

Layla gave Marsha an are-you-joking sneer.

"I'm sorry. But you asked," Anna said. "Take all the stuff when you leave."

"But that's too hard to do," said Marsha.

Steady

"Doing okay?" Caroline stood behind Reuben. She couldn't help herself. Her caretaker neurons were firing.

"Haven't you learned that's a worthless question?" Reuben, cross-legged on the stool at the kitchen counter, a stack of envelopes, the checkbook ledger open.

"That A.G. seems to be chanting." Caroline slung her arms around Reuben, and he leaned back into her but kept working in a frenzy, attacking the paperwork, his breath practically aerobic.

"Don't get me started," he said.

Caroline thrilled to get him started, to get that throaty growl out of Reuben.

"And listen, the neighbor lady, Susie, announced she's convened her church prayer group and they're working day and night for Anna's soul to go to heaven. So just stop believing you're the only one taking care of serious things, big guy."

Cadence

Every hug, every concerned look. Caroline's wrapping her arms around him and treating him like a sad sack. It was pathetic. He felt pathetic. A pathetic, sad sack. He sounded like a whiny guy. With a stupid to-do list.

Reuben wanted it over. Not Anna dead.

140

Jesus, he wasn't a complete asshole. But he wanted this dying to end. Wanted his life back. Was that terrible? Even this morning when he'd cleared time to get out on his bike, he'd spent most of the fifty miles humping the gravelly shoulder thinking about what he had to get back to and get done. He'd kept a brisk cadence on the brutal climb up Hilman Road. He pushed hard. Into the hill. Into the cut of wind. The metal blade of freezing air sliced down his throat. His quads powering. Every muscle in his legs twitching. Interval training. Wanted to push harder. Wanted to be lost in the sheer physical insistence. The azure blue of sky. The glacial boulders piled in the woods. But he couldn't get out of his thick head. Dug in on the pedals. Spun up the tempo. A brighter cadence. Tried to find that zone, that rush of the physical. He loved that rush. Loved it biking, clipped in, that joined power of pedal and foot. Loved it heli-skiing. Loved it years ago when he'd surprised Anna with skydiving. Back on the ground after their first static dives, she'd thrown her arms around him. "I've found my match."

Hell, being with Anna was a rush.

Or a shit storm.

Anna wanted it over, too. It was Anna who

kept asking for ways to speed it up. The pacemaker. What the hospice nurse, Kate, mentioned about not eating. Sometimes it seemed he and Anna were the only ones who were clear-eyed. Everyone else tiptoed through rooms. Or Ming burst into tears and hurried out of rooms. Or Helen in a fury, on the verge of hysteria. Last weekend Anna's brothers arrived revved up about some new experimental treatment. It took the whole weekend for them to understand they had no traction with Anna. The kids' upset was rough, but he'd cut them every slack.

Only he and Anna knew fully what the others partly knew. They'd lived all of it. The initial onset. Three A.M. fevers and the ambulance stuck in a snowbank. The code blue. Then her trudge back to health. And after, Anna insane to be alive. Frantic to make up for all the lost months. Staying up all night. Crisscrossing the state to play every gig and then getting up in the morning to go teach math. She was selfish and thirsty. For everything. Who could blame her? He blamed her. She had nothing for him. Pushed him away. Then another recurrence, and she needed him. If they were tenuous before the illness, it broke them. It made getting back together or moving apart equally impossible. He saw that now.

But now, oddly, it was Anna and him. It would surprise everyone that after the friends left, after her brothers with their unraveled sorrow staggered out, she'd ask him to stay. She could say anything to him. She could be nasty with him. He didn't flinch. However extreme. She counted on him for that.

She'd tried so hard with everyone. But not Reuben. She never tried with Reuben. Never had, that was part of the problem. But it was his gift to her now.

Tomorrow, after all the others had left, he'd sit in the chair by her bed and they'd sway from quiet to gossip. To quiet.

"So what was that bullshit of Helen's?" Reuben will say.

"I saw you caught that."

"And how do I get Ming to stop bawling?"

"Cut her slack, Reuben. Let her keep making soup."

"No, but —"

"Enough," Anna will snip. "Can't you ever let something be enough?"

She'll drift. Then startle — "No. No." Arms bunchy and twisting to fight something terrible off.

"Anna, it's okay."

"Oh, you're here? You stayed. Aren't we done with this yet?"

He'll tell her it will be done soon. He wasn't sure when. Soon. For both of them, he hoped he was right.

1982, the Valley

Once upon a time, before Anna and Reuben, Helen lived in the Valley, too. Just out of college, she'd stumbled into a sixty-five-dollar-a-month rental in a drafty farmhouse with four roommates. A painting studio nearby was another accidental story. Suffice it to say that life was dirt cheap in the middle of nowhere.

By February, Molly called crying that her girlfriend of two years had gone off to Chicago with an idiot finance guy. A room in Helen's house had unexpectedly opened. They hadn't begun interviewing potential roommates. Molly drove up the next week from Washington.

They lived that winter with plastic sheeting on the farmhouse windows, the thermostat turned down just to the point where the pipes couldn't freeze, and a woodstove that needed constant attention. One roommate played his stand-up bass till two in the morning and left cereal bowls stacked and crusty in the sink. Another roommate was a local organizer. Most nights a motley affinity group argued labor rights, making leaflets at the dining-room table. Helen could hardly justify feeling abandoned when, in June, Molly loaded up her car heading to Boston University's Ph.D. program in psychology. A generous research stipend and fellowship to boot.

Helen wanted to leave, but she had nowhere to go. Where else could she live on the paycheck from three afternoons teaching art in a school for troubled adolescents? She painted the woods and fields around the studio. In the summer she drove to Quabbin Reservoir to paint the shoreline. It was beautiful, but she kept thinking about the abandoned towns below the surface and the six thousand graves that had been relocated.

The following spring Anna and Reuben visited from California. They announced that they were getting married at the end of summer. They had the next five years planned out. Moving east, a wedding, starting right in on a family. "Finally she'll give me a baby." Reuben squeezed Anna close. Helen's stomach dropped as she watched Anna innocently looking up at Reuben.

Before they left, Helen took Anna and Reuben to the studio and asked them to pick out a wedding gift. Anna chose a large landscape from a new monoprint series where Helen worked over the prints with oil pastels and glazes. A field ablaze with ocher and crimson. Helen pointed to the field out the studio windows. "This is that."

Anna looked back and forth from the painting to the field, the tall grasses stalky and brittle from the winter, the browns dull and monochromatic.

"I love how twisted and mysterious you make a plain old field."

"I've got to get out of this old field or I'll be doing a full-on van Gogh, and it won't be pretty," Helen said.

Alternative Preparations

Marsha knew of a local death midwife, a deathwalker who worked energy, though rest assured it was gentle, nothing scary about it. A shaman called to offer an ancestral guide. The space needed clearing. There were residues of older sorrow in the room. The crystals that hung from the living-room windows needed washing. Dust clogged light, and that occluded the spirit. An altar was arranged with Anna's pearl earrings for wise emotion. Rose quartz for love.

The shamans, Marsha explained, differed from the Wiccans. That said, Wiccan perspectives were not all aligned — Norse differed from the Dianic, who differed from the Alexandrine and the Circle Sanctuary.

A.G. wanted everyone to draw next-life wish paintings in a copper bowl filled with sand.

The Friday Craft and Wine claimed that Anna's transiting spirit would be calmed by song.

Most of the Valley Jews were Ju-Bus or Bu-Jews and told Reuben they'd be reluctant at a gathering to recite the Shema or kaddish.

Anna's band offered to set up and rock the house.

Dog

Was that Zeus at the hill's crest, a dark, windswept mass hardly larger than a pile of leaves among the trees?

Princess

The band showed up. Big, clean scrubbed guys with day jobs — a carpenter, a tech guy, a gastroenterologist. The drummer, Jon, was a middle-school librarian. Jarrett, the lead guitar, handed Anna a CD he'd mixed.

"Hey, Princess," he said.

They all called her Princess.

The band wouldn't sit. Or couldn't. They hugged the walls. Kept their hands stuffed down in the pockets of work pants like they might break something. No thanks, each politely balked when Helen offered a drink.

Anna had been called Princess ever since that first night when she'd gone with Connie and Layla to what Layla had heard was a decent dance band playing the Shelburne Falls Grange.

"You're pretty good," Anna found herself telling the drummer and lead guitar during the first break, "but your band could use a little girl charm."

"And I thought being in a band would get me admired by women," the drummer joked. "So I suppose you sing?"

Before she could say no, that it wasn't what she'd meant, Connie jumped in. "Think Bonnie Raitt meets Phoebe Snow."

"She's got serious pipes," Layla added.

No matter then whatever Anna said to backtrack — that she didn't sing or she did sing but only acoustic harmonies with a woman friend — the band guys said, "Okay, then just get up with us and be charming."

Anna finally rose to their bait. "I'll be a hell of a lot more for you than charming."

Up onstage that first time, she was so nervous she wasn't sure she could get out one note, let alone charm. Then Jarrett, the lead guitarist, quietly said to her, "Okay, Princess, show us what big balls you've got." She howled, "You're on!" The music started, and when Anna reached for the micro-phone, she forgot she was basically a local math teacher and a mom. She forgot to be scared.

"How're the gigs coming?" Anna moved her gaze from one dopey-eyed, concerned guy to the next. Like something straight out of *The Wizard of Oz*.

"We're not gigging much."

They didn't lie well. There'd been a barn wedding in Colrain two weeks ago. They'd been hired to do all Grateful Dead.

"You know how that kind of night goes," Jon said.

"How's Theresa working out? Is she get-ting the parts down?"

"She's no you, Princess. That's for sure."

"Well, that's fucking lucky for you, ass-holes," Anna said. "Two dying singers and a band starts looking creepy."

The guys laughed. This was their Anna, rough-mouthed, a girl-guy kind of woman. No pity allowed. That was her only rule. She who came back, more than once — a blue wig and a black miniskirt — "Sugar Magnolia" sweet off her tongue. She made skinny-as-shit look hot.

"Give us the say-so, Princess, and Theresa's fucking toast," Jarrett said.

"Oh, you big jerk-offs, get with the program," Anna said. "There's no say-so for me to give. You're going to have to boner up for her like you all lust for me."

The men roared. She'd pay later for this much effort. But with these men Anna needed to make them feel good. To make it easy for them. She flirted, sometimes like an older sister, sometimes as if something could maybe happen in a snap if only everyone weren't so entirely married. Even in these odd, separated years with Reuben, Anna hadn't strayed. I love men, she told the band more than once. I just can't help that, ultimately, I love Reuben more.

"You should get some rest," Jarrett finally said. He looked like he needed to be tucked in for a nap. "We'll be back."

"No," Anna said. "Let's say the big goodbye now." She sounded downright cheerful.

They all shuffled up to her. The men were awkward and lumbering. She looked too breakable to kiss. But one by one the big guys leaned in and kissed Anna and said, "Later, Princess."

Lesson

This, Helen thought, this is what Anna will do. She will teach us all how to do this thing we don't know how to do.

4

The Hill

Helen and Reuben tramped up the back hill. The ground muddy and slick with ice crust. Their boots cracked through. Weak light splintered through the trees, laying down purple shadows like rhythm.

"I've wasted more time searching for a dog I never agreed to." Reuben pulled his wool cap over his ears. His curls tendriled out from the brim.

"He's Anna's. Always was."

"And I'm always out here hunting for him."

Cresting the hill, they stopped and looked out over the neighbor's field, still mostly glazed white. Scrubby tall grass poked through in bald patches where the snow had melted off. They stood for a long time in the quiet. Grasses stuttered with wind, but there was no sound of wind. The sky flat, milky, it looked like it might snow.

"Make her take medicine," Helen said finally.

"Why should she?" Reuben lifted his arm and pointed east. "Is that Zeus?"

"She'll listen to you."

"All I'm trying to do is listen to her now. Come on, Helen, isn't that what you've been telling me to do for years?"

"Not now."

"You really don't get it, Helen."

"What?"

Reuben whistled in three sharp blasts. The sound echoed, bent back across the open field. He put an arm around Helen, and her body gave way against him.

"You don't understand how impossible it's been. She puts on a good show for you when you call. Stopping is her choice."

Helen squirmed out of his hold. "She's also put on a good show for you."

They both turned and went back toward the lights of the house.

At the porch steps, Reuben stopped and told Helen what he'd held off telling her. Anna's wish.

Helen said, "No."

"You're going to refuse to lead her memorial? Really, Helen?"

He had no time for this. The memorial was just another thing to check off on his list of shit that had to get done.

"You're the one who should. She knows

it. I know it. You know it."

Helen grabbed the banister, then yanked back and picked out a splinter spiked in her palm.

"I'm staying outside till I find her damn dog."

Reuben started up the stairs.

"This porch is a wreck, Reuben. The whole place is falling apart. You really should take care of things."

Without stopping, without turning to look at Helen, before he slipped inside, Reuben called back, "Don't make it a big deal. Just do it."

Helen stood watching her breath. Silver bursts of breath. The whole place is falling apart. She'd sounded like a baby with Reuben. Nah-nah-nah-nah-nah. She'd had an impulse to go nastier. To have said the unsayable. You think you know her, Reuben. You think you know every last thing about her. Ask her about that summer. It was *her* pregnant. Not me.

"Hey, Zeus." She needed to put that practically feral teacup poodle on Anna's lap to ward off all the insane New Agers and their deities. Then say to Anna, You're not dumping out of this life with prayer flags festooning your house and a bunch of people chanting *om.*

Helen pushed faster through the pines she'd walked in with Reuben, up to the break, and continued beyond the scrub onto the open plain of the neighbor's land. She stormed through the field. Her body felt fierce. Like she could do anything with it. There were flurries, wet, icy clumps sticking on her face.

More than once when Helen's own mom was sick, she made Helen promise to speak at her funeral.

"Don't make it sugary," her mother warned. "I didn't have a sentimental life."

On the morning of the funeral, Helen had taken care dressing. She was twenty-two years old. She knew that was part of what her mother wanted. For her to look good, not as if she'd been up all night carrying on. She belted a navy silk dress she'd slipped from a hanger in her mother's closet and put on makeup from a drawer in her mother's bathroom. Correcting the smudge of a penciled lash line, she hated that her mother was right, that her mother knew she'd feel obliged to do it perfectly.

At the podium she found her friends in the back row. They looked terrified. Anna tried to smile encouragingly. But she wasn't even close. Later Helen imitated for her friends how, on the way to the cemetery, the rabbi had leaned close, whispering, "It's wrong to say under these circumstances, but I've never had anyone manage a room the way you did today. Extraordinary."

"He's right. You were." Anna couldn't shake the scared look. As if Helen had become someone different. Helen liked that Anna was impressed. Her mom had wanted her lady friends to be jealous of her composed daughter. The truth was, she'd been scared before she stood up. But standing in front of the room, she felt everything recede — her sadness, even her mother.

Now they were all the age her mother had been, and with each year Helen realized how young her mother had been.

The snow was driving hard. No horizon. The field and air dense and white. How would she paint both the seamless flatness and the impression of enclosing expanse? Pissarro's quiet snow on the road to Versailles, the brushwork visible strokes. Turner's snowstorm at sea, a turbulent, noisy whirl. Helen's old friend Arthur Cohen, who painted the Flatiron Building rising up out of the unplowed, snowy New York City streets. Monet's magpie on a wooden fence, alive with every kind of white. In all of those paintings, there was something — a bird, a woman walking, a horse and cart, the ship,

155

the city building — to mark a boundaryless world of snow. From here there was only field and sky, dark and snow-filled at once. Behind her the line of trees and behind the trees the woods down to the warmly lit house. How to paint the light that filtered up from the house? Helen knew she'd do whatever Anna asked.

Their Kitchen Window

"You're breaking up." Caroline heard Danny perfectly well. "You're breaking up." He repeated a version of what he'd been saying for the last umpteen minutes.

"I can't really hear you." Caroline leaned back in the Adirondack chair. It wasn't a full-blown lie. There was some static. She heard her own voice repeating. The branches of trees made an icy lattice overhead. The wood pressed damply through her jeans. The damp constricted through her. This grayness was enough for instant seasonal affective disorder. She watched her breath. There was nothing to say. She just didn't want to hang up and go back inside. She could see him. She knew he was talking to her while standing in their kitchen watching squirrels try to knock over the bird feeders. He was standing on one leg, the other foot scratching up his calf, his own funny yoga pose.

All Caroline wanted was to hear his voice as he repeated, "I've got it under control." She loved the sturdiness of their life. All that time she'd wasted embarrassed for everything she hadn't achieved. One panic attack and she'd fled the conservatory. Given up trying for a place on the stage. She'd hidden in her parents' home feeling broken, preparing for her life to become her sister's. Until she met Danny. And she'd been grateful for a straightforward suburban life. It had taken having children for her to start singing again. It had taken the children getting older for her to go back to college. Now she was considering a master's in counseling. Danny said with everything she'd learned taking care of Elise — from the hospital system to empathy versus practicality — she could practically run a psych ward.

"Are you still there?" Danny asked. "Have I lost you?" His voice was like bread crumbs on a path leading home.

"No, I'm all too here," Caroline said. "Tell me something good."

Seriously

Someone shouted, "Heli, Heli!" and Helen turned, trusting that Anna had run away from all the hubbub to join her in the snowy hush.

It was Layla. She labored across the field, trundling wide-legged in thick, furry boots, crunching heavily through the crusted ice. Then she was buckling into Helen's arms. Helen felt the trembling beneath layers of puffy down.

Helen tried to remember something about Layla. She and Connie were Anna's closest friends in the Valley. "My sanity duo," Anna called them. What had she recently told Helen about Layla? A new business? Something crafty, jewelry? Helen wasn't certain enough to ask.

"I'm looking for Zeus," Helen said. One side of her face was warm from Layla's crying, the other an icy sting of sleet. Each pelt a microscopic thud.

"Oh, God. He's been inside the whole time. He always hides out in her closet."

Always. Helen suddenly winded, betrayed by all the everyday things that Layla knew. She untangled and watched Layla swipe at her face with her jacket sleeve.

"She brags about you, you know," Layla said when she could speak. "Calls you her star." Her face was still a runny slick of snot, tears, and snow. "We've heard about every museum, every success."

"I need help, Layla." How many times was she going to need to ask?

The ice cut at their faces. Neither woman moved.

"I came out here with Anna the first time she lost hair," Layla said. "It was a perfect spring day. She started with a hairbrush and then her hands. It was everywhere. Clumps of her beautiful hair, tangled through the grasses."

Helen knew about that day from Anna.

Anna had never said that Layla had been with her in the field.

But now Layla had more. "The black hair against the green grass was brutal. The look of her, with these patchy places. But it was the sound, the sound Anna made, that was — I don't know how to describe it, Heli. Surreal."

Heli. There again, Anna's name for her.

Helen distinctly remembered Anna calling to tell her about her hair. Helen had been in the studio. Trying to meet two gallery deadlines. She kept painting, wearing ear-buds. Anna said she'd gone to the field to be all alone. Helen remembered Anna's insistence. "I went alone to the field behind the house. I had to be alone," she'd said.

Layla linked her arm with Helen's. Their nylon jackets scratched wetly.

"I won't fight her, Helen. I can't argue that getting sick every year is really a way to keep going. But that doesn't matter. You'll see. She's moved someplace far past us."

The sleet pelted Helen's face. Her cheeks bitten, raw.

"But I'm really going to need you, Heli. Anna's always said you're a rock. Will you be mine even a little?"

The slope back to the tree line was slick. Helen couldn't get traction. The soles of her sneakers were useless. Layla angled them up the hill, sidestepping. An arm hinged to keep Helen upright.

"You still think I'm the strong one to count on?" Helen shuffled, braced against Layla. "Maybe you should reconsider."

Dark Window

"You American girl now. No honor father." Anna imitated Ming's father's syntax. Ming had started the old story about their tripping fiasco and persuaded Anna to take over. The crowd hung on every word. Anna saw how happy her friends were as she talked.

Even with all these friends — more than

160

most people could manage or even want — she's had a loneliness. She feels it now. It had always been there. Certainly with Reuben, hadn't there been loneliness? She'd tried not to let her children see the hem of her loneliness, though they sensed it, the twins crawling into her lap holding her face between their baby hands. She tickled them and hid inside that delight. To be so loved and still feel the clutch of that ragged, tampered place. This was her shame. She couldn't be rid of it. Or wouldn't be rid of it. She clutched to hold it. This nub that often felt the truest part of her. Those secret hours curled small, shrimped into herself under the familiar blanket.

Maybe, always, that separation, that scratchy husk of loneliness was preparation for this. So she would not be frightened of leaving. She'd been frightened for so many years. And then she wasn't.

Helen slid open the porch door and, behind her, Layla. They ducked into the room, and Helen pushed the door closed. They were covered in weather. Ice hit the tall windows.

"I was so freaked." Anna worked to keep her voice bouncy. "I hid in Ming's room. But the bedspread was alive."

Her two dear friends, together. That was

good. Helen would be less lost with Layla.

Helen's lips were clenched. Look at me, Helen. Anna tilted her arms to show the wings of the dragonfly. Embroidered animals wandered over the red silk. She fanned her arms to imitate the emerald green dragonflies lifting to ensnare her. Her voice ran scales, glittery and excited, then plummeting gruffly as Ming's father like an ogre demanded more and more difficult tasks. Ming played along while Anna, in full-on faux Chinese, played the part of Ming's father commanding she kneel to honor him.

Helen gripped the door handle like she was on the verge of bolting again.

Look at me, Helen. Anna thought, She's punishing me. And there, again, her loneliness. A shadow that lingered until its presence became a comfort. Until there was less of her outer dark. Helen had been the easy friend, the good girl. She had an optimistic nature. That Helen had her own darkness always surprised Anna. The moody twist in her paintings. And there was Helen's spiral-down year. Men and drugs. Helen's recovery. Anna could never square how that was her good Helen.

Finally Helen smiled, and there it was — her friend's fury. Come to me, Anna thought, not because she needed Helen near to her. Not because there was anything she wanted to tell Helen. Not because she wanted to comfort or make any of this easier for Helen. But because Anna still needed to know she could.

The New Distance

Helen leaned against the door and listened to Anna trill on, entertaining with that stupid high-school tripping story, actually acting out parts.

Layla touched Helen's back. "Can you believe her?" Layla said and slipped into the room to become part of the rapt audience.

Here was Anna, vivid and clear, a roomful of friends appreciating her every phrase. This is what Anna loves, Helen thought, to be the center. Helen should feel grateful.

All she saw was that they were using Anna up.

Maybe it was worse. More selfish. Maybe she couldn't bear that it was on Ming and Molly's watch that Anna revived. So much has happened without her. It was Layla who was there when Anna pulled out her hair. That whatever bright star Helen might be for Anna, she was no real help. Anna had lied to her. Who had Anna really been protecting? It was too late to ask.

This dying was a new distance, unmapped,

and Helen felt how far apart they were. Still, she wanted to squish in close and claim her rightful place.

Phone

The mailbox was full. Everyone had a suggestion. A way they'd heard another family managed. They wanted the plan.

Reuben picked up for the kids. Always. Harper was threatening a leave of absence. Andy almost hit a deer on the road this morning. Julian yelled at Reuben. Hung up on him. Called back. "Sorry, Dad." They couldn't stand being at the house. They couldn't stand not being at the house.

Reuben listened.

Took three breaths before he spoke. Four.

Art History 2

Helen turned up the bedroom staircase and stood on the carpeted landing. On the wall was the wedding gift she'd given Anna and Reuben. She remembered it as more promising than the slur of color on paper that she stood in front of now. This was smeary — crimson, scarlet, and ocher. At best it was moody and decorative. Not resonant. Certainly not promising.

That late spring more than twenty-five years ago, when she'd taken Anna and Reuben to the studio, she'd felt — almost in equal measure — that she was already doomed to failure and equally certain of her success. While Anna was getting married and talking about buying houses, she was living for the slim chance of a painting fellowship. More likely Helen would spend another year in the ratty farmhouse with random roommates and dirty plastic sheeting finally untaped and stripped off the windows in May. But Helen had also felt superior to Anna. Anna, her bravest friend, had chosen the obvious, the safe and predictable. Anna might become just any woman in any town with a husband and children and a job that never mattered. In contrast, Helen, the ever-cautious girl, would willingly sacrifice everything to create a singular life.

That day in the studio, Anna pivoted sharply. "Helen, you're overthinking. It's obvious from a mile away. Cut it out. Just give me a painting and say you're happy for me."

Of course, Anna proved wild, fiercer always than Helen. There was a question Helen was inevitably asked in interviews or on studio visits. The young women painters asked her how she'd managed forging her life as an artist. She forced herself to say she hadn't managed that well. She reminded them that her marriage had failed. "I've been selfish, and yes, maybe all artists are selfish," she explained, "but my children suffered." The young painters laughed and shrugged, saying, "Jesus, who cares about marriage?" Being selfish in the service of art sounded virtuous. They were too young to understand the enduring shame, the endless shuttling of backpacks between homes.

That tension — what was an ordinary life? what was a singular life? what was happiness? — over the years, this became the subject of Helen's painting. How do you measure the sacrifices or the passions? How to compose the specificity of everyday surprise?

As she stood on the landing listening to the layers of conversation among Anna's friends, it seemed impossible that she'd ever painted this unpeopled landscape. That it ever held her interest. The wildness was right there, downstairs, when Ming hoped to put another bowl of warm soup into her friend, when Caroline and Anna sang harmony on Joni Mitchell's "River" and the local carpool friends, the can-I-borrow or can-the-kids-sleep-over friends, begged for another song. Each time Anna was sick, it was these women who rallied, coordinating, around-the-clock company so that Anna had to practically shoo them out when she wanted to nap.

"Of course I'm happy for you," she'd said to Anna that day years ago. And she *was* happy. She'd been young, new at balancing all the contradictory feelings within a moment. Was it really so much easier now? Now Helen was getting married. A ridiculous, middle-age extravagance, this hopeful desire. Also entirely ordinary. And Anna would be dead. Would that be the terrible tag after everything from now on — *after Anna died*? This was part of the unmapped distance. It was what she had never known and now would be part of the crowded canvas. If there was any weight in her paintings, if there was anything original, it was born out of surprise in the congested, jumbled foreground, some measure of confused compassion, this joy and loneliness, these limits of everyday choices.

Restless Everything

The hospice nurse took vitals. Anna didn't ask what the nurse wrote in the spiral notebook.

She'd stopped trying to remember the nurse's name.

The hospice nurse was petite, kind, soft of

foot. "We try to keep your body quiet. You'll sleep more and more."

Anna was good at sleep. Another of her great shames, her love of sleep. Reuben had always been up, up, up — pleased with everything he'd done in the hour or two before she'd risen from bed. It drove her crazy. She jarred herself into each day. Face scrubbed, teeth brushed, school lunches, jackets zippered, notes for teachers. She kissed the children; she kissed Reuben. While she cooked breakfast, she listened to everyone's last-night dreams and worries. She dreaded having to speak. On days when she didn't have to open the math center or didn't have an early tutoring session, she fought the urge to slink back into her darkened room. Once a social worker pulled aside the hospital curtain and said, "You look like you might be struggling with some depression." Without opening an eye, Anna lifted her hand and flipped the social worker the bird.

"Do you have pain?" the nurse asked now.

"Not pain so much as restless everything."

"That's normal," the nurse said.

There were more questions. Anna couldn't find all the right words anymore. The nurse repeated, "That's normal."

Everything she said, the nurse said,

"That's normal."

What seemed less than normal to Anna was a young, pretty nurse tending to the dying. These acrid smells. The soured blue of her skin. A job for old women.

Art History 3

The Gathering will be the first painting. All women. From all of Anna's worlds.

But no prayer flags.

And, So, Then. This is what Helen will call the next painting. A painting of Anna alone on the hospital bed. She thinks of Lucian Freud's studies of his mother. What Monet said about his painting of his wife, Camille: *I one day found myself looking at my beloved wife's dead face and just systematically noting the colors according to an automatic reflex!*

Or maybe the dog on the bed with her.

Helen will call it *Anna with Zeus.* The metallic railings of the hospital bed. That slightest disturbance of an off-white sheet that was both their absence and their shape.

Anna, Other Shames Known and Otherwise

1. She hadn't ever really read the newspaper. Forget daily, not even twice a month.

2. She hadn't always voted. Technically, she'd only voted twice. She'd no taste for politics. Greed and power. Why bother learning the names of despots?
3. She believed Democrats nicer than Republicans.
4. She never understood the Electoral College.
5. She'd only ever been tangentially interested in money. She wanted to have its security, but she couldn't be bothered with investing or saving. What was a 401(k)? She'd let Reuben do all that. And the daily management — electric, phone, heating oil, credit card — he wrote every check.
6. She'd lied. To Reuben. About that summer, the child they did not have.
7. She bought shoes at thrift stores. She never bought bottled water. Yet she saw a chandelier in an antique shop and didn't think twice about spending fifteen hundred dollars on it.
8. She'd preferred attractive people. A lot more. When she'd made friends with a woman who wasn't beauti-

ful, she felt embarrassed to be out with her. But also a little proud of herself. As if that showed largesse.

9. She hadn't read enough books for someone who considered herself cultured. There were years she didn't read at all. She wasn't interested in difficult narratives. She liked stories where you got close to a character.

10. She saw everyday situations hierarchically. Whose kids were smarter? Whose kids struggled more socially? Who were the athletes, the artists?

11. She didn't care about being rich, but she didn't want to be the poorest of her friends.

12. She didn't return phone calls. Sometimes she lied and said she hadn't gotten the message. Sometimes she erased messages without even listening.

13. She had no sense of direction.

The Scribe

"Do you want a scribe? Someone to write down any notes or wishes. A letter, even." The hospice nurse packed up.

There seemed so little in her bag. A blood-pressure cuff. A thermometer.

A scribe, wasn't that ancient! Anna saw
the unrolled parchment, deckle-edged. A
long beard and a quill.

She thought she was done having any last
words. Still, she tried it out. In her head.

Darling children.

Dearest Reuben.

No. What she wanted them to know, she
believed was known. But still there was
something she wanted to say.

5

Worn

Anna's rockaRoo went to Caroline, then to
Helen, who gave it back to Anna when she
had her second. There were strollers, out-
grown, circulated till a wheel fell off. Travel
cribs traveled between homes, and the green
vest Helen knitted for Ming's first was worn
by most of the other babies. Onesies, draw-
string gowns, snowsuits, winter boots, pull-
ups, snap-legged overalls, T-shirts, sweatpants, jumpers — all the clothes sorted,
washed, boxed, and sent on till they were
sorted, washed, boxed, and sent again.
Cotton pj's worn to almost-worn-through
silky perfection, until worn wholly through,
reluctantly tossed out. A dress with appliqué
lilacs was a favorite of each of the girls, and

who knew where the navy velvet blazer first came from, but it came in handy for more than one school assembly. Even this year Caroline had sent the group a photograph of her youngest, abroad in Prague, wearing the hand-me-down woolen peacoat of Helen's son. Helen wrote back, *It fits yours better than it ever did mine.*

Next Generation
Here we go. Rico, Lily, Julian, Harper, Andy, Lucinda, Rusty, Tessa, Shana, Lewis, Maggie, and Eli. Who could keep all the names straight? Who didn't — calling out for one kid — wind up mixing it up and rattling out another kid's name? Sometimes even the dog's name. It was enough when they were all together, running berserk, the littlest chasing the big ones through rooms, everything verging on toppling and crashing — it was good enough to shout, "All of you numskulls into the backyard!"

1994, Donor
"We've got a situation." It's Molly, her ultra-uptight, serious voice.

Anna hears Serena in the background. Maybe laughing. But maybe not.

"It's Tim," Molly says, sotto voce. "It's all gone wrong, Anna."

173

"Slow down." Anna motions for Reuben to pick up the second phone on his side of the bed.

"Hey, Moll," Reuben says. "What's up?"

"What's up? Tim's bonkers. And he's downstairs. In our house."

Originally Tim was part of Anna and Reuben's college gang, but Molly and Tim had been pals since the summer a motley crew chipped in for a house on Lake Winnipesaukee. So it wasn't out of line that when Tim visited Anna and Reuben, Anna mentioned that Serena and Molly were having a hard time finding a known sperm donor. Reuben held up his barbecue tongs and declared it was a royal waste of time and the donor bank was obviously a much cleaner way to go. All through dinner Tim argued that a known donor made good sense, genetically speaking. So no one was surprised a week later when he stepped up to say he'd help. It made sense. And not just because Tim had solidly maintained he had no interest in ever having children. Solidly, as in since freshman year. "It also makes sense," Molly explained to Serena before the first face-to-face, "since as far as we know, he has no interest in sex — not with animal, vegetable, or mineral."

Reuben maintained his donor-bank position, but Anna insisted he was being a predictable pessimist, unable to consider that some people can actually make selfless gestures.

It seemed perfect. As for the genetics. Tim was a computer genius and handsome as all get-out. He was a racial blend that he liked to call a what-am-I-not. His brother and sister had brilliant, gorgeous children. Tim was solid. Responsible. And not looking to co-parent. Unlike earlier prospects, Tim hadn't raised the worry about what he'd feel if the baby looked like him. He never even mentioned sharing holidays or a special uncle role.

"You got to understand everything was set. He'd shown up with his health papers like any good stud." Serena was clearly enjoying the lesbian comedy aspect of whatever drama was unfolding.

Suddenly — and here Serena and Molly, crammed close to the phone, talking practically in unison — at the eleventh hour, at the pre-conception final-checklist, candlelit celebration dinner — health and genetic testing done, plans to sign the legal agreement scheduled for the next morning — declared he'd gone weird on them.

"Pretty much out of nowhere, while we're eating the strawberry tart, he announces he needs full responsibility for the spiritual upbringing of the baby."

"Tim? When did he go spiritual?"

"Exactly. How had Mr. Computer Tim, Mr. Logical Tim forgotten to mention over two months of conversation that he's had a religious conversion and become Mr. Spiritual Tim?" Molly says.

"Apparently he hasn't just taken refuge with the guru," Serena chimes in. "Turns out he's a one-man world religion — some creepy amalgamation of Buddhist, Mennonite, Catholic, Sufi, and Native American."

"Where is he now?" Anna says sufficiently creeped out.

"Downstairs." Molly's back to a whisper. "We argued for a while. Then we said we had to call it a night."

"Yeah, we sure did. In the middle of us insisting that he would not ever have any responsibility, spiritual or otherwise, he takes out a hand-stitched suede bag with God only knows what inside it. 'This is my medicine bag.' He waves it and says in this super-serious voice, 'A baby comes forth from great cosmic energy,' and then declares that right there in our living room he wants to actually show us how he plans to bless his precious seed gift."

"Whoa, he whipped it out?" Reuben says,

his delight way too obvious.

"Stop it. That's gross." Anna falls back into Reuben's lap. He slips a hand down the V of her T-shirt and palms her breast, mouthing, *This is getting me horny.*

Anna rolls her eyes, and he nods goofily. *Super horny.*

"Oh, yes, my dear, I plan to stop it. I'm driving him to the train station in the morning." Serena hams it up. "With my mother insisting we bring our baby up Methodist in the AME and Molly's mom sending us pamphlets quoting Pope John Paul's position against circumcision, we sure as hell aren't going to have a donor who goes religious psycho on us."

"That is if he doesn't do some ritual cult-murder impregnation tonight." Molly tries to sound like she's joking, but they all know what a squealing slasher-film fan she is.

"Ladies, I'm not saying the obvious 'told you so,' but can you now promise you'll go anonymous donor?"

"This is not about you, Reuben." Anna sticks her tongue out at him. Then, vamping, lazily drags her tongue across her upper lip.

They all know how much Reuben loves to be right. And Anna knows how much Reuben wants to get off the phone and jump into playing medicine man.

1995, Potion

The child parade is led by Ming's and Anna's eldest boys, Rico and Julian, hauling a bucketful of half-used bottles gathered from the bathroom cupboard.

"It's important," Ming's son, Rico, declares. "Not just a game." Rico is always the leader. "The benevolent dictator," the moms all call him. He declares that the kids want — no, they need — to use calamine lotion, a long worm of Neosporin. There's a blue bubble bath and shampoo. The younger children nod with proud intent as the older kids make their case for potions. "We need certain potions," Rico says, twisting open a container of baby powder, a cloud of talc poofing up.

The children scan. Everything in the kitchen looks necessary, absolutely essential for the sake of scientific progress. Is there anything that could be taken from the refrigerator? Cheese? Mustard? The jar of olives on the table?

The mothers sit at the round table — cheese and crackers, a bottle of wine — the afternoon reward. They've been talking about — what else! — the lives of these very children who tangle together looking keen and expectant.

Yes to mustard. No to olives. The mothers manage a unified serious face.

"And no tasting any potions," Helen says which the other mothers punctuate by eye contact with their respective offspring.

"Absolutely no tasting," Caroline cautions her daughter, who's snatching a cereal box off the shelf. "And remember, you big kids are in charge of the little ones."

"To our Einsteins," Helen toasts while the kids pack like puppies through the doorway.

"Or Strangeloves," Anna says, and they clink glasses. They can't get over how lucky they are. To go through this together. How else could they figure any of it out? No need to appear like they know what they're doing. If disaster is coming — and which of these women ever breathes a breath free of impending disaster? — it isn't here yet.

Down the hallway the kids chant, "Pour more, pour more!"

And then there's Lily and Rusty marching back into the kitchen.

"We need two eggs," Lily announces, wrangling her fiercest smile. How very canny those older kids are, sending out these two cuties. The mothers can't resist Lily's dark eyes, her tangle of curls, her limping, determined gait. Brave Lily, twice-a-day doses of Tegretol, still seizures breaking through. Yet always insisting herself into the center of the big-kid games.

Of course the big kids have sent Rusty as Lily's protector — a perfect choice to show that mad scientists though they might be, they have some wits about them.

"Why eggs?" Anna asks with scientific formality. "And why two?"

"The egg is our binder. We're interested in watching bubbles react with a binder." Rusty raises his hand in mid-lecture.

Can they, the women, refrain from bursting into laughter?

They want to hold Rusty there forever, their little scientist, his voice with the springy lilt of a four-year-old. This boy of theirs — not just Helen's younger child — because these children are all their project, their great potion, something these five friends dreamed up as teenagers, all those evenings debating questions of nature and nurture — this boy of theirs who protects Lily and follows the older kids — squinching up his pretty lips and setting his face not to cry.

"It is important," he announces.

"Well." Anna nods respectfully. "You've made an excellent case. Actually, I'll give you three eggs. On the condition that you alone break the third one."

Always Anna who bolsters a child's courage. Who believes it will all work out. "Just give it time," Anna says when one of the others worries about getting a child to sleep on schedule or give up the bottle or later when a teacher voices concern about late reading or class behavior. When Helen points out Anna's hypocrisy that she fretted about both Julian's and Andy's quietness, Anna holds up her hands. "Shoot me if I'm inconsistent."

Anna whispers to Rusty and hands him two eggs. He nods solemnly. "I promise."

Then she kneels and puts the third egg into Lily's hand, helping close Lily's stiff fingers around it.

"What did she say?" Lily bumps close to Rusty as they head back to the big kids.

"Yeah, what did you say?" Helen asks watching the proud set of her son's back.

"Nope. My secret with your boy," Anna says. "Right, Rusty?"

"What?" Lily whines. "I want a secret."

"I can't tell." Rusty glances mischievously back at Anna. "But I promise that it's good for both of us."

181

Those Years

On blankets, in slings, strollered, nursing, put down for naps, waking, hungry or never hungry. There was the messy child, the fussy child, the incessant talker, the drifty child, the one who cried over nothing, the milk-spilling child, the tantrum child, the silent, the fevery, the rashy, the easily startled — angels each of them when they slept.

1997, Lily

Before Lily's brain surgery, there had been two months in the hospital, Lily's head fitted with a plaster cap, probes drilled into her brain charting seizure activity and location. Ming and Sebastian alternated weeks staying in the hospital. Sebastian turned over the restaurant's kitchen to his staff. Ming ran her law practice from the waiting room. "Steady wind and lightning," the young doctor said. The data showed seizure activity like lightning across a lake. Miles of printout, jagged lines of storm in the right hemisphere. "It is astonishing, really, Lily's attention span, not to mention her sense of humor and charm, if you consider the constant static distraction."

Ming saw a wide, murky lake and began to cry. She would not have the strength to paddle out and save her daughter as the lake roughed with swells.

"We can do this," the doctor said, and explained how the hemispherectomy gave Lily a chance to live seizure-free. "The child's brain especially has such plasticity that we really can expect many left-lobe functions to be integrated by the right side."

Ming scribbled down what the doctor said. She kept notes every time she spoke with the doctors. She had to. Hemispherectomy. Corpus callosum. Just the words terrified her. Now she grabbed Sebastian's hand with her free hand. Maybe her daughter should stay right there, safely attended to in the hospital, playing birthday party with her lilac and turquoise My Little Ponies.

Sebastian clutched his wife's hand but kept his eyes eagle-fixed on the man whose hands would cut out half his daughter's brain.

1997, Bright Future

"Go to the movies." The doctor stood. "I'm in with Lily twelve hours. Probably more."

Sebastian put up his hands as if to physically push back the suggestion. He wasn't budging until his little girl was in recovery.

The surgeon shrugged. "I'm a father, too."

"Let's follow doctor's orders." Anna took

183

Ming's hand and pulled her to her feet. "We're out of here."

Sebastian started to thank Anna for coming to the hospital, but she flashed a don't-be-an-idiot look. This was planned. She'd shown up to keep them company till the surgery was over. Helen was on call to show up once Lily was out of recovery.

But once outside the hospital, the women seemed lost, the day too bright, too calm. And an odd part of the city, no reason to be there except for the hospital, and neither knew anything beyond the two blocks to the parking garage. Central Park was blocks and blocks away. There were no shops to browse. A no-man's-land with a lot of people in scrubs. Ming insisted she wouldn't go far from the hospital.

"I can't eat," Ming said.

"Let's walk," said Anna, but when the light changed, they seemed unable to move.

Finally, somehow, they drifted a few blocks. Took a left. When they passed a salon called Lily's, they took it as an omen.

"Is this weird?" Ming said. "It actually seems like it might feel nice."

"Lily loves pretty colors. You should have bright nails when she wakes in recovery."

Starter Wife. Madison Ave. Kimono. They read through the names of enamel polishes.

Ming decided on a red called Bright Future. Anna chose a hot pink called Hi Maintenance.

"Well, these two pretty much sum it up." Ming laughed, and the women in the salon chuckled along as if they were in on the joke.

One woman ran hot water in the footbaths. "Are you going to a party? It's good color for a party."

Anna said, "Sure, a big party. The party of a lifetime."

"Then you have extra scrub and massage?"

"We want extra everything," Anna said. "We've got plenty of time."

Ming pressed buttons on the side of her chair, and a rolling began from the base of the seat to her neck. Her body rippled as the chair heaved and surged. She leaned back and closed her eyes.

Anna laughed. "You look like you're in agony."

"It's pretty much the most uncomfortable thing ever. But I hoped it might get better."

They watched as the manicurists cut and filed, trimmed their cuticles and pumiced their soles. Then there was scrubbing and exfoliating. The women laced tissue over and under between their toes and smacked the bottles of polish against their open palms.

"You like this color?" The woman checked after she'd painted Ming's big toe.

"She loves it," Anna said.

Ming looked over at Anna with such gratefulness.

"While Lily was having half her brain removed, I was having my toenails polished. This will be part of the story. How weird is that?"

"Only a really small part of the story," Anna said.

2003, Have Lovers

"Don't marry again. Have lovers," Ming commands in her instructional voice. She levers another log onto the fire. "Marrying is for having children. You did that. So onward."

Ming, Caroline, Anna, and Helen lounge in front of the fireplace in Ming's living room. A whole weekend visit of rain that won't let up. The husbands have swept up the restless kids for bowling. All the husbands except for Helen's, who after a year's separation is now officially a not-husband. Even Ming, the traditionalist among them, believes that Helen's marriage couldn't have lasted through Helen's ambition as an artist.

"Don't all you creative people burn through marriages? Just don't go for that again," Ming says.

After a glass of wine, they have it all worked out for Helen. She'll have a glamorous life, they insist. More shows, more galleries, more museums. Helen will become more and more famous. Have more and more lovers. Everything about Helen has a "more" in front of it.

"It will all be very discreet," Caroline says, stretching out into her best languid sex-kitten pose. Caroline describes how, when Lucinda and Rusty are at the Ex's, Helen will see her many lovers. How quickly they've all begun to call Paul the Ex instead of Paul.

"Clandestine is good, raunchy is much better."

"And you'll report in and tell us everything."

"But we're not interested in the downside. No singing any pity-me-I'm-lonely ballad. You should have thought of that when you were still married." Ming sounds a little too excited by the whole prospect of Helen's swinging-singles life.

"Someone needs to have lots of fun for all

of us," Anna says. "Let's remember how late Helen was to any fun."

"There's a French lover. You met at a vernissage on the rue de Whatever." Caroline rolls her *r*'s extravagantly.

"A Greek lover with a sailboat works for me."

"Wait a second, Ming. You were the one with a Greek?" Helen asks. "Wasn't that anthropologist Greek?"

"Ming was the romantic globe-trotter," Anna says. "That was Alexi, her mad Greek. There was Belgian Maurice. And, of course, don't forget she picked up Sebastian in a restaurant in Ecuador."

Ming pours out another half glass. "And now, ladies, I'm a lawyer with a ranch house in the Berkshire boonies. Which is why I really need Helen to go crazy for all our sakes."

2006, Dark

It was better that no one asked. Helen was convinced it was better for all of them. Let Ming think it was a life of romantic flings in faraway cities. Let them conjure interludes. There were men. They were right about that. But so little of it ever romantic. Maybe at first. Then it went dark fast. Whom did it help for Helen to describe the lost days, the high wire of night? The tinselly powdered lines of whatever the men brought with them. Soon the men hardly mattered. What good was it for her dearest friends to imagine her kneeling over a hotel desk desperate and licking the slick creases of unwrapped paper, tonguing for some last bitter coke crumble? Outside in some city, the sun rising. How had that even happened? And then it had. Before each gallery opening, she'd promise to keep it about the art. But there were afterparties, someone grabbing her arm, saying, "If you want your name remembered with the big boys, you have to party like the big boys." Reviews lauded her with just her first name. Helen. Helen as the new name to follow, as the return to figurative painting that honored depth of subject and technique and a welcome end to post-anything irony. She liked being a single name. That was like the big boys. Picasso. Matisse. Basquiat. Helen. She didn't bother questioning why she wasn't known by a last name. "You must come with us, Helen," and someone took her by the hand. Then there were rooms and rooftops, always a man saying something that first sounded like praise and, after that, the streaky dawn light and her wasted in a city she didn't know. There were men. One left her in a closet. One doubled around her ankle the gray pearl choker he was bringing home to his wife.

Anna figured it out. Not because Helen offered. "What's going on?" Anna said. "What are you doing? When are you getting back to pick up the children from Paul?"

Helen lied. At least at first. Then she stopped answering Anna's calls. Anna pushed and pushed. She didn't stop. Then, finally, Helen called back. She was in a steep fall, in a sweaty, staticky jangle.

"Where are you, Heli?"

Helen looked around at the large television screen, the orange curtains drawn shut. Berlin. Maybe it was Munich.

"I'm in a fantastic hotel," she said, as if that answered any worried question Anna asked. Then she turned nasty. "You think you're me, Anna, having to collect you from another drunk high-school party?"

"Is there a writing pad next to the hotel phone? There's an address, Heli."

"I'm not an idiot."

"You are. With idiot people flocked around you. Your kids are beyond worried. They're calling me. Now *I've* got to get *you* home."

Helen tried accusing. "Having fun feeling superior? I'm not you, Anna, with your perfect life. Perfect mom."

190

She yelled into the phone. "I'm not the perfect anything you are!" She yelled and yelled. Everything. The drugs. The men. The hospital in Milan where her gallerist brought her. The attempted overdose.

"See?" Helen's voice flattened. "I'm not perfect you."

She'd done it. Calling Anna's life perfect after the hell of diagnosis. How far up her ass could her own head fit? Now even Anna would leave her. And Anna should. She'd used Anna, too. Crying over Anna, a sob story she'd hoovered up her nose. Or wept into some man's arms. She deserved to lose Anna. She'd basically lost Lucinda and Rusty. They stayed with their dad. "It's just easier," the kids said, at first blaming it on her schedule. When she pushed, Rusty shouted, "Mom, why is it about you? I just need a normal parent who takes care of normal stuff!" Then Lucinda stopped talking to her.

She was losing everything. But she was a painter. The art world referred to her by her first name. Helen. Up there with the big boys.

"I'm not whatever you think I am."

"You're not whatever *you* think you are," Anna said into the silence.

"What's wrong with this picture?" Helen asked after she and Anna said their good-byes to the group that loitered smoking after the meeting. Anna had driven down, insisting she go with Helen to the noon meeting.

"Wasn't I supposed to be dragging *your* skinny ass into recovery?" Helen fingered the ninety-day chip shoved into her coat pocket.

"There's something to be said for getting the big-time drinking and drugging over with by eighteen, Heli. You had so many years of being the good girl to make up for."

Anna slipped her arm through Helen's. She steered them off Hudson, veering toward a shop on Bleecker Street where she'd spotted a perfect T-shirt in the window. They'd each buy one and give it as a gift to the other. An old tradition.

Anna took her time, then asked about the kids.

"Lucinda still isn't talking to me. But she allowed me to come to her last volleyball game. And Rusty just looks terrified whenever I leave the room."

"It will work out."

Helen kissed Anna on the cheek. "Tell me that about a thousand more times before you drive home today."

2006, Celebration

The invitation said, *Come to Our Wedding* and, in smaller type, *the one we couldn't have eighteen years ago.* Molly joked that they might have also written, *the party we definitely couldn't have afforded.* The inn was swanky, with a low-key, restored-chintz elegance. Everything about the inn — the airy rooms, the mowed lawns, the stone-path gardens — had that lovely low-key, effortless feeling.

Caroline and Danny arrived first, posted themselves on rocking chairs so that as the rest arrived — Helen alone, then Ming and Sebastian, who'd given Anna a lift — they gathered, bogarting all the other rockers on the inn's front porch.

"It's all a wonderful ballet," Caroline said, watching the last of the tent being set up on the lawn.

"You really are too excited to be away from our kids," Danny said. According to Caroline everything all day had been perfect — the lack of traffic, the cloud shapes, the lobster roll at a clam shack down the coast.

"You should have heard her ranting about the poetry of basil mayonnaise."

"I'm sorry, but if I can't think this is pretty much perfection, then I don't know what is," Caroline said.

One perfection they all admitted to was the kid-free weekend. Except, obviously, for Tessa and Shana, who were maids of honor, they'd agreed not to force the tribe's attendance. At first Ming, brandishing her lawyerly authority, argued it was essential to have the kids. To witness Molly and Serena's marriage. This was American history in the making. But she was promptly overruled. It was too complicated with high-school sports teams and proms and studying for college finals. Not to mention that Helen's kids were barely talking to Helen.

Sitting on the porch, Bloody Mary in hand, Ming admitted, "Okay, kid-free is already a lot more fun."

Down at the tent, Molly and Serena were in deep conversation with a woman holding an armful of magenta peonies. Dressed in scrubby T-shirts and sweatpants, they looked more like women heading out for a day hike than women who in five hours would be gussied up and standing with their daughters at a marriage celebration. The unsaid perfection, the one they'd promised would not upstage Serena and Molly, was that Anna was there. Right up on the porch. In the middle of the conversation. She had survived what they said she would probably not survive.

"Pretty much perfection" became code for the afternoon, for the pre-wedding hike to a waterfall, for the service where Molly and Serena in taffeta gowns managed to weave their traditions so that Boston Irish Catholicism and New Orleans Black Methodism seemed an inevitable twining for even the most reluctant of the relatives.

And "pretty much perfection" was the surprise that Molly had cooked up for Serena when, after dinner and toasting and dancing to DJ SureShot, she directed everyone up to the log house behind the tent. There was a fire blazing in the great stone fireplace. And set up in the other corner was Vince Welnick — the actual ex and last keyboard player from the Grateful Dead — right there, in person, with his road band, playing "Truckin'."

"I'm not sure how anyone actually dances to this, but please join us!" Molly shouted as she led her bride and partner of eighteen years onto the bluestone dance floor.

Serena was a self-confessed Deadhead. She loved the music, but she also loved that nothing about it fit with her image as a black lesbian orthopedic-surgeon mother. She liked to brag she was probably the only southern black girl in an Indian-print skirt swaying to "Sugar Magnolia" back in the day. Now Serena, shaking her head with equal parts joy and incredulity, had her arms wrapped around Molly. Tessa and Shana rushed close, and the women let their daughters slip inside the hug.

"I told Molly about Welnick!" Anna shouted as the friends danced in a loose circle. "When I learned he was out playing joints, like roadside dives, I knew he'd be game for a wedding." Anna looked almost as thrilled as Serena.

The snare drums started whisking, and the band funked up for Stevie Wonder's "Superstition." The crowd lit up happy for a groove easier than the Grateful Dead.

"Who's that?" Caroline pointed to a girl swaying alone in the corner. She looked eighteen. Tops. Even with her blond hair scraggly in front of her face, there was no mistaking how high the girl was. Wasted was more like it.

"She came with Welnick." Molly slapped her hands over her face.

"His daughter?"

"I wish I could say yes. I'm trying hard not to think about her."

"Shit, that's just wrong." Danny looked furious, like he should do something. Between all of them, there were a lot of daughters. "That hurts," he said.

Caroline put her hand on his back to remind him it was Serena and Molly's night. They deserved an undisturbed night of joy.

Later Vince Welnick scanned the dance floor. "Where's Anna?" — as if he'd been looking for her all night.

"Anna," he said formally when Molly lifted Anna's arm. "Will you please join us?"

Without much convincing, Anna stepped through the crowd and hopped up onstage in her layered skirt and cowboy boots. The band hit the opening chords, and Anna shrugged her shoulders and blew a kiss to Molly and Serena. Then she slid her hands up the mike and started hitting perfect harmonies with Vince on "Friend of the Devil."

"I was scared she'd refuse." And the others knew that Molly meant because of the god-awful wig with its thick, blunt bangs.

Anna hadn't played with her own band since the onset, but up onstage it was as if there had been no hiatus, no months in the hospital. She could hold her own. Deep in it. Snapping her fingers while the band segued into the Four Tops to sing backup on "Baby I Need Your Loving."

Molly had arranged it with Vince. But, clearly, whatever Molly had assured him, it was obvious that Anna was a surprise. The songs kept rolling.

Then the guitarist handed Anna his other Gibson acoustic for Lowell George's "Willin'." She closed her eyes. She set the easy strum, and a harmonica joined. Anna took a sharp breath. *I've been warped by the rain, driven by the snow, I'm drunk and dirty, don't ya know, but I'm still . . . willin'.* The band paced with her. She took her time. Let go and went down into the full lament and grudging hope of the lyric. When she shook her head, the wig was fixed in place like a thick helmet. She let pauses fill the room as she came up to the chorus, where Vince joined her.

When she'd finished the song, Anna walked over to Vince. She crouched beside his keyboard and started into an intense conversation. Like she was in mid-argument. Her hands gesticulated in blunt stabs. She stared across the room. And back at him. Then pointed to where the girl was sloppily propped against a wall. He listened, vigorously nodding his head. Then Vince took both of Anna's hands, holding them tight to his chest as he bent into his microphone.

"Whoa. Force of nature, this little woman. I suppose no one messes with her. And now here's two more Anna's asked for. The first by the one and only Laura Nyro. For those of us who've needed it."

His hands started jazzy and loose on the keyboard, and Anna drifted over to her microphone. The band hung back, listened while Vince and Anna sang "Gonna Take a Miracle." And they slid right into John Prine's "Angel from Montgomery." All of her struggle to stay alive pressed up in Anna's throat.

Ming and Sebastian danced, Sebastian fitting his South American rhythms effortlessly to the song's country beat. Danny hugged Caroline from behind as she swayed and cried, singing along on the chorus, *Just give me one thing that I can hold on to. To believe in this livin' is just a hard way to go,* her un-miked voice braiding with Vince's and Anna's.

Helen came up behind Serena and Molly and put her arms around them. "Damn," she whispered.

Molly turned her teary face to Helen's so they were wet cheek to wet cheek. "She really knows how to mess with a crowd."

Fathers

Three weeks later Vince Welnick killed himself. Cut his own throat. As gory and violent as they come.

"I know it's not all about me," Molly nervously joked. "Still, it kind of changes the vibe of our wedding album."

"It explains how damaged he was that night," Anna said.

"People get really lost sometimes," Helen said.

But they all admitted it was the girl they kept remembering. Her stringy blond hair. The swimmy underwater motion of her young body as she danced. Or how, at the end of the night, Ming found the girl curled on a pile of cushions in a corner of the log house, and then Danny and Sebastian walked her around and around the tent as the guests filtered out and the inn crew broke down all the tables and chairs.

6

Black Ice

Outside was noisy. Ice pelted the tall windows. Crack and snap of trees. Something big hit the roof. The plan to stay the night had always been the plan, but now it seemed like foresight. Out there was a treacherous mess. Black ice, the interstate impossible.

And though Molly had earlier announced

she needed to switch plans and drive home given the Tessa concerns, the others vetoed her leaving.

"You're staying," Ming said with finality. "You'll wind up dead in a crash first. No surprise disasters. That's more than the rest of us can bear right now. So chill out."

Anyway, inside was downright cozy. Lamp-lit. The woodstove stoked. Reuben had stacked plenty of wood before leaving for his house.

"And we can drink," Caroline trilled, pouring Molly a full glass of cabernet. Fixed a seltzer with lime wedges for Helen. "Or at least some of us still can."

Restore

"I'm all lid." Helen pinched the skin above her eyes. "Remind me why we're against the knife."

Finally in comfy sweats and oversize T-shirts, the women grouped close to the bathroom mirror. Crow's-feet, they agreed, made the disaster around the eyes sound cuter than it truly was.

"It's all about revive, reverse, restore," Ming said, offering a tube that promoted cellular growth.

"Try this." Caroline dabbed a pot of eye cream and patted in circles close to her lashes. "And it better do all that and more, given what I paid for it."

"I'm ravaged with lines, but every second of sun was worth it." Molly stuck two fingers into the pot of cream.

Molly borrowed Caroline's toothbrush. Like back in the day. But back in the day they'd crashed, sleeping two girls, even three, to a bed, a mom popping her head in the door, feigning surprise: "How many of you can fit on that bed?" Another girl dreamed easily on a beanbag. Back in the day, it was all easy sleep.

Tonight Helen will sleep the night with Anna. The other women have divvied up the spare bedrooms. Ming and Caroline brought their own pillows. Everyone has sleep issues. Melatonin, or a half of something prescribed, but surely still there will be middle-of-the-night reading. They've confessed to snoring. Mornings arrived earlier and earlier.

Man

Then there was a man.

The women froze, but he seemed even more surprised to see them sprawled on the couches. "I just thought I'd stop back." His voice faltered. Shaggy, wet, he dripped all over the dark pine floor.

"Anna," he said softly.

"She's resting, Jarrett," Ming clipped.

Oh. Jarrett. The others relaxed. This was just Jarrett, from the band, the one who played lead guitar.

"I'd like a moment alone with Anna."

"She's wiped out from all the company today." Ming remained firm.

"That's why I came back. Just to play for her. Some songs to help her sleep." He seemed unbudgeable. And lost. Wet beard, wet wool plaid jacket, water puddled by his work boots. Like a derailed Paul Bunyan. No, a drenched Cowardly Lion.

"We're spending the night, Jarrett." Molly stepped in. "Swing by tomorrow, Jarrett." Her voice set at another assertive register, kind and limit-setting — her shrink voice — the way she repeated his name, Jarrett, asserted professional control.

"Maybe just one song." Jarrett looked like he might cry. Actually, he looked like he'd been crying for a while already.

They knew that Anna would have invited him in. Made room for his big wet self to soak the couch. Poured him a glass of wine. Let him stumblingly talk about his feelings. Play the guitar. Did that mean *they* had to?

Molly pulled up from the couch and walked over to where Jarrett stood.

"Tomorrow." She reached her hand to his shoulder. He crumpled when she touched him. This broad, solid man, his whole body seemed to break apart at her touch, and then, out from him, a ragged, wounded sound. Crying like braying? Like falling rock? Like something trapped? Like something none of the women had heard before.

After Molly had guided Jarrett out the door, after Ming had checked on Anna, after Caroline had topped glasses of wine or seltzer, the four women were quiet. Not a good quiet. Not a relieved quiet after the all-day scurry — boosting, hosting, fending off — and definitely not the quiet of being alone together they'd been waiting for all day. It was emergency quiet. They couldn't shake that desperate vision of Jarrett soaked and dripping, that primitive sound that issued from him or the way he toppled, disassembling like Jenga blocks. The four of them not so much speechless as adrift. Each alone, shipwrecked. Then they gathered themselves and clambered back to one another.

Caroline lifted her glass. "You're practically a national hero, Molly, pushing that lumberjack out the door."

Molly took a grateful, thirsty drink of cabernet.

There was a rush of agreement.

Praise for Molly.

Praise for Ming for remembering that Jarrett's name was Jarrett.

Praise for all of them for not screaming and having massive heart attacks when he suddenly appeared. "Like Bigfoot from the wild," Helen said.

Praise just to hear their voices together in the room.

"He's definitely in love with Anna."

"The whole band is Anna gaga."

"Has there actually been some hanky-panky romance Anna's never copped to?"

"Who exactly was that Betsy from work?"

"Did anyone else see how deftly Caroline managed the crazy neighbor chick?"

"Crazy, right?"

"Certifiable."

"No more chanting ever."

"And we've got to talk about the prayer flags."

"Can they be globally outlawed?"

"Except for maybe in Dharamsala."

Hunger

"Hey."

Like that, Anna. Awake, up on her own, angled against the bathroom door frame. Flushed, wisps of hair loosed from her braid, soft around her face.

"Any food left?" She looked beautiful. Maybe it was just edema puffing her, but tonight she had no lines.

"See?" Helen nudged Ming. Forget Reuben's assholic sign on the fridge. "She's still interested."

Reheated eggplant parm. Salmon. Goat cheese and crackers. The possibility of her asking this very question was what the jammed fridge was all about.

Suddenly they were all ravenous.

Ming lit candles.

"Tell me about Tessa," Anna asked Molly as she walked unaided to the long farm table. "Is there any ice cream left?" she asked, and — like that! — five pints appeared before her.

"It's more than weed. I'm scared it's really serious, what's going on with Tess." Molly sat beside Anna as the feast assembled on the other side of the kitchen island. Happy for time alone with her. Molly tried to fit everything in before the others came to the table. "I feel something's seriously off."

"Sweetheart, slow down. Remember us back then. You got to try and remember how off we were," Anna said, spoon deep in the chocolate chocolate-chip ice cream.

"It's helpful to have you remind me. This

kid thing is tough."

"You didn't have the best parenting model," Caroline said as she sat down and spread goat cheese on two crackers. Molly felt electricity snap down her back as the others nodded.

"Yeah. I didn't have the best blueprint to follow." It always stung to realize they'd noticed even half of the damage.

"I'm happy we got this night," Anna said and worked her spoon around the softened outer circle of the pint of butter pecan.

They couldn't stop watching her eat.

"I'd decided to stop," she said. "But I woke up craving ice cream. What the hell, there's always tomorrow to get serious about the hereafter."

Caroline laughed. "You're wicked."

"You bet. Right to the edge of no return, Carrie."

"What are you trying to be?" Helen slapped her hands over her face. "The Joan Rivers of hospice?"

Anna nudged Helen. "Come on, Heli, don't be your old party-pooper good girl. Have a little fun with me."

"I wish I could." Helen peeked through her fingers, then let her hands sift down. "Do you actually feel this easy?" There was no anger in the question. She didn't feel the anger she'd felt all day.

"It's the oddest thing. I spent all those years refusing to be defined by illness. I was so insistent, so ferocious about it. Now I see I wasn't. I have the sweetest life. The kids. My family. All of you."

"Do you feel ready?" Molly asked.

"It's not a matter of being ready. Who'd ever be ready to give all this sweetness up? It's that I'm not really here anymore."

"But you say you're happy to be with us tonight," Helen said. She was so relieved that they were all finally together talking. Not about kids. But this.

"I don't know how to explain it. I'm sorry."

"It's bittersweet." Ming licked the spoon's metal. She made no attempt to wipe the tears off her face.

"Just sweet," Anna said, and picked up the next pint of vanilla bean.

On the Bright Side

She'll never have to floss again.

Or shave her legs.

Art History 4

Helen had always loved that *The Last Supper* had been painted on the monastery's refectory wall, that the monks of Santa Maria delle Grazie dined each day among da Vinci's twelve apostles. As if the apostles and Christ were right there at a table behind the monks. And all the men were in various states of response to Christ's question. She loved the painting's movement, the control of the essential drama. Helen's *Supper* will be five braless middle-age women at a cluttered late-night table — pints of ice cream, bottles of seltzer and wine — talking like they have for decades. Instead of da Vinci's bucolic landscape out the rear windows, Helen will create this furious storm, wind and ice unrelenting. The danger will be entirely outdoors. In the warm light of the house, the women will gather to eat and talk. Layers of history. Secrets. The old hurts and alliances out on the table among the plates and glasses. The women animated, teasing one another, threading from one story to another, like there is no tomorrow.

Bloom

"Tell me all about Lily, Ming." Anna wanted to know, but she mostly wanted to drift. They were still at the long wooden table. She couldn't imagine being able to get up from the table. She closed her eyes. Lily in college, who could have guessed that? She thought she nodded. Now honors. Oh, Lily. Every day earned her name — great durable bloomer. "And if that wasn't enough," Anna heard Ming say. Ming described Sebastian fitting the Subaru with special adjustments. Lily passed her driving test on the first try. "And there's a boy at school. She wanted me to tell you that, Anna." Then Anna was driving with Lily on a narrow road. It was summer. Lily was driving, saying, "He's crazy about me." Bright orange tiger lilies clustered abundantly on grassy slopes. They were looking for the pond. The pond was sheeted in ice. "We'll swim in High Pond," she said to Lily.

Somewhere nearby Ming shouted, "Grab a blanket! Quick! Something bad is happening! Anna's shivering like crazy!"

Temperature

It was fast, the shaking. Like a leaf. Literally. She was leaf thin. Brittle. Anna tried to speak, but her mouth couldn't make words. Her teeth sounded like they were breaking.

"She's burning up." Molly lifted Anna like a child in her arms. Carried her into the bedroom.

"It's freezing." The words came out jumbled. Anna looked up at Molly. She shivered so violently that all the skin on her face trembled. Like it might come off in sheets. Was this all from ice cream? Should they have considered that ice cream was danger-ous? They circled close. But when they wrapped her in blankets, she kicked out of the blankets. Her body thrashed with a force they hadn't seen all day. They didn't want to put up the rails because she would crash against them.

"It isn't a seizure," Ming assured them. At least not like any she'd seen with Lily.

They bracketed the bed. Put hands on Anna to keep her jerking body from sprain-ing. Reuben had said to call if something went horribly wrong. Where did this fall on the scale of wrong? The women made eye contact across the bed. What if it was hap-pening? If this was it. If this was dying. On their watch.

Tylenol? Was it against a rule to give Tylenol for the fever? Were there hospice rules?

"I'll call John." Helen had Connie's num-ber.

"Don't." It was Anna. Her voice bleary and far away. But her voice. "Don't call anyone. This happens. Then it stops."

"Can we do anything for you, honey?"

"Talk about warm places."

Sleepover

"Anna," Ming said, "remember windsurfing."

Helen spooned behind Anna. Caroline slid in front. Helen scooched forward until the backs of Anna's legs penciled against hers.

Ming put up the rails to hold the three of them on the bed. Anna was a sliver between Helen and Caroline. They were afraid to press too tight. The sound of her teeth, beyond chatter.

"Tell them the story." Anna's voice reed-like up between them.

But they all knew the story. It was one of the hospital stories, a story Anna liked to be told waking up out of a neutropenic fever or in the jangly, crawling-out-of-her-skin hours coming off medications. A beach in Spain where Ming, Sebastian, Anna, and Reuben once vacationed with their kids. It had been told and told again during treatment. By now they'd all memorized Ming's version, Reuben's version, and even the kids' versions. Of course, there was Helen's annoyed version about having been excluded, since the trip was planned for a time she couldn't have possibly joined. Caroline, who also hadn't been on the trip, told a version to a nurse when Anna, hallucinating on medications, insisted Caroline's family *had* been on the trip. They all could describe that winding coastal drive, the sheer cliffs, and every one of the kids carsick. Domino vomiting. How much vomit could there be in one car? They all described how Sebastian and Reuben were idiotically determined to drive the coast and then turn up to Seville, where Sebastian's cousin lived, until Ming and Anna, hours beyond furious, revolted and they stopped in Tarifa, which turned out to be the windsurfing mecca of Spain. Not just windsurfing, there were coves for naked windsurfing, which, yes, over the course of three days all of them, even Ming with her well-known modesty, tried. Then there was Azul, the hotel and café where Sebastian and the very handsome chef Roberto made dueling paellas and lamb roasts and, after dinner, Anna sang "Hotel California" with Roberto and his band.

"Anna, remember those gorgeous blue tiles in the lobby?" Ming said. Ming folded laundry she'd collected and washed earlier in the day. She kept asking Anna to remember. A trellis of orange flowers. The smell of jasmine. Sebastian's cousin furious that they blew off the visit to her in Seville. The children, a happy band of sand-encrusted savages that roamed in a pack.

213

Ming described the lopsided bundles of driftwood the kids dragged up and the dry vanilla scent from the wood-fired stove. And how, on their last night, Chef Roberto and Anna sang flamenco.

"He had such a thing for you, Anna." Ming reached over and put her hand against Anna's forehead.

"So what's new?" Molly said. "Did you see the band tonight? They're all in love with you, Anna."

"Anna, remember I said Reuben would forgive you if you strayed? He'd have to, Anna. That flamenco was so sexy, and Roberto was that gorgeous."

"You have enough room, Anna?"

"Let's all go back to Tarifa," Ming said. "Okay, Anna?"

Every sentence had Anna's name.

11:11

11:11 on the bedside clock. Everything aligned, upright numbers, singular and paired, palindromic time. That lucky, twice-a-day. 11:11. Wished on for years. With each emergency, each recurrence, she wished Anna alive. Helen also wished for her sobriety, for the kids' forgiveness and understanding, for her painting. She'd wished herself a man she loved. For a good life with him. Had she overwished? Was there any wish left? 11:11. Anna was a palindrome. Asa was a palindrome, too. Helen placed her cheek against Anna's back, sliding against the sweatshirt fabric until her chin hooked under Anna's pointy wing blade. The shivering stopped. Anna's breathing was slight, slow motoring breaths.

The stove clock clicked to 11:12, but Anna's breath steady on the bed was its own hour.

Anna did not smell like Anna anymore.

The Quiets

Now she is quiet, her body slowed. Her thoughts quiet. Her dreams quiet. Her breath like sips, not breaths. Even her farts are quiet. This amuses Anna.

Scribe

And look at that! She does not even need to wait for the scribe.

Dearest One. That is what Anna calls the unborn child. This one will be a girl. *Dearest One* will tell all the boys and girls that follow.

Others are in the room. But she is talking only with the not-yet-born child. She is writing a letter. She is writing a long book to *Dearest One.*

Dearest One is much closer than the others.

Look, they are standing together at the gate, Anna and that beautiful tenderness, the secret, the first child of her first child.

■ ■ ■ ■

APRIL 2013

■ ■ ■ ■

1

Mud Season

They came back with the crinkle of paper bags, the rasp of plastic, the click of screw-off tops. Dropped shoes in a clomp by the back door, dirt in the lugs of boot soles, the angled heels of work shoes, still always a scratch-scratch brooming of mud tracked inside. Mud season they couldn't keep outside. They came in smelling of outside. They shuffled through rooms in worn cotton socks, asking, "Does Anna need anything?" They sat near the bed or lay next to Anna on the bed, smelling of town — shop and sidewalk — car oil and a lavender wash. They wore the aftertaste of restaurants — ginger and garlic, a smeary trace of deep-fry. Food was a holiday she'd taken years ago. Places she could no longer exactly remember. Or what she remembered was off camera, the white porcelain handle of a café mug, the clank of metal hangers in a shop where last summer she bought a dress. She must give that dress away. Give away all the dresses in her closet. She imagined her dresses flouncing through town, a flutter of hems waiting at a crosswalk, an A-line flare pressing a code at an ATM. She knew still the sounds of this house, the squeak of the cupboard by the sink, the stuck jostle of a dresser drawer, and the uneven stairs up to the children's empty bedrooms. The children, they had been back in those empty rooms, wandering in to lie next to her. "Momma, can I tell you something?" "Please," she would say when she could speak, or she would nod her head and nod again when they asked if she wanted them to keep speaking. They went on interviews. They saw films with subtitles shot in countries where the film could never be shown. "See you in a bit, Mom," they said, and then they were back. "You won't believe who I bumped into," they said. She tried to imagine running into someone unexpectedly, but it was confusing how anyone got anywhere or why and where they went. Someone left and someone else came back. The nurse said, "Are you comfortable?" They brought in flowers from the yard. "Here's the garden," they said, so that even with her eyes closed she saw Ball jars of daffodils and tulips. "What a spring," they said. "We could carry you outside." Soon there'd be lilacs, they promised. Your favorite.

She shook her head no.

They're not your favorite?

No. Outside, April. Anna is shaking off the possibility of May.

Scribe

She wants a greater eloquence. What Anna needs to say is simple. Still, it sounds like slogans. Have courage. For everything. Look closely at flowers. Listen to wind. There is comfort in numbers. To make a strong, clear whistle, stretch and slick the blade of fresh grass along your thumbs. Then blow. Be foolish. Goofy is good. Be diligent about brushing your teeth. Love abundantly. When your courage fails, and it will, find courage again.

Connie and John

"It will finally be her. Her will. Not any hospice protocol." John lowered the rail to sit on the edge of the mechanical bed.

Now John was just John all the time in Anna's room, even two days ago when he'd successfully shut the defib, leaving the pacemaker on.

"Not that she was ever a patient who went

by the book."

"What are you saying?" Connie snapped defensively, her knitting needles clacking like punctuation.

"What are you saying about her?" Connie was fried. She'd spent the last two nights at Anna's. "Are you accusing her of having done something wrong?" Anna's nights were increasingly restless, legs cramping, dreams uneasy. The sharp hallucinations and sudden bursts of energy.

This morning John came by before heading into the office with coffee in a thermos and Connie's yellow iris mug. Connie was grateful for the coffee. But she was more grateful to behold her husband's face. Two nights, and their life, their house, the first buds on the trees in their garden, seemed so distant, something almost in a rearview mirror. Everything now shrunk down to ice chips, to moistening peeling lips, to managing unseen hallucinations.

But here was John. Still she wished he were just her beloved husband and not the doctor.

"Just that she could be frustrating from a doctor's point of view. What can I say, Connie? She wasn't an ideal patient. She was her own kind of stubborn. On the other hand, denial's probably what's kept her going."

Connie pulled at the skein of yarn in her knitting bag. She'd taken on an elaborate pattern that involved actual concentration. Multiple yarns as well as cables. But the mistakes she kept making were basic — dropped stitches, botched stitch counts. A complicated project seemed like the right idea to focus her mind. Now Connie wished she'd opted for mindless, shuttling her needles in steady rows of knit and purl.

"You think I don't know her?" Connie knew this wasn't what John was saying. Her voice had gone all squirrelly. A better friend would have forced Anna to show for every appointment, to obey all the medical instructions. "Sometimes she just needed not to be a patient," Connie said.

"No, Connie, I know you know. It's just helpful to understand that her dying is going to be like her living."

"Hello, I'm still here," Anna piped up from under a pile of comforters on the bed. "At least technically I'm here."

John and Connie burst out laughing, Connie bordering on hysterical. It was clearly too important to both of them that out of nowhere Anna still cracked a joke.

She this, she that — another thing Connie

knew that Anna hated about being a patient.

"Jesus, you're a pain in my ass," John said. He windshield-wipered his hand, flattening folds of the comforter looking for Anna's arm. "An unpredictable pain in my ass."

Connie rested the knitting in her lap and lifted her mug of coffee. Here was her husband holding Anna's hand. And then — Connie knew he couldn't really help himself — John's fingers slipped up to Anna's wrist, and Connie watched as his eyes narrowed in concentration while he took Anna's pulse.

Scribe

Pick a number, Dearest One. Double it. Add 9. Subtract 3. Divide by 2. Subtract the original number. Your answer will always be 3.

Not memories. In her head. But math. Math tricks.

Pick a number. Double it. Add 10. Divide by 2. Subtract the original number. Your answer will be 5.

Dearest One, pick a number, Anna thinks. Square it.

2

Ming, Getting There

"Well, what exactly do you think?"

"Give me a moment to consider." But instead of actually thinking about her client's divorce negotiations, Ming thought about walking straight out of the conference room. She'd drive directly to Anna's. All week she'd been deep in an argument with herself. Helen was right. She'd yielded too easily. Been swayed by emotion. Given up the fight. In her law practice, she prided herself on keeping steady when her clients were ready to throw in the towel. She'd counseled not to let circumstance force an easy settlement. Hospice was the easy settlement. How hadn't she grasped that earlier? In the week since they'd been there, apparently Anna not only had voluntarily given up food, she'd shut down her pacemaker. Still, Ming could turn this around. Anna would eat again. Have the pacemaker turned back on. She'd convince Anna. Her logic would work better than Helen's bullying. Even if Ming's steady logic hadn't always triumphed over Anna's impulsivity, Anna usually admitted that she should have listened to Ming.

"How's that considering going?"

Ming steeled herself against the sneer of the opposing counsel's tone. She felt practically giddy. Just to consider rolling back the dilapidated swivel chair and stand from these negotiations to go to Anna's, where Ming's skill as a negotiator was more crucial than arguing for her client's alimony and the payment of children's summer camp.

Yes, the idea of bolting made Ming feel better than she'd felt in weeks.

All she had to do was stand up.

Instead she sank deeper into the rolling chair and palmed the scratched-up teak conference table.

"I think we should move forward and not try to reopen what at our last meeting both clients figured out so successfully," she said.

Because, however wonderful her fantasy was, there were two serious fantasy busters that kept Ming at the table.

The first was that she was notoriously dutiful. A dotter of *i*'s. She'd never bolted from any meeting. Thanks to her father, she seemed genetically grateful to be overworked, never able to switch off the anxious DNA from when she'd first hung her shingle, certain that no one in this small upstate community would hire a woman lawyer with a Chinese first name and an Ecuadorean surname. She still panicked that clients wouldn't keep coming. For that reason Ming remained of counsel at Winters and Trell, her old Albany firm. Sebastian tried reminding her she'd spent twenty years uselessly worrying, that her practice flourished, that it was his work in the restaurant business that was far more fickle. What did he know? With his Latin blood, Sebastian was wired so optimistically.

But the real truth — who was Ming kidding? — was that there was relief in work. It was comforting to put her head down and focus, her vision narrowing so tightly that it occluded Anna. Hours passed. Looking up, she would have accomplished something. Even with a divorce like this that trailed on, at a certain moment from the tedious tangle of human pettiness she'd see the path to close a deal. You can't count on human decency, she'd learned, but you could count on the legal process. She believed in the law. It was what distinguished her as a lawyer — that she actually believed that the logic of law helped manage human foibles. She would triumph in this divorce negotiation. And even if she failed, who really suffered?

Failing with Anna was different.

"It's too late now to turn things around," Helen said yesterday, reporting that Anna was hardly awake. In and out. Though mostly out.

"It's not," Ming countered. She'd work on Helen, woo her back. "I'm sorry I didn't back you up last week."

She'd finish — get the ridiculous negotiation about summer camp and college tuitions done — and then leave this meeting and drive east out of the Berkshires to Anna in the Valley. She'd use all her logic to steer Anna. Sebastian had prepared a lunch and dinner in the hopes that Ming could convince Anna to resume eating. There was a cooler and a wicker hamper in the car with foods that would be easy on Anna's system. Wild mushroom and garlic soup again. Honey and pollen from his bees.

She's so sorry she lost any time. Ming can't lose her. Anna is her firecracker of joy. It was Anna who burst Ming out of the rigid order of her strict parents. Years later it was Anna who had Ming making jokes while Lily's brain was severed. Sitting in the stupid massage chairs getting pedicures, Anna looked at Ming, and Ming instantly felt lighter. There would be no one who could unfasten her so easily.

"You hanging in?" Ming touched her client's arm. Her client, Jenny Hyde, had her stiff meeting face painted on, an armor of pancake and lipstick. In contrast, last week Jenny showed up at the office for a meeting with lunch. She'd been at the stables — no makeup, in riding clothes; she was a beautiful woman. The two women sat on the back porch of Ming's office taking in the spring warmth and eating turkey sandwiches. "I actually miss him," Jenny said out of nowhere. "I woke up this morning remembering this thing he used to say that was guaranteed to crack me up. I'm not sure why I stopped finding him funny." Ming took off the top piece of bread and quietly ate her sandwich. Best not to offer commentary. Jenny was talking to herself. Could be the spring air. Could be something lasting. Ming couldn't guess with any certainty, having seen people get back together who had knuckles hard against each other's windpipe. It wasn't all that different from staying married. Any given day Ming found herself furious with, annoyed by, thankful for, attracted to — oh, the list went contradictorily on — Sebastian. Ming recalled a law professor who provocatively declared that every married couple has grounds for divorce. Ming then was twenty-four, newly married, and thought the professor a cynical asshole. Still it stuck in her mind. Twenty-five — no, twenty-eight years later, just seeing Sebastian's socks in a threadbare crumple every night on the bathroom floor made her want to slit his throat. Still, moments later she loved the way he roughly slid close to her in their bed and they slept folded in their own well-creased origami.

What Ming knew with certainty, having negotiated too many divorces, was that when kids are involved, the marriage goes on after papers are signed. You don't live together anymore. You don't have sex together anymore. Though Ming can point to those who continue living together and those who continue having sex. But it doesn't matter if the grown-ups can't abide one another; they still remain responsible for the children. She and Sebastian have weathered a sick child; all the pivotal-event divorce statistics were against them. Every day there were challenges so far beyond the cost of music lessons or camp. Ming believed in the known challenges of marriage.

"Useless!" Suddenly Mr. Hyde was shouting. "You're useless!" He bucked up, the chair tipping in a clatter behind him. Hyde's voice was a razor. "I have no time for this!"

"Control your client." Ming watched the opposing counsel swivel toward the curtained window to signal that he neither condoned nor condemned.

She needed to stay put. It was a game. Who bolts first?

Instead Ming pressed the recording device on her phone, preserving the full onslaught of invectives spilling from Mr. Hyde's ugly mouth.

"I'm done here," she said when he paused.

And, like that, Ming was done. She was up and walking out of the conference room, Mr. Hyde's voice a harsh wind at her back.

Opening her car door, she remembered another moment from the vacation in Tarifa — a chubby nudist family on the beach and their chalky flesh rolls going lobster red as day after day they nakedly bounced about playing netless badminton. She was counting on the story to make Anna crack up. And Ming will use that openness — however momentary — to step-by-step show Anna the path back to food and medicine, to another round of living.

Even before Ming snapped her seat belt, she was prepping her case. Anna had relied on her before. Anna respected her pragmatism. From the first illness, Ming had made sure there was a living will and a health proxy. "It's the best way to ward off disaster," she'd insisted when Anna said a last will and testament seemed like giving up. She'd overseen every update. Ming had managed Anna's recurrences with practicality, as if her logic and diligence, her order and reasoning, would trump each advance of illness. As if there were always a way to negotiate.

It would work again. Helen was right but tactically wrong. Caroline and Molly would back her. Today, together, they'd navigate correctly. Ming felt confident. She knew how to win.

Helen, Getting There

This morning when Asa carried in two mugs of coffee and settled back into bed with Helen, he said, "You've had an unexpectedly good week. Think about that on the drive? Tell Anna. She loves hearing about your life."

Helen leaned against Asa. "I will." But all of it — the perfectly brewed coffee, the week's surprises — seemed more twisted than good. A stellar week if Anna weren't dying. A stellar week if she hadn't learned that Anna had stopped eating. Or had the pacemaker or whatever it was called shut off, even though Layla kept repeating over the phone that that actually didn't speed anything up?

Now, here, at the New Haven rest stop, as Helen angled against her car, the gas pump clicking at full, she thought, Good things come in threes. She crammed the pump handle back into its slot and pressed YES for a receipt, but she couldn't wait for the receipt, buckling into her belt and throwing the car into gear in one move, she accelerated in a fast swerve onto the interstate.

Helen knew that if she said out loud that she was suddenly positive Anna was going to live, she'd be accused of magical thinking. Superstitious. That was a dirty little secret of Helen's. Nonreligious, down-to-earth Helen secretly checked her daily horoscope, stepped onto airplanes with her right foot, was a sucker for chain letters that promised good fortune or bad luck. Helen, who shook her head over any New Agey hocus-pocus, was in fact driving like a bat out of hell ready to pronounce the inevitable future like she was goddamn Tiresias.

But there it was. *Good things come in threes.*

First was the confirmation of the show. A twenty-year retrospective, at the Art Institute of Chicago slated for fall 2015, including the negotiated sale of two paintings to the museum.

Second was last evening. When Helen walked from a Prince Street meeting to join Asa for dinner at Café Select, she took a call from a number she didn't recognize, and fifteen minutes later, as she heaped horseradish onto an oyster, she swore to Asa, "When he said, 'Hey, Helen, Larry Page here,' I had zero idea who Larry Page was, and then after he said, 'We'd like you to be our 2013 inaugural recipient of the Google Arts Prize,' I stood on the corner of Lafayette and Prince shouting, 'A hundred and fifty thousand dollars! No fucking way, Larry!' But honestly, Asa, I still have no idea who Larry Page is."

Asa tipped an oyster into his mouth and shook his head. "Ever heard of the Internet, Helen?"

So that was one.

And two.

Now, with the speedometer well above eighty, it was obvious to Helen that Anna was number three. It made perfect sense.

In an old-wives'-tale kind of way.

In a three-is-a-mystical-number kind of way.

It was obvious — as in inevitable. It didn't matter that the defib thing had been deactivated or whatever Layla had told her. The proof was suddenly everywhere that Anna was going to have a comeback and be fine. For example, if Helen looked left and watched the light bounce staccato through the trees in sharp diagonals, that was a sign, because Anna always said that it was Helen who taught her to notice light and the play of light and speed. Okay, maybe light and the trees weren't 100 percent proof, but Helen wanted to fly to Anna's. Be the first to arrive and share everything. Not share her own good news with guilt but with giddy certainty that Anna was about to feel better.

Helen might not even have to do any convincing. Maybe Anna woke this morning feeling strong and, without thinking twice, wandered into the kitchen and took all her medications and ate a cheddar cheese omelet. She'd probably find Anna out in the living room. Hey, Helen, Anna will say, looking a little sheepish when Helen walks in. There's a new plan.

Helen heard the shriek of the siren before she saw the triplet lights. She was driving almost ninety miles per hour. Helen veered onto the shoulder, the car thumping against the grooved surface.

Helen unrolled her window, then watched the patrol car in her rearview mirror. She looped through ways to get out of a ticket. How many points was too many?

The cop was slow getting out of his car.

State police, light gray hat with the Connecticut blue band. Matching blue tie. He adjusted his belt. His wide stance, the slow walk were clearly deliberate, as if to provoke more guilt. Helen's adrenaline spiking, she felt guilty of more than speeding. It seemed he slowed even more, kicking loose gravel with his boots until he'd stopped at the back of Helen's car. Close up he looked practically pubescent. Helen was probably too old to smile her way out of this ticket.

The patrolman tucked his head and leaned in to speak. The brim of his gray hat pitched low. His hands were crossed, resting on the wide belt as if for emphasis. He checked out the inside of the car. Took in the bottle of water, the cup of coffee. The overnight bag in the backseat.

"Where you going, ma'am?"

"Massachusetts."

"What's there?"

Helen suddenly choked up. Swallowed hard. "My friend."

"Any idea how fast you were driving?"

Helen managed a weak smile. "Too fast?"

"Well, ma'am, ninety-one miles an hour. Pretty important getting there?"

Helen wanted to blurt it all. He'd understand. She'd enlist his concern, and he might even offer a full-on siren escort blazing right to Anna's driveway.

"License and registration, please."

Helen fished out the registration, the current one at the bottom of five expired, and fumbled in her wallet, tearing a corner of her license, then watched the cop make his slow way back to his patrol car. She was still pumped, needing to get to Anna's while this child cop made grand theater of her speeding.

She needed to breathe herself down into calm. She closed her eyes, and she was back in the hospital room, Anna's third New York treatment, the one when she met Asa. Anna argued she could easily do the same treatment in Springfield, but Helen kind of liked slipping back into their old hospital routines — walking her son to the crosstown bus, stopping to buy Anna containers of fresh egg salad and a soup, a bagel with lox cream cheese, and taking the subway uptown. She'd emerge up the stairs at 168th Street, each day surprised by the acrid tang of fried food, and walk the long block past food trucks where orderlies lined up for breakfast sandwiches and sweet rolls. Early mornings the hospital rotunda was quiet, the security guards nodding Helen past. She ran the five flights, the grocery bags banging against her shins. It was critical to take the stairs to prove she wasn't also sick.

Another belief: if Anna died, Helen would die, too. It was the twisted logic of superstition. She'd never been without Anna, thus she wouldn't exist if Anna didn't exist.

"Well, for now you're the complete winner," Anna said at the end of treatment. "I stay alive, and you get the guy."

But before Helen could find a return quip, Anna said, "Hang on to Asa. He might prove more reliable than me."

"Ma'am. Ma'am."

"Yes, sir." Helen blinked her eyes open. The officer was back, and if it were possible, he seemed even younger, a splash of acne along the jawline, the overly wide stance a cover for his coltish body.

He handed her the ticket. "Your friend'll still be there if you go the limit."

"Yes, sir," she repeated. She watched his bouncier gait and even the kicked rock as he headed back to his patrol car. He was feeling okay. Doing his job.

He shadowed his car behind Helen until the next exit. She kept cleanly on the speed limit. Even when he was long out of sight.

"Yes, sir!" she shouted out loud in the car. "Yes, sir!" she shouted louder.

She'd done it. She'd shut up. Didn't say anything, not one stupid thing, so that the kid cop might take pity on a middle-age lady and give her a break, letting her off without a ticket.

In which case the state police of Connecticut would have used up Helen's third good thing.

In which case Anna would have died.

You owe me, she'll tease when she describes the speeding ticket. How when the officer said, "She'll still be there," Helen refrained from saying, Yes, sir, thanks to this ticket she will be.

Helen can't wait to say, You really owe me, Anna. I took points on my license for you. All you've got to do is come to my wedding and make a toast.

Parked at the bottom of Anna's driveway, Ming was already there. Helen would have preferred to be alone, but she didn't really care. Anna will be fine.

Zeus barked from the top stone step.

"Hey, Zeus." Helen filled with momentary goodwill toward the dog.

As she opened the car door, her phone rang. Lucinda. Helen's eldest.

"Hey, cookie," Helen said. She was happy for the call. For the unlikely clear reception, for the chance to hear her daughter's voice, for the sheer grace that Lucinda has returned to talking to her, for the chance to brag to her kid a little about the Google prize. Maybe she'll take Lucinda on a trip. Rusty, too. She owed them a whole lot more than a trip.

Lucinda shouted "Mom!" with such delight that Helen's stomach instantly constricted.

Helen wanted to disconnect. Let it roll to voice mail when Lucinda called back.

She stuffed the ticket into her bag and stood from the car. She slammed the car door and leaned, looking up at Anna's house. The prayer flags drooped along the roof peak. A bit of clothesline dangling from the eaves.

Lucinda was about to say something wonderful, and Helen, who only wanted everything wonderful for Lucinda, who was grateful every day for the way her daughter generously forgave her, needed Lucinda to stop. To shut up and stop speaking.

Or Helen wanted to jump in faster than Lucinda, wanted to say, Let me call you right back, cookie. Let me get inside, check on Anna and call you right back.

But she couldn't get off the phone. And Lucinda, her beautiful daughter, her daughter who had taken so much time trusting Helen again, was already bursting forth,

"Mom, I got it! The job, Mom!"

Lucinda's voice bell-like, her joy so complete that Helen felt it. Painfully.

"You said I would, Mom. Thanks for that faith. It's like you made it happen, Mom."

And there it was. Done.

The third good thing. Claimed.

While Lucinda talked about schedules and benefits, Helen wandered over to the side yard. The bucket swing on the rusted metal play set rattled and clanked, the chains twisted so the canvas seats hung sideways. Helen untwisted the seats so they swung freely.

"I'm so proud of you," Helen mustered, suitably enthusiastic.

"The office culture's super chill," Lucinda said. There was going to be a conversation about salary. She was going to thrive. And flourish. "Those are words they use, Mom," Lucinda said. " 'Thrive and flourish.' "

Her daughter's voice was a song in her ear. And Helen responded. Out of that most fundamental place, Helen sang the praise that was the mother praise song — the song of praise for crawling, then walking, the praise of all the watch-me-Mom-I'm-swimming-underwater.

Then Helen made her way to the bottom of the granite-slab steps leading to the front door. But there was no rush anymore, no reason to go inside. Instead she veered to the side of the house where the land hilled up. It was too late to have a take-back, too late to have a full-sweep do-over to untangle this day from her superstitious, idiotic thinking.

"You deserve this, Lucinda. I knew it would work out." Helen stood on her tippytoes. She reached, stretched, then jumped until she snagged the end of the clothesline that dangled from the roof. She tugged. She tugged and watched the arc of rumpled prayer flags unfix. Helen moved below the pitch of roof. Angled back out into the yard so there was traction and momentum to her yanks. She swung and tugged with one hand, the other hand holding the phone to her ear as Lucinda chirped and Helen chirped back.

"This is such wonderful news," she said. She jerked hard on the line that held the prayer flags.

She made her way around the front and sides of the house, pulling and tugging, flicking out when the line snagged.

"Great things will happen for you. I know this." She felt awed by the big unknown life still ahead of her daughter.

Helen was under the last of the flags. They

hung flat and limp. She yanked with a final jerky whip and watched the last of the string of prayer flags drift in slow motion, sagging down to the muddy ground.

Molly, Getting There

Route 2. Soon after the Concord Rotary, spring had barely arrived. It was like driving back into March, by Fitchburg and then Leominster, where it was February gray and bare, the edges of woods grimed with a last layer of snowplow crap. Depressing.

Everything near Molly's house popped and shouted April. Daffodils all funny-faced in the garden bed, clusters of other bulbs poking up. It seemed overnight the furry husks of magnolias have dropped and scattered on the ground, and the tree by the yard swing was a riot of pink flowers in various states of bloom.

A hawk swooped. Cut low close to the car, plunging down for roadkill. The whole shoulder of Route 2 looked like one long roadkill diner for hawks and turkey vultures. But despite how bleak Route 2 looked, Molly was glad to be alone in the car. She wished the trip to Anna's were longer. Like North Dakota longer. Even keeping to the speed limit, she was almost at Millers Falls and the turnoff onto 63. On a good day,

Molly loved the in-between, the no-one-can-find-me limbo of being on the road. Now there were phones. Now people expected that you were always findable. Everywhere. The car outfitted for hands-free phone usage. But Molly and Serena have made a decision not to talk and drive, modeling behavior for the whole family now that the kids were driving. Molly hated thinking about the kids driving. Especially now.

The message Molly left on Helen's phone had been a lie. She wasn't running three hours late because she'd been called in for an emergency session with a suicidal patient. She'd give anything for the known world of patient emergencies, the calm that settles through her limbs as she manages a crisis, sets up therapy protocols. She'd give anything for that confidence.

Sitting with Serena and Tessa in Dr. Drake's office this morning, the principal in a primped voice that tried too hard to sound appealing, too modernly unfazed by lesbian moms and down with the kids, suggested they address the situation. "Let's really tune in to what's happening here." Molly was actually surprised at how little confidence she could conjure in herself. She was hopeful that she didn't look like a complete shaking mess. But she didn't look like a health-care professional, that was for-fuck's-sake certain.

The car banked on a steep curve. Molly felt heated and queasy. Thin saliva flushed through her mouth. She cracked the windows. She might actually have to pull over.

Last week when they were at Anna's, her friends had pooh-poohed her concern. This is what kids do. This is what we did. Kids get high, had been the consensus. They shared the use-and-abuse phase of each of their kids. Then they teased her. Do we need to remind you, Molly, of a certain teenager's unabashed love of Thai stick back in the day?

But this situation was different. This was not about Molly's having forgotten any of the fun and stupidity of sixteen. Or that she had forgotten her own mother's scotched afternoons of pills and booze. Or that she had to argue with her wife, since for Serena marijuana was practically a nuclear panic button, her having scraped out of a childhood with addict brothers. This wasn't even because Tessa was such an idiot that she brought weed with her to school. (Thank God, Dr. Drake did not believe in what he called "oversharing" with the authorities.) Or that Tessa sat through the meeting with a not-nearly-hangdog-enough look on her face.

It was what Molly had seen. Just as they'd all settled into the circle of scuffed plastic chairs, Tessa shrugged off her peacoat and Molly saw the tattoo. Right there on Tessa's waist. Before Tessa yanked her sweater down and gave it a quick tuck into her jeans. Molly had sat through the meeting straining to focus on the principal, talking about priorities and accountability. She worked to pull herself back into the conversation. "Absolutely," she said, providing parental-sounding observations, clear and concerned, neither minimizing nor inflating the situation.

But the whole time, Molly kept sneaking looks at the edge of where Tessa's angora sweater met her jeans and prayed she'd been wrong. She knew she hadn't been. A tattoo was bad. A tattoo of a heart with a slash was really bad. But it was the two words Molly had seen in that flashing peekaboo of a millisecond that was killing her. FUCK LOVE. She'd seen that. She thought there had even been a period: FUCK. LOVE.

Her daughter. Their daughter. That same loving kid who just two weeks ago had spent a whole Sunday flopped on the den couch with her sister, Shana, watching their old favorite videos, crooning along with Sebastian in *The Little Mermaid.* This same nervous child who freaked at the mention of a shot at the pediatrician's had gone and gotten a tattoo. And not just that she'd gone off to some ratty tattoo parlor, subjected her perfect skin to the prick of who-knows-how-well-sterilized needles (wasn't there a law about minors needing consent?). But that the image Tessa had chosen was sad and cynical. The words even sadder. And permanent.

What was churning in Tessa's heart that would make her choose that slashed heart, those dark words? How was it that without any real preparation, in an instant, a child seemed unrecognizable? And how had Molly not understood that something — some sorrow, some something really bad, really dark — had taken hold in her daughter?

The phone rang in the car. Serena. Molly didn't pick up. Then she didn't pick up the second time Serena rang. She'd blame it on reception. If Serena called again, she'd be forced to pick up. Serena didn't know about the tattoo. Hadn't seen it. Molly wasn't going to tell her on the phone.

There had been agreements made at the meeting. Weekly drug tests. Counseling.

"Let's remember that Tessa is actually excelling in her schoolwork," Molly said, turning to her daughter. She wanted — no, she *needed* Tessa to smile. To shrug. To do anything that acknowledged their bond, that said, I know I messed up, Mom, and I love that you still believe in me. Instead Tessa glanced back with a don't-patronize-me look.

Molly fought an urge, right there in the principal's office, to stand up and say, Stop. To burst into tears and say, Whoever you are, I want my daughter Tessa back, and I want her back with that stuff washed off her.

What was so fucking great about being a parent? Why, knowingly, did any right-minded person take on the anxiety and uncertainty? Would anyone do this if it could possibly be foreseen that the adorable baby, that crawling, walking, running, finger-painting, reading, laughing, cuddling, clowning, miracle of a child, this I-love-you-Mommy-so-much of a child became this person who would break your heart with a sullen, nasty, I-don't-have-time-for-this-bullshit glare.

Molly swerved off the exit into Millers Falls. It had once been a small but busy mill town, powered by the falls. Now it was scrappy. A dingy place with no industry, no anything but sagging buildings where every shabby last person in the town probably had tattoos. Multiple tattoos. It wasn't that she and Serena didn't have friends with tattoos. They had friends who were always finding some occasion to mark with a new tat. But this was permanent. FUCK. LOVE. Could the period between FUCK and LOVE possibly mean a declared philosophical division between sex and love? Hookup mentality? But it's Tessa who taught Molly that periods are used for emphasis in texting. This body marking was nothing she wanted her daughter to live with for a lifetime.

Then Molly was through town, the road narrow and steely blue with pine shadow, the houses set back from stone walls. She had only twenty more minutes alone, driving past the Bookmill in Montague. Should she just stop for a coffee, look for a book to give Tessa? No way. Too easy for any book to be misinterpreted. Then past the house where she and Helen had lived a million years ago, when all they had to worry about was keeping warm in a drafty house.

When she arrives at Anna's, she'll undo her lie. She needs to talk. Tell her friends about the school meeting. The weed. And the tattoo. She needs help. This was where

Anna was always perfect. The best of all the friends at balancing what was actually worrisome in parenting and what was Molly's anxiety confusing the situation. Anna always cut through Molly's perfectionism and insecurity, discarded the extraneous in a flash, always supporting Molly's solid judgment.

"Go easy," Anna had said at so many crucial moments, and it released something in Molly.

Molly needed the afternoon alone to take a long walk with Anna. I get it. It's a little worrisome, she imagined Anna saying. But I swear it is eighty-five percent just stupid teenage shit, Moll. Like blue hair back in the nineties. Or pierced eyebrows. It's honestly not a whole lot different from you and me and all the messing around we did with drugs and boys. They've got to push against us. It's their job.

But Helen told her not to expect much on the visit. Anna was sleeping most of the time. Often not responsive. Molly didn't entirely trust Helen. She might not have that long walk, but they'd talk.

The car phone buzzed again.

She was not going to be able to avoid Serena.

"Hey, honey." Molly heard Serena sobbing. Serena never cried. Not her MO. Serena was cool in the face of problems. She had a surgeon's calm. Molly knew when Serena panicked, because the more she panicked, the steelier she became.

"What? What's happening?" The sound of Serena crying was tinny through the car speakers. "Do you need me to come home? Where's Tessa?"

Molly slowed the car. Too many disaster thoughts all at once. All of them outdisastering the tattoo.

"You've got to talk to me, honey." Molly sharpened her voice. "Is Tessa okay?"

"You tell me." Serena's voice was taut, almost accusing. "You're the shrink."

"I think she is."

Molly turned in to a random driveway, a ranch house in the middle of renovation, a man up on the scaffold, two trucks in the driveway, a log swing set and slide in the side yard.

"We're the parents. We have to believe in Tess so she can believe in herself." Molly heard the steadiness of her own voice and all the right things she told Serena, things she might tell a client during a session. Still, it felt far away. She wished that as a parent she felt even half the clarity she felt as a therapist. Looking out at the man up the scaffold, the way he torqued his whole body to one side, leaned out bracing himself against the post, Molly thought, He's an idiot trusting that flimsy structure.

"Thanks, honey. I love you." Serena sounded calmed, even a little embarrassed. "Say hey to the gang. Give Anna a big kiss."

Molly made a smooch sound and pressed DISCONNECT.

She put the car in reverse, then slammed her foot on the brake. She was dreaming even to hope she'd take a walk alone with Anna. Not today. Not ever again. She had to trust her instincts. Molly rooted her cell phone out of her bag. Texted, Tess, we need to talk. It's your body. But. No. More. Tattoos. I don't care if I sound like a hypocrite. I love you. Call. And she pressed SEND.

Caroline, Getting There

Throughout the week Caroline had been calmed — it worked as an instant chill pill — by imagining just how she'd set up the story. She imagined her friends' stunned, openmouthed gasps as she recounted how this time Elise had flown down to St. Martin and checked in at La Samanna under the name of Jacqueline Bouvier.

Honestly, their gaped mouths might almost make it worth the whole insanity. And it was truly nonstop insanity between convincing the concierge not to throw Elise out of the hotel until Caroline could get a flight to the island; paying barrels of gold for Elise's oceanfront suite, the room service, and all the unbelievable room damage; then the return flight where Elise, in full-blown psychosis, unclipped her seat belt and paced the aisles ranting Kennedy conspiracy theories, from the obvious "There was a shooter on the grassy knoll" to the more obscure "It was a joint endeavor of the Russians and LBJ."

Elise never entertained predictable delusions of the Jesus or aliens variety. It's the fabulous she tended toward. And this one was the biggest doozy. Caroline couldn't wait to make everyone guess just how much this St. Martin extravaganza of nuttiness has cost her and Danny.

Always classy when Elise went off her meds. You had to give her that.

Let's not forget the two-hundred-dollar beach hair braiding with semiprecious beads.

But Jacqueline Bouvier!

Shouldn't that have been a tip-off when Elise registered at the hotel that all was not exactly right? Could they really feign shock when she showed up for her dinner reservation wearing a strand of pearls, gloves, and high heels?

And, yes, ladies, that was all she wore.

If nothing else, at least it was a good story for her friends. Caroline would enjoy repeating, "Just the strand, the gloves, and the heels."

Though there was nothing funny when she arrived in St. Martin and saw that familiar hypomanic arch of Elise's face. Her tongue every few moments swiping at her chewed, chapped lips, like a cat. Her tweezed-to-pencil-stroke eyebrows twitching in some come-hither madness.

Definitely not a good story so much as a sad old story now.

But it will be worth it, back in Anna's living room, Caroline playing all the parts — French concierge, fussy flight attendant, batshit admissions nurse — and watching the horrified delight on her friends' faces. A desperate move using Elise's insanity. But what was the point of years of her sister's insanity if at the very least Caroline couldn't get some bang for her buck?

Driving through Hartford, the city skyline on her left, Caroline decided she'd hold back and pay it out slowly — the blue organza silk drapes that Elise cut up for a matching bikini and beach robe, the words she finger-painted with ketchup and God knows what on the suite's stucco walls. Elise so bonkers, so manic beyond pain, that when Caroline describes the vine of bruises and lacerations on her legs as she still begs to go out disco dancing, Anna will say, Carrie, you've got to admit, Elise always makes crazy seem fun. Come on, Jacqueline Bouvier!

Driving north, Caroline felt bouncy. She gauged the drive in twenty-minute bursts — Hartford to Springfield, Springfield to Northampton. Actually a little manic herself. But twenty minutes later, driving through Springfield, the Memorial Bridge spanning the Connecticut River on her left, she felt drained, numb, exhausted all down her limbs, only the loop in her brain a speedy, furious calculation of how many thousands and thousands of dollars she and Danny had spent on Elise's medical care and maintenance. How many hours she'd spent trying to keep her sister safe.

It was the other part of why she needed to get to Anna's and see her friends. She's told Elise antics God knows how many times. And they always let her. Let Caroline be funny and compassionless and mean and angry and philosophical and hopeful and outraged and just plain sad. She's so sad for the increasingly worn, chipped life that is the life her brilliant big sister has led. And Molly, Helen, Anna, and Ming allow her the whole complicated range of what it is to be Elise's sister.

And then Caroline was hanging a sharp left onto Anna's road and skidding down the muddy driveway to park next to Helen's car.

"Hey, hey, ladies." She called, propping open the kitchen's metal door with her foot. She hefted her purse and three bottles of chardonnay onto the kitchen counter. There was no sign that anyone was there. The house was weirdly silent. But all the cars were in the driveway. They'd gone somewhere? Without her? They knew she was running late.

Caroline jammed the wine into the fridge. She didn't really believe they'd leave without her. No, actually, she did believe they'd leave her. And this was proof. That having pulled away sometime in high school, she'd never fully been allowed back in. As if the group had reconfigured and she'd never really be allowed into the core again.

She made it all the way into the living room before she noticed Ming and Helen bunched low on the couch, a braid of limbs among the pillows.

Helen's eyes were closed.

Ming nodded at Caroline. "You're here." Ming's voice was so quiet and flat that Caroline thought Helen must have one of her migraines.

"Where's Anna?"

Caroline saw Molly outside on the porch, talking on her phone, her free hand gesticulating in wide slicing arcs of emphasis.

"Is everything okay? Where's Anna?"

Was she too late? Was it possible?

"Go in, Caroline." Ming nodded in the direction of the bedroom. The words, the nod, seemed to take reserves of energy Ming didn't have. "When the nurse is finished rolling her, Anna will be awake. She's in and out. That's what it is now."

"No worries, ladies. I'll get her up." Caroline had no room for Ming's negativity.

"She hasn't been out here in the living room since last week when we were here."

"I've got the you-can't-top-this story of the week." She had been to the Caribbean and back. She'd saved Elise, and she could save Anna. Anna will giggle, Jacqueline Bouvier. Caroline will show all of them how essential she is.

"Go in. She likes hearing our voices."

Helen's eyes fluttered open, then slipped back closed. "At least we like thinking that."

3

Beautiful Certainty

At 9 times 8, she drifted and woke at 14 times 7.

"She said ninety-eight." Someone hovered. "Anna, did you say ninety-eight?"

Ming. Behind her, Helen. "It's me, honey. I told you we'd be back."

Such comfort still in the tables. The beautiful certainty in numbers. She wants to tell them this, but she is drifting again and here, now, 16 times 9.

Wonder Women

Have no fear! The Old Friends have special powers. A wonder gang. Middle-age action-figure ladies, with hormonal floods and touched-up roots.

They take turns on the bed, smoothing Anna's hair, her neck, her arms, and not so much speaking to her as she drifts but including her on these first mini-forays into — *the slog the crazy the scary the unbelievable* — each of their weeks, none of them quite prepared to step into full spotlight.

When they start a second loop, Helen saying, "Just now, as I pulled in to the driveway, Lucinda called. She's been offered a huge new job, and — drumroll, please — it's in London," Anna shifts a little, not with that horrifying spasming they'd witnessed when they first came into her room but a feline stretch, languidly twisting her arms into the air, circling kinks out of her wrists and rolling her shoulders, then asking Ming to prop pillows as Helen helps her upright.

"Lucinda said it was me. My faith in her," Helen manages to choke out before she breaks down in tears.

Anna nods, her eyes still shut.

"Okay, ladies, I'm only sending out this teaser." Caroline poses, voguing her arms dramatically. "Yesterday morning I was on a Caribbean beach, and Elise had Bo Derek cornrows."

Anna winches open an eye. Then, cartoon style, pops the other eye. She rubs flakes of crust caught under the lashes. Caroline hands her a warm washcloth. Anna spreads the terry-cloth square on her flattened palm, moving it slowly across her face.

Anna looks over at the open window, the cloth balled against her cheek. "We should go outside."

"That's just what Ming thought," Helen says, as if this were the simplest idea. "It's gorgeous outside. You up for it?"

"What's the worst that can happen?" Anna laughs.

Maybe Paris

Molly drove through the winding back roads of North Amherst. It was like high school. Afternoons they'd done exactly this. Molly driving, the rest of them scrunched together, sometimes even two squished in the passenger seat, no set direction or plan, maybe winding up at the Farm, where they'd hang for a couple hours before piling back into the car, and Molly would drop them off one by one at their homes.

She veered to avoid potholes, but the dirt road, gouged from a harsh winter, was pocked with deep cavities and troughs. She slowed, taking the road at five miles an hour; still the car bumped heavily, like a horse-drawn wagon on wooden wheels and not a fancy German import with hydraulic struts. With every rut Molly glanced into the rearview mirror. Anna's head bobbling even when they were on steady ground. She was like a child buckled into the backseat, her eyes barely clearing the bottom of the window as she peered out. Helen scooted close, wrapping an arm around Anna to keep her from slipping down or hitting her forehead with each jostle. It seemed downright crazy that they'd taken her out of the safety of the bedroom.

Molly turned the car onto paved road. When they gained speed, Anna pressed the button, and her window slid open. A sudden lash of wind like an alarm.

"This feels wonderful." She tipped her face, gathering her hair from where it whipped and caught between her lips.

"Not too much?" Helen held Anna tighter. She seemed breakable. This wind alone could snap her. "It's cold, isn't it?"

"Open all of them."

"Where are we going?" Molly shouted over the thrum of air.

"Let's just bomb around." Anna looked delighted, impish, chin lifted, angling to take all the wind and sun across her face.

When she pressed to slide up her window, the others quickly copycatted. Then a silence as sudden and contained as the wind had been unruly. They passed the middle school where Anna had taught and, farther on, the horse farm where her younger son, Andy, had learned to jump, taking home a wallful of dressage ribbons, breaking his collarbone and an arm and getting a couple concussions along the way. Then Puffer's Pond, where for years they'd sprawled on the raked sand beach watching all their kids cannonball off the float.

Ming pointed to an unmarked turnoff, and Molly swung into the lot, parking to face the pond.

"I brought a picnic," Ming announced. "Sebastian says it's his way, Anna, of coming to visit."

Helen suggested a fire in one of the cooking pits. But nobody moved. Wind ruffled the pond. Even the blue of the sky seemed a chilly blue.

"Maybe let's eat in here?" Ming said.

"Let's take a vacation." Anna looked out her side window toward the boarded-up changing rooms. "Can we?"

"Of course, Anna." Ming hadn't even begun her argument. Maybe she wouldn't need to. What a relief to hear Anna speak of a future. She gave Helen a light shove on the shoulder, and Helen shrugged a hopeful, *Maybe you're right.*

"We always said we would," Helen said. It was true. They always planned to go away together. Women, not nearly as close as they were, celebrated birthdays in Paris. Come on, stupid book groups went on reading retreats in Turks and Caicos.

"Let's not bother with why we didn't get it together," Ming said. "Let's plan."

They went giddy with options.

Yoga in Tulum.

Skip the warrior poses, just margaritas, please.

Ski Park City.

Think Easter in Rome.

Sail the Greek islands.

"No," Anna said. "I mean right now. Let's just get out of this stupid town."

Chant

Layla let herself in through the kitchen door, the wood and metal chimes clanging. She heard Zeus yapping up a storm in the back of the house. Probably Anna's room. She'd be quick. She knew how jumpy these friends got about their sacred time. She didn't blame them. But she had to talk with Helen.

"What does Anna want after?" the Valley women asked Layla two nights ago when they'd gathered in the living room for a prayer circle. Anna had refused both the offer to carry her out or for them to circle the bed. When Layla admitted she didn't know what Anna wanted, they acted like she was a delinquent friend. Connie didn't know either. Right then Layla broke out of the circle and went to the bedroom.

"What do you want?" Layla hated that she couldn't stop crying while she asked. She wasn't sure how much Anna still understood.

"Everyone asks me this," Anna moaned. "Helen'll take care of it. She won't let it get boring. I don't want to bore everyone to death."

Layla held off discussing the service on her now-daily check-in call with Helen. She had her marching orders from the Friday Craft and Wine group. But Layla knew that the word "chant" wasn't going to go over well with Helen. All those childhood friends seemed seriously uptight against anything they'd determined was Pioneer Valley New Agey. She'd say, "We want to sing one song." When they spoke last night, Helen said, "Please, stop by. I'd like to see you." It felt close between them. Most nights the calls ended with both of them in tears as Layla charted Anna's decline.

Whatever Helen thought, Anna loved this chant. Layla had no doubts. However cringeworthy or boring Helen might think it was, the fact was that Anna asked to close every Friday Craft and Wine with that chant. In their years of singing together, the women had created intricate harmonies. It meant something. Actually, it made Layla's blood boil. It should be enough to say, Helen, it was my kitchen or her kitchen pretty much every day for twenty years. I also know some things Anna wants. But why justify? The whole thing made Layla feel like she was back in seventh grade. And not quite in the right crowd.

"Hey, killer," Layla called in response to Zeus's incessant barking. She waited for him to race down the hallway to circle and yap at her feet.

But it was odd. No one shouting at Zeus to shut up. Nothing cooking. Not any of the food extravaganzas the friends had brought last week. None of Ming's soup on the stove.

Maybe they hadn't come? Couldn't take it when it got really tough. Not for them if they couldn't be big heroes swooping in with their self-congratulatory smiles when Anna rallied and told childhood stories.

Now, with Anna barely conscious, they'd chickened out of the tough stuff.

"Coming, killer."

More likely a simple delay.

Layla could stay until they came. She'd take any time with Anna. Even when Anna slept. Her light, motoring snore was a comfort.

But in the bedroom there was only Zeus.

Zeus alert, up on all fours, barking on the hospital bed like his manic, teacup-poodle self.

"What's going on?" Layla bent to let Zeus hop into her arms. "Where's everybody, killer? Where's Anna, Zeus?" She tried to strip any alarm from her voice. "Where's our Anna?"

Anna's clothes, the ones she refused to change out of — the purple sweatpants, green Billabong T-shirt, and blue ski socks, each a castoff belonging to her kids — were clumped on the bed.

Layla spun in a circle. Where was Anna?

She eased Zeus down. He raced to the pillow, grabbing it up with his teeth, gnashing and shaking it.

She spun again, as if she'd missed something. "Where'd she go, Zeus? Just tell me." Layla didn't want to be crying. She was crying.

She folded the sweatpants and T-shirt. She balled the socks. Piling them neatly on the armchair. When she looked back to the bed, she felt dizzy. Her saliva ran thin in her mouth. A flush of nausea. She might actually get sick. The bed was so empty.

"What's the deal?" Layla forced a singsong lightness. "Where's your crazy momma?"

Connie had stayed over last night. There was a schedule. Connie would know. If anything had gone wrong, Connie knew. And John. He'd know.

Zeus turned in agitated circles on the bed, the sheets making tangled whorls, finally catching his paws as he fell over. For days he'd stayed curled next to Anna, barking when anyone touched down on the bed.

"It's fine, Zeus."

But nothing felt fine. The house felt electric. Like there were frayed wires, trip mines everywhere. Through the open windows, the air piney and crisp. She felt the dangerous vacancy of the big timber house.

She needed to call Connie and John.

But even the phone seemed dangerous. She couldn't touch it. Or pick it up. If she did, what would she hear?

She needed to get out. Get to Connie and John. Once she got to their house, it would be okay. She'd find Connie crouched in the garden. Connie would rise, pulling off her gloves. Want some tea? she'd ask, and they'd stand with cups of green tea, surveying the lettuce beds, the newly planted pear trees.

She was spooked, but it was probably fine.

Still, she had seen this. The room without Anna.

"Come on, killer." Layla held out her arms. Zeus yapped and chased his Rasta tail. "Come on." Layla leaned over the bed and tried to grab Zeus by his rhinestone collar. She couldn't bring herself to touch the sheets. Something horrible would happen if she did. He growled, low, back-throated, like tumbling gravel. She reached with both hands. He snapped. It was fast. The bite sharp. She felt the clamp. Layla knocked him hard with her free hand. He skittered across the bed. The blood beaded up on her hand. She grabbed Anna's sweatshirt, wrapped her hand with it. Zeus stood, wagging shaggily. She had to leave. She shouldn't abandon him there on the bed. Anna wouldn't want that. Wherever Anna was. But she couldn't get herself to reach for him again.

Lotion

The car aimed down I-91, swung west below Springfield onto 90.

Toward Stockbridge.

Toward Otter Brook Inn and Spa.

Key word: "spa."

They loved that word: "spa." The open-throated vowel. Just saying it, they felt refreshed. None of them had been to Otter Brook before, but they'd heard that it was fancy-schmancy. They didn't bother calling ahead to see if there were day passes or if they needed to book in advance.

They were on vacation. Who would dare turn them away?

Plus, they were too busy. Each woman envisioned her health-spa dream — steam room, sauna, deep tissue work, mud masks, massages, body scrubs, pedicures, an endless supply of luscious body creams.

"I want to use lots of Egyptian cotton towels and drop them for someone else to pick up," Caroline said, twisting her wrists flamenco style.

"Sebastian's heard the restaurant is phenomenal but phenomenally expensive." They laughed at how hard it was for Ming to ever cast off fiscal caution.

Anna pulled out her credit card. "That's why God invented plastic. What bill collector dares follow where I'm heading?" Not at all garbled, Anna's voice was so strong, the joke so on point that even Helen laughed as if just the word "spa" had already had a group tonic effect.

"I'm a beauty mess." Anna pulled at her forearm. She'd thrown off the thin blanket. "Forget topical applications, I'm drinking all those gorgeous little bottles of body lotion while I'm there."

Molly turned in at the spa entrance. They allowed a last group peek at their phones (Ming: three messages from Mr. Hyde's lawyer; Asa: Tell Anna you'll buy her a front-row seat in heaven with all your Google moolah; Tessa: nothing, not even SHUT UP. MOM). Then they switched to airplane mode and drove slowly down the long wooded driveway.

They drove past the gentle slope of lawns, trimmed paths, arbors, and gardens recently pruned back in preparation of summer splendor. And there, of course, loomed the mansion. They'd pictured exactly this — a vast structure, multiwinged, brick and locally quarried marble. Why accept anything less on their spa vacation than a mansion restored to its original gilded glamour? And it was here at a spa that Anna would begin to get well, get back on path. Everything felt possible. The Old Friends would work their magic and bring her home with rosy cheeks.

As soon as Molly put the car in park, there were men opening car doors.

"Welcome, ladies." They fluttered and greeted the women as if they'd been eagerly waiting all day to serve them.

Ming wedged in front of a valet to take hold of Anna while Helen slid behind, an intricate ballet, partnering her up and out and past the men. They practically lifted her an inch, wafting her through the front doors, all the time keeping up a sprightly chitchat with Caroline.

Molly winked at the handsome valet as she slowly stretched one long leg, then the other, from the car. "No, no baggage. No worries." She winked again and tossed over the keys.

Five Minutes

"Helen? Ming?" He felt like an idiot calling out. It was immediately clear that nobody was in the house. Unless he counted the dog, who'd slipped through his legs and zoomed out the back door as soon as Reuben pulled it open. Obvious as it was that the house was empty, that Anna wasn't in her bed, why was he rushing two steps at a time upstairs to yank open the kids' bedroom doors?

What did he fear he'd find?

He'd parked next to Helen's car. Ming's and Caroline's were there, too. Their overnight bags lined up in the front vestibule.

So what was going on?

He looked for a note on the kitchen counter, the dining-room table. The obvious places. Simple courtesy. A note. Could it be that hard? But it was typical, wasn't it? The way they swooped in, as if nothing had been happening the whole week while they were back in their lives. Amazing, actually, the way they thought they were above all this, all the massive everyday effort.

Each day there had been some alarm. Five times in the last three days, he'd gotten a call — "Reuben, you got to get here" — or a text — Come now, need help. If there's not an actual crisis for Reuben to address, there's a forest fire of the soul he's being asked to manage. And it's not a metaphor. The kids are ablaze. Her brothers again challenging hospice. And then calls about the goddamn dog. One day Zeus was picked up five miles away. The next day he'd tried to bite the nurse when she was turning Anna.

And then nights, Reuben falling half comatose into bed, certain he'd conk in less than a second, yet two hours later he's adrift, recalling Anna's sunburned face on a family vacation in Belize. They're on the motorboat returning from their first scuba dive. He's counting all the shades of blue he sees in the ocean and sky. "There's a whole world down there," Anna's practically singing, her face exalted and splattered with new freckles. "You told me, but I didn't believe you. It's as beautiful as this one." Or he's jolted awake, pinned by nightmare panic, and she's on a hospital bed, shrunken to a newborn, pleading, "Promise me. Just promise me."

He walked back into the bedroom. Maybe he'd missed a note. Ming was usually conscientious. A goddamn lawyer, for God's sake. But no. Nothing. No note on the pillow. No FYI. No simple acknowledgment that he might actually walk into the house, find Anna gone, and freak out.

The only clue was that Anna's throw blanket wasn't on the bed. The one she always wants around her shoulders or over her legs.

Instead Reuben noted bits of blood staining the sheet. That looked fresh.

He knew there was no reason to freak. They would have called him. Even the blood was obviously from something minor. Her skin was so thin that sometimes her cotton clothes abraded it. Still.

Reuben began to straighten the covers, untangling the sheet that had knotted at the bottom of the bed. He pressed the bed control and watched the mattress unhinge and flatten. Reuben lay down on the hospital bed. He fiddled with the control knobs. Like a kid riding it up, then back down. He jammed on the button, making the ride fast, then slow. Then faster. It was something he'd wanted to do since he first set up the bed in the room. No hospital bed, she'd insisted. That was always Anna's first tack.

Her go-to was a quick, dismissive, "Don't want it. I don't need it."

"Okay, you're right." She smirked at him when she first pushed the controls and the bed levered her up to a seated position. "But don't get cocky about being right."

He jiggled and hoisted the rails up. Like a crib. What if someone came in and found him? Who cares? This had been his room, too, though with all the extra furniture dragged in, it hardly looked like their bedroom at all, the room their children padded into from nightmares, the room he tried to hold it together that first year of her illness, the room where they fought and fastened to their separate, stubborn ground.

Reuben rolled to his side, pulling the comforter over him. He didn't have that much stubbornness left. Five minutes. He'd give himself five minutes. More than a ton to do. Still, he was going to give himself these five minutes. Everyone else seemed to take time to get their heads straight. Shit, Anna's brother Michael had signed up for yet another marathon and spent most of his last visit on training runs rather than hanging with Anna. Reuben needed five just to get over how pissed off he was. Fair or not, mostly he was pissed at Helen. And Anna. There it was. That anger. This room empty.

How could she do this? There had been so many years of sickness it was hard to remember his life, their life, before sickness. It wasn't that he couldn't remember, but it hurt more remembering. The first years, her fierce prettiness. He'd wanted her all the time. For years, that. Their private play. Her sweet, drowsy smile after sex. It was terrible to watch what sickness and medicine had done to her. To her face. Her perfect copper skin, etched, blued, crepey. Her tiny ears bulbed wide, the lobes droopy. She never wanted to be this. He bunched the comforter in closer and squeezed shut his eyes.

Glow

"I'm Mindy." An adorable young woman glided up. "May I be of help?"

Mindy radiated easy health, a smooth outdoor glow. Even her smile seemed limber and toned. The promise of everything offered. The room behind Mindy was large and light-filled. A table centerpiece of green apples in a wide glass bowl, an immediate offering of health.

"Oh, Mindy, we'd love treatments," Anna chirped before anyone else. "Just skip the wellness program."

"Do you ladies have reservations?"

"Be here now, baby," Anna sang out with

full-on hippie exuberance. "That's our man-tra."

"We'd like the day passes." Caroline stepped in, primed after her week with Elise to take quick control of any potential situation.

"I'm sorry, we have a two-night mini-mum." Mindy kept her smile professionally supple.

"I don't have two nights." Anna waved her credit card in one hand. "I'm the poster child for don't put off for tomorrow what you can do today."

Her breezy song had decibeled up.

Gone screechy.

For the first time since they'd taken off on their vacation, since they'd hightailed it out of town, Jack Kerouac–ed it across the state, it became evident to Ming and Caroline and Helen and Molly that all of Anna's enthusi-asm — all that bubbliness they'd been tak-ing girl-power credit for — was something else. Maybe the morphine restlessness Reu-ben reported often looked like an energy surge.

No maybe about it. Watching Anna in the lobby of Otter Brook Inn and Spa, both spindly arms swaying like tentacles above her head, her credit card dangling between two fingers, it was obvious that she was wasted.

They watched Mindy take a quick defensive lobby scan.

She wasn't okay. She was higher than a box kite with tails. They'd been such idiots.

At the front door, a band of hikers — trekking poles in one hand, hot chocolate lofted in the other — stopped yodeling "This Land Is Your Land." They stared at Anna. Horrified.

Two women in matching yoga outfits stood in the center of the lobby, palms raised to hearts. They stared at Anna. Horrified.

Of course everyone was horrified. What had they done dragging her anywhere? What was Anna — all of seventy or eighty pounds? She looked like a tiny, shrunken, teetering child.

Too late.

And too late for Mindy. This situation was not in any hospitality handbook. Give us your anxious, your depressed, your anorexic, your bulimic or fatty. Give us your fitness-fearful, your fitness maniac, your high-strung or strung out.

But here was Anna — her narrow face a glazy, eggy blue, her emaciated arms waggling in the air, her whole shriveled body

277

moving like spongy underwater seaweed, and — compassionate reception be damned — who was anyone kidding? — this hallucinating, wobbling creature was definitely not in any handbook.

And just forget liability.

This was way beyond a wellness-center buzzkill.

The yoga ladies gawked in mountain pose.

Mindy was visibly trembling when two hulking men shouldered close. Clearly a silent wacko alarm had been triggered. The terrified nod Mindy gave said, *We're way beyond wacko. We're at 911 level.* But before Mindy or her freaked-out trainer henchmen had a chance to lead the women into a back room where everything might be efficiently taken care of outside the view of guests amply paying for tranquillity, Anna reached out, lowering both her arms, the credit card dropping from her fingers.

"Maybe we'll come back another time," Caroline said and put out her hands to steady Anna. Anna slipped out of Caroline's grasp and lunged precipitously forward.

"How thrilling." She flattened her hands across Mindy's stomach. "I've just noticed. What are you, six months? My little babies are all grown up."

In an instant Mindy's trembling shifted.

She was gulping. Stuck, trapped, she tried to push back, to wedge Anna's hands off her body.

"Oh, it is so, so beautiful, Mindy." Anna's voice was soft and otherworldly. Her hands clinging on Mindy's belly.

"You're pregnant, and suddenly, Mindy, women tell you their pregnancy stories. Then birth stories. Then the baby has colic and there's a woman in the checkout line, a stranger, telling you to put a warm towel on the baby's belly. Each step of the way, there's women opening the next gate." Anna closed her eyes, her hands orbed on Mindy's stomach.

"Dearest One," she said, and began whispering. Like an incantation under her breath. A blessing?

Dearest One? Ming mouthed, and looked from Helen to Molly to Caroline. Eyebrows raised, they didn't know what "Dearest One" meant, but they'd all heard her mumbling the phrase. Even back at the house when they'd thought she was asleep, they'd leaned over the bed and heard her murmuring, "Dearest One."

They had to get her out of here.

Mindy was gasping, a frozen cry. Should they wait for Anna to lift her hands off Mindy? Or intervene? Of course Mindy was skeeved. It seemed time for a swoop-out rescue. Exit stage left.

Then, all sparkly and confident, Anna's eyes shivered open. "It's a roller coaster, Mindy, but get ready for some massive joy."

"She's actually right," Helen said. "Don't worry, Mindy, we'll get out of here." Helen continued quietly, "We just wanted to take her on a nice vacation."

"I'm so sorry," Mindy sobbed over and over as the four women closed in to catch Anna as she swayed and then, like a soggy piece of paper, began to buckle and wilt.

That Kind of Life

Standing in the doorway, her hospice bag and knapsack cushioned against the door frame, Kate watched Reuben sleep. He was curled, the blue comforter wrapped tightly, his hands in a fist around the welt of fabric. He had the look of an exhausted stray. It was deep, the sleep. A magic-potion sleep. Like something from the storybook she read to her son at night. Reuben was a dark-haired Goldilocks who had wandered in. Or, with that gruff snore, more a kindly wolf, if any of the stories had a kindly wolf. He snored a steady, thick engine. Clearly he'd broken his nose more than once. She recognized that deviated sound.

The bed rails were up. He'd done that? He must have. Yes, he'd put the rails up. And looking at his fingers, their twitchy release and grasp of the coverlet, she remembered that it had once been his comforter, too. And the room, yes, this had been his room. His room with Anna. How long ago? She couldn't quite ever get that story straight. Even as simple as were they still married or not? So it was less Goldilocks testing the bed than a return. Which tale would that be?

Watching Reuben, she'd completely forgotten about Anna! Who was where? Had it happened?

No, if it were the end, Kate would have been called. That was a clear part of the protocol.

When she arrived, she'd been glad for the quiet. It was hard to have a moment alone with Anna. She never knew who'd be camped out in the room — some new woman friend insisting on relaying old escapades or looking cheerful and asking confused, increasingly desperate questions. There were the two brothers every weekend, and sisters, or maybe those were the wives of brothers — she couldn't tell. And children, Anna's grown children, of course, but also nieces, cousins, grown kids showed up and wanted to hold her hand. Once Kate had arrived to a crew of middle-age men jamming an acoustic-rock show in Anna's room.

Everyone acted affronted when she'd ask them to clear the room. The brothers hung around saying they were doctors. Always challenging her, challenging hospice as if hospice were her invention. She had to explain it again and again. There were things best done without family and friends. Even after she insisted, she'd hear them linger just outside the door, wanting to reclaim their place.

Of course, she'd been doing this work long enough to know that this overflow, this bounty of love, was infinitely better than the apartments and houses where she'd helped men and women die mostly alone. How many times had she sought out an adult child, paging through local phone books, working hard to sound neutral? "Even an afternoon's visit would be calming. I think he'll sleep better after you visit," she'd said to too many daughters and sons.

Yet with Anna it might finally come to shooing the whole swarm from the room, their buzzing vigil of insistent love.

Reuben rolled onto his back. His arms flopped out. He spittled forth a throaty gasp. Kate backed out of the doorway. Did not want that awkward moment. Did not want to be caught watching him sleep. But she couldn't take her eyes off him. It was nice to watch a well person sleep. It had been a while. And a man. That, too. To see the long, healthy stretch of his body, his easy, good sleep. Easy, that was the word, his breath easy. His muscled arms flung wide. Nothing labored. Even the thick snoring was the sound of a healthy man snoring. Stunning. Why shouldn't she want to watch? To watch his vulnerability. Sure, each night she looked in on her boy. This was different. It was pleasurable, it was intimate watching a man.

The other morning when Kate had been in the room, out of nowhere Anna struggled to remember a line from a book she'd quoted in her wedding vows. She'd become increasingly agitated, fixated that she couldn't even retrieve the name of the book it came from.

"It's about shells. But not really." Anna's face scrunched and bothered.

And later her mouth struggling, as if it were just there, on the verge. "A gift something."

Now Kate has the book. She's certain it's the book Anna meant, right there in her knapsack along with supplies for restocking. She'd been on her rounds, at another home hospice visit. After showing Tom how he could regulate the pump himself, he'd asked if she'd bring him over the second volume of the Dune trilogy. A couple weeks earlier, he'd declared the hope of rereading his entire library before he died. "But Pynchon might send me to an early grave," he reconsidered. She'd scanned his makeshift plywood-and-cement-block bookshelves for what he'd wanted and seen a narrow blue spine with the simple capital letters, *Gift from the Sea.*

"Screw borrowing. Take it," Tom said in his burly way. "I don't remember which girlfriend left that shit behind."

But before she left, he said, "Actually, if she kicks first, I'll take the idiotic book back."

Kate had looked forward to giving Anna the book. After putting her son to bed, she'd read a little of it. She liked holding the blue book in her hand. The simple line drawings. It was beautiful, even if she couldn't stay awake and then woke with the light on and the book next to her. She'd tried to guess which passage Anna had used in her vows. What she'd said to Reuben. No shortage. The whole book was quotable. If you had that kind of life. The book assumed everyone had a marriage that might endure.

Really, it stung to read the book. All that reflecting, taking time to nourish a life. All that getting away from a life Kate had never had. Frankly, she wasn't sure anyone ever had.

What had Anna wanted to say to Reuben? It was hard for Kate to imagine Anna young. Impossible to imagine her well. When she conjured a wedding, she could picture Reuben in his twenties — same curly hair, thicker, no gray — but he stood beside an old, gnarled stick of a dying woman.

There it was again. It was her failing as a nurse. She couldn't ever see the young face inside the dying face. Even those patients she'd cared for, the ones who'd fully reverted, pulled back into the sturdy safety of their childhood — babbling to mothers, talking to little sisters, at family tables that hadn't existed for sixty years — she saw them only in their diminished, frail, dying bodies, the baby talk coated in the drool and stench, the gummy toothlessness of last days.

It was terrible, a lack of empathy, this, when she was in the job of empathy. But watching them die, she couldn't spin the dial of time and muster an image of the once-fully-vital self. Even all the pictures inevitably clustered bedside — that lineup of prior selves dressed smartly or rafting wild rivers — seemed invented. It was her secret failing, this lack. It's not like it killed anyone.

Maybe she could leave the supplies and the book for Anna with a note. On the bedside table. No, that was way too creepy; Reuben would know that she'd been right there in the room, seen him sleeping in the hospital bed. She'd stood just beside him arranging the vials of pills. Even if she left supplies organized on the kitchen counter, Reuben would figure out she'd been in the house.

Maybe it would be a kindness for him to wake and find the book, to know that Anna had wanted to recall words she'd once said to him. Or he wouldn't like it at all. Hard to tell with Reuben. He was so wound up; he was in a perpetual twirl of doing, always a task at hand, always in his pocket a scrawled list of questions. "What about something for the sadness?" he had asked, and it took a minute for Kate to understand he meant Anna's and not his own. Kate had freaked herself out by putting both hands on his shoulders and saying, "Reuben, is there anyone here giving you support?" It wasn't the gesture, or even the hands on his shoulders, it was that her tone sounded unprofessional. What was she actually offering? He'd been gracious saying, "Do I look like a guy who has time for support?"

Reuben juddered, half hoisted himself toward the door. She held her breath, expecting his eyes to blink open. He groaned, still sleep-blind, shifting back into a fetal tuck.

She was out of there. Down the hall, past the wall of framed family pictures. Wherever Anna actually was, there was enough of everything to get her through the night. Kate couldn't imagine who'd dragged her anywhere but with this crowd anything was possible.

Kate would come back. Try to fit it into her rounds. But she'd promised her son a game of catch, help him break in his catcher's mitt. After throwing, she's planned to teach him how to soften a glove with oil and twelve-minute-interval heatings in the oven.

The book will wait till morning. She'll kick everyone out of the room and even convince stubborn Anna to use the oxygen tube. Then she'll read aloud to Anna. Stay a little extra. Wait for her to remember the passage from the book. Ask Anna to read it to her, encourage Anna to say the passage aloud. She'll watch Anna's face carefully as she recites the vow. See if she can bring herself to see something in Anna's face, to learn whatever hope exists in a woman who believed love might endure.

Next Stop

"Next stop Machu Picchu," Molly announced as she parked close to a picnic table.

Ming sprang into motion, pulling bags and a wicker basket from the popped-open trunk. "Brought to you by our chef, Sebastian," she said with a deep bow. Indeed, he'd packed pretty much everything but the actual donkey that would carry the basket up a mountain. She wasn't ready to give up. This was when she'd begin arguing her case with Anna. Maybe they'd pushed too far going to the spa. Still, Anna had wanted to go out. Had wanted to go on vacation. That meant something.

Ming shook out a red gingham tablecloth. She wafted it and let it settle on the picnic table. In the basket Sebastian had neatly stacked metal containers — empanadas, spinach frittata, sliced tomatoes, melon, soft

288

goat cheese, and grilled breads rubbed with garlic.

While Ming set out a feast — right down to cloth napkins she folded into fans on each of the blue metal plates — Helen picked along the pond's shore, gathering dry branches and limbs, breaking them down, and going back to collect twigs and brush for a fire in the cooking pit beside the picnic table. After the initial high flare, while the fire burned steady and solid, Helen and Caroline locked wrist to elbow, making a chair of their arms, and Molly slowly lifted Anna from the backseat, adjusting the blanket around her shoulders.

"You doing okay?" Even as she asked it, Helen could not imagine what that meant. But still, hadn't it all sort of worked out? Maybe not the full turnaround that Ming claimed could still happen. But didn't some of the magic she hoped for happen? Anna rising from the bed, insisting they go away. Anna taking them off on an adventure, another Anna adventure even right down to — God bless her — Mindy crying and Anna counseling Mindy to take the episiotomy, take all drugs offered when she goes into labor.

Molly kept one hand on Anna's waist and the other braced around her neck as they stepped their way to the picnic table. They lowered Anna to the bench, and when she tilted, listing unsteadily, Molly wiggled in right behind her on the bench, holding her in a clasp.

"I've got you," Molly said quietly. Seated behind Anna, Molly knew, was the most alone she'd have of her. "There's something I need to tell you." But before she could begin to describe the principal's office and that brutal fraction of a second when she saw the ink on her daughter's cinnamon skin, she heard the stutter thickness in Anna's breath. Anna struggled with each inhale. Molly tried to breathe along with her. Anna would say, Don't be so dramatic, it's just a stupid tattoo. Molly shaped the wool blanket around Anna's shoulders. You're not losing her. You're a great mom, Anna would say, turning her head with that confident, certain look. For now, with a cheek against Anna's back, hearing the effort of her breath, it was enough just knowing what she *would* say.

"Eat up, ladies, this is Michelin-rated," Ming crooned. "What do you want, Anna?"

"I'll watch. The smell of food's still good."

"Okay, are you all finally ready for the story of the week?" Caroline said and leaned forward, positioning both arms theatrically on the table. She waited for Ming to serve Molly and Helen to sit back down from poking at the fire pit.

Around them a soft spring light hovered, haloed over Puffer's Pond. The jumble of marsh wren and spring peepers chorused, the staccato of woodpecker — the air was a dense sound fabric.

"No contest, I have this week's winning story," Caroline said, and the others waited for her latest situation to unspool. This is what they have always done together. Talk and listen. And any vacation, however exotic it might be, would finally be that — talking to make sense of their lives, the necessity of saying out loud, This is what happened. Talking for the sheer pleasure, the hilarity. To be one another's witness to the stunning accumulation of a life.

"It starts last Thursday," Caroline began, "with a collect call from Jacqueline Bouvier."

Deadline

"I might need help?" Anna folded back in Molly's arms.

"You bet. What do you need?" Molly stayed close to Anna while Ming packed up the picked-over food and Helen doused the last logs in the fire pit. The light on the pond had shifted golden — magic hour — the birches and pines along the shoreline glowing, the colors saturated and alive.

"I've set a deadline." Anna sounded official. "If it's not over, then I want a drug that can finish this. Can Serena help?"

Caroline froze holding the melon rinds she was dumping into the trash.

"It's illegal." Ming snapped shut the picnic hamper. If she'd lost the moment to make her other case, she'd hold ground with law.

"I know what it is, Ming," Anna shot back. "I wanted to keep Reuben out of this loop because of the kids. I'm asking whether you four will help if I need it."

"Serena can't," Ming declared officially. "She can't. I can't. I'm a lawyer." Ming looked to Helen. Helen kept crouched by the fire pit, her back to everyone. The wet wood hissed, and the gray smoke twisted vaporously.

"I'll ask Serena." Molly knew that Serena would say no. Adamantly. But Molly knew other doctors, colleagues from Fenway Community Health, who believed in assistance and had taken the risk. "And yes, Anna, I'll do what you need." Molly was glad to be the first to say yes.

"Whatever you need." Caroline's shoulders tensed up to her neck. "This is hard." Every muscle in her caretaking body was trained to rescue.

"It's a lot to ask," Anna said. "But not knowing if there's two days or three months is stupid. Saying good-bye is getting old."

"Helen?" Ming's voice vibrated stiff and friable. It was two to one.

"Whatever you need," Helen said quietly. A wave roiled through her. She understood. They wouldn't need to secretly assist Anna. It was days, not weeks. That was clear. What Anna needed was to know that she wasn't alone. It would help her.

Helen went close and wrapped her arms around Ming. She buried her face in Ming's soft hair.

"Whatever you need, Anna," Helen said again.

Lucky

Jarrett was driving up Bull Hill Road when he saw the baby skunk. Odd in the daytime. Not impossible — he'd seen a few. But a baby? Now, that was something unusual. Maybe it wasn't a skunk. From the distance he couldn't see white markings. A mink? A marten? No, this creature was bushy. Not sleek at all. He slowed the truck. Probably just a stupid cat. It was stopped in the middle of the road. He heard a car coming down the hill. People took Bull Hill as a shortcut. Took it too fast. Teenagers liking to churn up dust on the curves. Like they were in their own video-game chase. Every year some idiot rolled.

He slammed on the truck horn. Warn the car. Warn that skunk. Really, he didn't have time for this. For any of it. He was late already. And he couldn't be late to pick up his son. Most of all because Daniela wouldn't let him hear the end of it. Two late school pickups and she was calling him a deadbeat dad, throwing the phrase around like she actually knew what it meant. Deadbeat nothing, the back of the truck was piled with wood for their house. The house he'd built for his family with his own two hands. The house on which he paid the electric and the mortgage and every other bill. The house she'd said was her dream house. The very dream house she now seemed on the verge of asking him to leave. Everything with her these days felt like a test that he was failing. Every cup left on the counter. A clump of mud on the rug. And that was just the surface. It seemed like suddenly there was a ten-page list of problems. Or worse, there was a list but he wasn't even allowed to see what was on it. He wanted to say,

Come on, Daniela, we have a good thing. But these days he couldn't say even something that simple without flubbing it. Okay, he wasn't the most talkative guy in the world, and he certainly wasn't some poet. Okay, he had plenty of room for improvement. Who didn't? If she wanted him to do more of the house stuff, he'd try. She'd said she was sick of taking care of everyone's food. Okay, he'd try, but he couldn't promise gourmet anything. Nothing like the amazing meals Daniela rolled out as if they were nothing tough. Was he wrong for having believed she enjoyed cooking? He was the first to admit that right now he couldn't do a lot more than a breakfast-for-dinner meal. Eggs and bacon, toast and potatoes. But that didn't make him kick-out-able, did it? And she wasn't quiet about any of it. Couldn't she see that their kids had the willies?

Yesterday when he'd pulled in to the circle at school, Owen hopped into the cab of the truck and turned to Jarrett. "No worries, Pop. I just got out here. I'll tell Mom it was my fault. I was helping Ms. Brown clean our bunny cages." The poor kid's face looked stricken.

Then a car rounded the sharp bend ahead on Bull Hill. It barreled down, a red flash of speed, and it looked like it couldn't brake fast enough to avoid the animal right in the road. Jarrett could tell it was a lady driving. Would she spin out into his truck? Or would she pull hard right where a dense bank of white pine shouldered the road? Neither was going to end well. He kept his hand flattened on the horn. Watched the car brake, the woman's wrenched face. The animal crouched. He understood then it was a dog. Not a skunk. A small dog. "Don't turn in to the tree!" he shouted. The car windows were closed. Then the car slipped past, a slick red ribbon of motion, skidding to a stop below him.

He was out of his truck. Breathing like he'd been sprinting. His chest thudding. The damp air filled his lungs and started him coughing. Took three long steps, scooped the dog up in his hand. Clutched it in. Its heart skittering madly against Jarrett's palm. It was Anna's. Anna's dog. Her hardly-even-a-dog creature she brought to practice, that the band gave her shit about. What was it doing out here? At least three miles from her place.

"You're okay, idiot." He tucked the dog in like a football. It would relax in that safe hold.

Jarrett made his way to the red car. He

recognized the woman. Her blue plastic glasses. Her thin hair tied in two bunches like she was still a kid. She was local. The food co-op? School? Didn't know where, but from somewhere here he knew her. He knocked on the glass. The woman's hands clenched the wheel. She hunched in her fleece jacket, stared at Jarrett like she couldn't trust ever letting go of the wheel. He motioned for her to crank open her window.

"You did good," Jarrett said when the window was halfway down. "You okay?"

"Jesus."

"You handled it like the Indy 500. You professional?" He tried to keep it light.

"I'm vegan," she said and looked plaintively at Jarrett. Her glasses askew. Her fingers still gripping the steering wheel.

This was trouble. Too much trouble.

"Vegan. Interesting. So that makes you drive faster?" He wanted her to laugh. Reset from the panic. Make sure she was steady to go forward.

He needed to bolt. He needed to get to school. There was a chocolate milk shake waiting for Owen in the cup holder. Then they'd stack wood. He'd cook dinner. Maybe even get Owen to help. Call it boys' dinner for the girls.

"Well, no worries," he said. "I'll take care of the dog." He loosened his grip and petted Zeus. Let the lady see that the dog was fine. "He's fine," Jarrett said. "Not a scratch."

The woman squinted at him, her blue frames tilting on her nose.

"The dog's traumatized." Her eyes went all gooey. Humorless. Made him want to push it. Match idiocy with idiocy. Say he was a survivalist. Loved roadkill. Didn't discriminate. Squirrel, yes. Dog, too.

"The dog's traumatized," she repeated. She was about to go weepy and fog up her glasses. He'd have to soothe her. Listen to her animal sensitivities. He had to get to school.

"Well, it's pretty darn lucky. You really did great."

"Dogs know when a person's dying. They react."

It smacked him then. What she was saying.

Shut up. He needed her to shut up. Small town. Every person needing to be in the midst, making it their drama. Thinking they were entitled to have feelings. And an opinion. On everything. This reckless lady had better shut up before she said something so stupid that Jarrett lost it. He wanted to lose it. Wanted to bait her. All day he'd been riding that edge. It would be great to press past the point of containable. Stop worrying about getting right all the things he seemed not to get right. Stop trying to be a good citizen, a good husband. It would feel terribly amazing to tear this lady more than one new vegan asshole.

Until, of course, it felt ten times worse.

"You're one lucky lady." Jarrett forced a grin. He hitched the dog higher into the crook of his arm and ran back to his truck.

"Hey, idiot, sit right there." He plopped the dog down in the passenger seat. The dog pawed himself in a circle and settled down like the car was his old home.

"Hey, idiot, we're going to get Owen." Jarrett could just see his son's lit-up surprise. A chocolate milk shake and a dog. What could be better? Pretty basic. Basic was good.

"I'm on my way," Jarrett sang out loud once, then wailed it again with a big bluesy push. "I'm on my way with a hound named Zeus. Got me a hound, his name is Zeus. When he wags that mangy tail, my heart lets loose."

That felt good. Thank God for the blues. Singing. Got a lot of people through a lot worse days.

Maybe he'd be a few minutes late, but he'd get to school. He could already see his son's shiny smile. The boy would be bonkers with happiness when he stepped up into his dad's truck and saw Zeus.

Secret

Reuben woke to the vibration and ring of his phone. How long had he slept? It was dusk in the room, mossy gray light filtering through the windows. There was a dream. He couldn't quite hold the thread of the dream. But it had ringing, too. A bell?

And now the buzzing again. He rolled over, fishing the cell phone from his jeans pocket. Reuben considered — for just a moment — letting the call go to message. But it was Julian. He's promised the children he'll always pick up. The least he can do. Reuben didn't have anything new to tell him except that Mom wasn't home. God knows where. God knows how. She's barely been able to stand up for two days. And hasn't spoken in a day. But hey, her friends, her supposed best friends in the world, apparently decided it's a grand idea to whisk her away. Who knows where they are? When they're coming back? They haven't answered the text Reuben sent. *Did* he send the text? Or did he just think about that Where the

300

hell are you, Helen? text before he shut his eyes.

"Hey, buddy." Reuben was glad his son couldn't see him sitting in the hospital bed.

Julian was quiet on the other end, so quiet that Reuben held the phone away to see if they'd disconnected.

"What's up, sweetheart?"

"I have to tell you something." His son's voice was so much like his own. It has always been that way, even when Julian was a child, the boy's voice had Reuben's inflections, the trilly laugh, the nervous dip and rise, the occasional stutter, so that Reuben, despite being wrong plenty of times, has always felt he knows how to read every emotional nuance of his son's speech. Now there was a knot of anxious seriousness. But there was also something from a different depth. Different from the "How's Mom, Dad?" anxiety calls. Or the calls where Julian tried to manage an adult steadiness, "How are you doing, Dad?"

"Okay, I'm listening." Reuben pulled a leg out from under the comforter. He felt hot, trapped with the rails up, but he didn't want to interrupt the call to try to lower the side.

"I told Mom something. A secret. I didn't tell you."

Reuben wanted to stop him. Wanted to

say, No worries, that's fair. He also — he felt like such an asshole — felt the old jealousy, that stab of fury when Anna knew things about the kids that he didn't. She always had. "It's a mother's right," she'd say with an imperious smile. "Is that fair?" he'd say, and she'd barely deign to shrug. "This isn't about fairness. It's about I'm the womb."

"You don't have to say anything, Julian. I don't need to know."

"We lost it, Dad."

Reuben looked around the room for a focus point. The light filtered duskily, the shapes of things a little borderless.

"We were having a baby. I told Mom."

"Oh, Jules, I'm so sorry."

Reuben needed to be on his feet. A sudden urgent necessity. Had to get out of this bed, but the rails seemed locked or stuck. Or just complicated to lower from this inside-the-bed position.

"We lost it. And I don't want to tell her."

Reuben knelt on the bed and then clambered out, one leg at a time, the metal wobbling against his jangled, unsteady movement. He hopped his back leg from where it caught between the rails and walked to the bank of bedroom windows. The yard needed raking. The hydrangea needed cutting back. He should get out there later. And what about the old tree house? Half the ladder was rotted.

His son was describing the trip to the doctor's office. Julian used all the new language: sonogram, fetal heartbeat, D&C.

"The doctor says we can try again."

"Everything's going to be fine," Reuben said, knowing that that was not the point.

Reuben hasn't thought of his son as a father. Or if he ever has, it's been abstract, in some future order of things stretched far in time. A future that wasn't now. But now he saw his son's lean frame, that shag of curls bent over the tiny swaddle of a newborn. It was an image Reuben already knew. An image from a framed photograph taken of him, Reuben, holding Harper and Andy, not an hour old, a little package of infant in each arm and Reuben's head bent close as he welcomed them into the world.

"I don't know how to speak to Mom."

"Yes you do. She loves hearing your voice."

"So that's okay? To lie to Momma?"

There it is, "Momma," the word his eldest child had forced himself to grow out of when he was ten.

"It's not a lie," Reuben said.

He opened random cards from the cluttered windowsill. *See you soon.* Funny

303

notes of hope. There were so many notes sent from Anna's old students. From all over the country. Word had really spread. Even the ones who were grown up wrote, *Dear Mrs. S.* They thanked her for their love of math. Sent pictures of themselves on top of mountains. Reuben flipped one card open, and tiny writing darkened everything but a thin border of hearts. Why would anyone write that much? Why would they think Anna wanted to read all that?

Reuben straightened two stacks of envelopes Anna hadn't bothered to open.

Sorry

Before they turn out of the pond's parking lot, the women switch on cell phones. It's a sound bomb, a mad pinging frenzy of messages and texts, screens jammed with increasing desperations. And unpleasantries.

"We're in big trouble," Helen announces.

"You're always worried about getting in trouble," Molly says, and the others yowl, comparing forty years' worth of Helen's goody-two-shoes apologies.

"They're waiting at the house for us. They've all but alerted the National Guard."

"This is excellent. It's like eleventh grade again," Ming says. "I hope we get grounded."

"Laugh all you want. Do you want me to read Reuben's texts to you?"

"After we get in trouble and we're grounded, I need to ask everyone for some talk time. I need help," Molly says. There's been a text and then two more from Tessa.

"He's furious. There're a lot of mad people."

"We double-dare you not to say sorry to anyone," Caroline teases Helen. "Try not to even *look* or *smell* guilty."

"What are you afraid of?" Anna slips her hand into Helen's.

"We should have at least left a note."

Anna laces fingers one by one with Helen's. "What are you really afraid of?"

"A world without you." Helen blurts it before she can stop.

The car goes quiet; even the motor quiets.

"And that I'll be able to live in it." Helen wants to shift to look directly at Anna, but she can't. Instead she looks out the car window. There's almost no light left. The last colors nearly all pulled from the day.

Up front Ming moans, a sprained sound.

Anna's hand is cold against Helen's. Helen reaches her other arm across, sandwiching Anna's hand between hers, fighting an impulse to clutch.

"It will be good, even your sadness," Anna says.

The road, the mowed hills, the row of trees, the rectangle and the square barn — everything at this time of day is shape, soft edges more than specific lines, the palate so contained, still bits of red and blue and green shine inside the great density of dark.

A World Still with Her will be an almost-black painting.

That's another reason Helen can't look at Anna. Because Anna knows. Whatever goody-goody, accommodating, worried apologist Helen is, she's also ruthless. Helen has always joked that artists are cannibals. Pillagers calmly regarding the composition of disaster. And Anna knows that Helen is already doing exactly that, making a Donner Pass of the sadness. Already this great texture, this corduroy of darkness. The hillside with the dark swell of land. The simple geometry of a barn. A car on a road, the headlights cutting a muted path, the shape of heads in the car.

"Are you afraid?" Helen asks.

This was what Helen has never asked, what over all these years of treatment and periods of health Helen and The Old Friends have trained themselves not to ask. It was a tacit agreement. The answer too

306

obvious; it loomed in each moment's specific worry. When the tumor wouldn't
shrink. When there would be no donor
match or the body would reject the match.
Or when there was staph infection, sepsis,
pneumonia, congestive heart failure. Each
complication in the treatment. Each shocking recurrence. Even in the months when
Anna was radiantly healthy. The unspoken
answer never left; it was there — like the
petulant wallflower, like the delinquent
fundamentalist playing Nintendo just waiting for the call to jihad — it was there just
breathing on the edge of the party when
Anna overfilled her healthy dance card. Yes,
I'll hike Mount Washington, yes, I'll drive to
Amagansett, yes, front and center, I'll clap
not only at my own children's graduations
but with Ming at Lily's graduation. It was
there with every yes, with every chance to
be alive.

"Are you afraid?" Helen repeats. And now,
above everything, Helen needs to hear
Anna's answer. Ming tilts her head, and
Molly glances in the rearview. Helen sees
they all genuinely don't know. They've been
so busy with their own fear. None of them
have dared to ask her.

But Helen knows the answer. She's known
it since she arrived two weeks ago and began

her adamant petition to pull Anna from hospice. She knew it back at the pond when she agreed to help Anna if Anna asked. Helen's job all these years was to keep Anna away from fear and close to the yes. But Anna is not afraid. Again, Anna is doing something before Helen. It has always been this way. Boys. Drugs. Marriage. Children. Even the pregnancy that Anna ended. Over and over, Anna went first. Now this.

Anna begins whispering. Is it her breathing? Has she fallen asleep? Is this what they've each heard throughout the day, a wisping from Anna, that pale cirrus of utterance in a register outside their frequency? Helen sharpens toward the murmuring, but even just next to Anna she can't make it out.

"I'm sorry." Helen flexes her fingers gently against Anna's. "I don't know how to do this."

Magic 9

There is so much magic with 9! I must be sure to tell you all about the Denmark and 9's trick.

Oh, you will dazzle everyone with this number 9. It really has magic.

Here, first, is one puzzle that is quick and easy:

Take a number and multiply by 9. Add the digits in the answer, and voilà, the number 9. I'm sure you understand, but let me show you: 356 times 9. Equals 3,204. 3 plus 2 plus 4. Equals 9.

Or here's another. Take any random number — 345 — scramble it — 534. Subtract the lower number — 534 minus 354 — add the final number — 180 — to a single digit — 1 plus 8 plus 0, and voilà, Dearest One, the number 9.

Now you try.

Hey

Helen angles sideways through the kitchen door, Anna cradled in her arms. She warned the others, but none of them are quite prepared for the crowd or the thick smell of cardboard and pizza. For how harsh the vibe is. It's clear they've already been charged, tried, and hanged.

"Hey! Looks like we missed this whole rockin' party!" Helen goes bold, goes boisterous. Stupid exclamations in her voice. She's determined not to lose the double dare, to be something different from what her friends expect.

"Hey, hey!" Ming sheepishly copies Helen.

Molly and Caroline chime in "Heys" too, contrition bleating out the vowels.

Helen feels a ca-ching ca-ching of her slot-machine victory. She can't wait till later to mimic their *heeeeeys*. You actually sounded like sheep, she'll gleefully taunt.

Still, it hurts to look at Reuben and Layla and Connie and John. The crush of their worry. And there's Jarrett in the corner, mopishly picking a melody on Anna's guitar. A couple other Valley friends whom Helen's met over and over but can never hold on to all their names. One is also an Anna. A.G.

Let them all be named Anna. Anna bird and Anna bunny one and all.

They all look horrified, mouths cast in wounded, Munch-like *O*'s.

"Anna's wiped from our adventure. I'm going to get her washed up and into bed." Helen ducks from the damning glances, pivots to shake a grin at her friends. Let the other three answer questions and face judgment. They've sworn not to reveal anything about their holiday.

She smiles at Anna, folded in her arms. Anna is still doing that whispery thing, but even if she's off in some somewhere else, Helen understands that she's also taking this in. She knew that Helen would rise to a challenge, that it was part of — not opposite — her good-girl behavior. This Anna knows best of everyone in the room.

Take a Party Bag

She feels the shape of her house. Even with her eyes closed. So many beloveds in the room. All that ampleness. The ampleness of her beloveds and the ampleness of her home. With her eyes closed, she scans all the pretty things in her living room. Her pretty things. They do not know that she is just ahead of them. Lovely friends, lovely things — so insistent. All shiny brightness. All insistent. She who loved a party could not be at this party. There should be goody bags. So many things to put in a goody bag. Take something home. Please. Take a party bag, she thinks, before you leave.

Privacy

Helen helps settle Anna onto the toilet, wiggling her cotton leggings down. Then stands at her side.

"It can take a while," Anna apologizes, propping herself against Helen.

"I've got all night." Helen kisses the top of Anna's head. "That was a great vacation."

"Was it?" Anna's lids flutter, but her eyes stay shut.

Then a sprinkling, a faint tinkling of pee.

A smile pencils Anna's lips. "That still feels good."

Helen hands her some folded squares of

311

toilet paper. "I can't imagine."

"That's what you're good at, Helen, imagining things." Anna swipes lightly with the toilet paper and lets it drop.

Night Dose

Anna fidgets, thrashes, all knob and jut; there isn't any comfortable arrangement of any limb. Helen shuts the window, drapes a cloth over the lamp, hoping the muted green light might help. She wishes Ming and the others would come. All day she's wanted time alone with Anna. Now she needs the others.

"How can I help you?" The question itself so unhelpful. It's probably time for more of whatever Anna's been taking. Just feed a bit under her tongue the way Helen saw the nurse do earlier. She isn't sure exactly what or how much. She won't go out and ask for help — especially from Reuben.

"Your mom." Anna flicks her wrists. Her fingers jab and retract, like she's poking at something in front of her.

"My mom? What?"

Helen wedges a pillow under Anna's leg. But Anna kicks her leg out from the blankets — the pillow dropping to the floor — then squiggles it partly back under.

"Tell me. About it," Anna says.

Helen isn't sure what's needed. Anna knows everything.

"You remember — she knew I was angry with her. That haunted me for years. But when I became a mom, I understood the passing angers of my children. And realized Mom did, too. When Lucinda and Rusty were so angry, I'd remind myself that she put up with my rage that she was sick. Mom used to drive me crazy, saying, 'You want me to help you pack your bags?' Now when I'm having a hissy fit, I say it to myself."

"I thought you'd never be okay. We were too young."

Helen sees how hard Anna's working to form each word, to shape this thought.

"But you've had a good life," Anna says.

"I was okay." Helen had been the same age as Andy and Harper.

"They'll be okay?"

Helen eases down onto the bed. She adjusts, slipping partly under Anna to be extra padding. She feels Anna's vertebrae sharp against her chest.

"They'll be more than okay, Anna. They're already okay."

The bedroom door opens partway, and Helen waves them in. Ming and Caroline drop into chairs. Molly bends over the table, preparing the nighttime doses.

"Really?"

"You know they are. Anna, you're inside them."

"Even after I'm dead, keep telling me that."

Divine Proportion

The total of lines 9 and 10 was line 7 multiplied by 11. Hello, my friend Fibonacci, meet Dearest One. And always, too, 1.61. The quotient of line 10 divided by line 9. Hello, Euclid. Anna keeps the leapfrog-springing forward always toward the golden ratio.

STILL APRIL

1

Patriots' Day

Was he there? Had anyone heard from Michael? The calls came to Anna's house. That made sense. Someone there with her all the time. But at Anna's, the television off, unused, might as well have been unplugged. Same question. Same question. Had he gone to Boston? Everyone knew he'd been training. He'd made a big enough deal of it. Flat-out saying no, when people asked if Michael was honoring his sister. More than flat-out. Like they were morons for asking. "I run for myself, thank you very much." Sounded selfish. His point exactly. It *was* selfish. For the self he pulled on running gear every morning, ran intervals and fartleks, just to loosen the spiral of the mind, have the singular, pure focus of body. After a long run, no matter how messed his body was, always that final shot of adrenaline. Can't beat it. So alive. "That's the risk," he'd said, handing his phone to his wife, Felicity. He was leaving his phone with Felicity so that he could run outside of time. Time out from the vigil. Any day. It was hour to hour every day. "Perspective," Michael said. He'd accepted it might happen while he was out of touch. Everyone else needed to get a life. It was unbearable — keeping up with their lives only so things would be in order for them to leave when the final call came about Anna. Now the hanger-rigged, antennaed television in the living room was switched on, volume down so Anna can't hear. How much was she hearing anymore? Still. Skin powdered, rolled, a pillow wedged to keep her on her side, and then sometimes, out of nowhere, she was up, sitting up, lucid. "I'm not entirely sure," the broadcaster says. The puzzled jigsaw of a developing story. Broadcasts of jerky sprints toward and away. What bits of news, known, repeated. Twenty-five thousand–plus runners. Oldest marathon. A handheld video. Body down. Filtered chalky light. Thick curtains of shouting. There are injured. Barrier fences crumpled, raked aside. Make a lane. Coming through. Let them in. Get them out. "He'll be fine," they say with each call. "It's Michael," someone says. "He's got to be fine."

Paired

Felicity looked at the phones — hers, Michael's — on the table.

Orientation

Inside the Gatorade tent, it sounded like stadium risers collapsing. That happened a lot. Sideline mishap — there was even that official unofficial name. Sideline mishap. Always someone's fat uncle or a kid positioned to cheer on Mom wound up in the local ER. From heatstroke to busted limbs.

"Or it's a knucklehead with Roman candles," the lady said to Michael. "Breathe." She palmed light downward strokes on Michael's chewed-up left Achilles. Felt to Michael like she was moving concrete, but in a seriously necessary way. Food. Massages. He'd been psyched to have tickets to the Gatorade VIP tent. Even if this lady was more granny than belly dancer, her hands felt spectacular. He'll play this rubdown back to Felicity in a way that will have her eyes crinkle with jealousy. Facedown in your tiny little running shorts and her hands all over you? She'll say head waggling, voice testy. Way cute. He had reason to feel proud and give himself a post-run thumbs-up. Shaved two minutes off his time. Beat his running partner by twenty minutes. Poor

Jack bonked on the fourteenth mile but stayed in and limped to the finish. Now they were both princes on massage tables enjoying the Gatorade tent spoils.

Second time — "What the . . . ?" Michael sat up — wasn't any collapsed bleacher or domino of trash cans. It wasn't fireworks. Swung his legs over the side of the table. Up, but stuck, bolted to the table. The air sharp, stinging.

Jack was on his feet, bouncing, official, pointing at monitors hung throughout the tent. Right there, right outside, the scramble and screams, two men kneel. "We need someone."

"I should . . ." Michael wanted to say, Help, go out and help. He's a doctor. But he couldn't speak. He couldn't move. He jabbed his chest. "I should . . ." He could hardly breathe.

Jack tensed. "Forget it, man, we're out of here." Pulled Michael up. The drifting smoke on the screen was the powdery chemical bite inside the tent. Then they were out in it. Jack pointing them into a stream of moving bodies, foil-caped shoulders, crowds pressing forward, then left. Jack's hand fixed on him, a slight pressure with every step, using Michael to crutch himself forward. Michael couldn't keep track of their turns. Jack talking. As if to maintain orientation. Little stuff. Of no consequence. But it matters. It counts.

2

The News

Michael was home, safe. Still, they kept channeled, fixed to numbers and situations. They listened to radio news on the way to Anna's. Came home tuned to radio.

All vigil. All the time.

An aisle of a grocery store, a dentist chair, pouring a glass of orange juice — where would they be?

At home, red light green light, they went about their lives. Or tried. There were always more errands, appointments, pay stubs. Held off to the end of the day, then checked in. How is she? How's Anna? Admitted, "I don't know about you, but I'm barely in *my* life."

At Last

Reuben hooked his feet under the rungs of the hospital bed. He was glad for the quiet. For the rinse of morning light through the room. For a book he recognized and pulled from her table. "Go, go," he'd said to the others. "We can't bunch around all day watching and waiting," then pushed away the mishmash of chairs collaged bedside. Now, finally, this quiet, the only sound the watery gurgle lacquering Anna's each breath. He'd made sure of her comfort. He looked up from reading when her breath shallowed, caught, then huffed thickly, puffing openmouthed. He watched her sleep. She looked as he had seen her look all the mornings he'd watched her. He spoke quietly. "It's only me. Just us."

3

April 20

From the front of the meetinghouse room, creamy April New England light fans through the tall windows. Helen looks out at all the faces for whom Anna is their Anna. A *my Anna* for each person sitting in the main pews and for those that fill the upstairs balcony, that wide kaleidoscope of Annas. That shaping through time, that shifting specific story she's been for everyone in this room.

And she was, also, of course, none of those Annas.

Helen welcomes everyone, explains how the afternoon will unfurl. "So many of you asked to speak," she says quietly. "But Anna made me promise to keep the service short. And we all know better than to disobey Anna." Actually, she'd rather announce, Anna made me swear this won't drag on till we all wish we were dead.

"And starting out," Helen continues, "it's important to know that whoever we each think we were to Anna, however special, there were three that were her essence, were essential — no, *are* essential — above anyone or anything — her shining lights, her enduring Sparks." Helen slips to the side bench to let Julian, Harper, and Andy come forward.

Next Anna's brothers, Michael and Robert, stand up together, arms around each other's waist. "Our big sister," Robert begins, and Michael crumples, his taut runner's body crunched into a knot. Robert, with a sweep of his arm, smooths Michael up to standing and carries on in his gentle, clear way. "When my brother and I were little punks, our big sister admitted us into her club. She let us have girl magic. That made us better men. That was my sister's gift. She made each of us better versions of ourselves."

Michael starts, "I have seen unbelievable things this week." He gathers himself but doesn't speak of the bombings, the images that repeat and repeat these last five days. He doesn't mention that just yesterday the second of the two brothers responsible for the bombing was caught hiding inside a boat. Instead, with depth and humor, Michael catalogs phrases and gestures he's observed this week in his children, in his nieces and nephews, in all the gathering friends, in Anna's returning students — all wonderful, recognizable bits of his big sister. "She gave herself to all of us," he says, and snugs closer to his brother. "It helps me so much to see her in each of you."

Helen calls up the Friday women's group — arm in arm, bangled in sparkling jewels and scarves — they sway. The chant goes on. And on. A lot of verses. Of hope and rain and love and tides. And more verses. Of wind and ocean. Layla had insisted this song was Anna's favorite. Really? Really, you loved this song? Helen thinks, and then the blow, this electric new fact — there'll be no postmortem, Helen won't be privately conferring with Anna, there's no going over the service with Anna later.

Helen does a quick spot check for Asa. He's right there straight-backed at the edge of the last row. She knows he's busy in his mind, making irreverent jokes to Anna, making Anna laugh. Asa believes that sad speeches have no place in this room. There's his slight smile, which also, Helen knows, is for her. Keep steady. But mostly Asa is busy wisecracking, working to keep Anna's soul entertained.

Then Helen calls up Reuben, the official not-husband husband, who three mornings ago, in the room that had for years been their shared room, was the one alone beside Anna, holding her hand well beyond the last moment.

Helen invites the stem-cell donor to stand. He's reluctant, then stands, still grasping his seated wife's hand. Helen had spotted them before the service began, people crowding to shake his hand. A man with a goatee pulled the donor into a big bear hug. When Helen greeted them, he asked if she might point out Anna's children. He needed to apologize. He was Anna's match. No donor rejection. Still, here they are. "I need to apologize." Helen knew she should say something nice. Wasn't that part of the job Anna gave her? Would it hurt to say, Because of you we got all these extra years? Instead she pointed out Anna's children hiding together in the front pew.

For a moment she enjoys the donor's discomfort as the hall fills with applause. But that dissolves, and she's overtaken by her own gratefulness. Helen describes his correspondence with Anna, the funny aliases created in the first year when the hospital insisted they remain anonymous. "Of course," Helen says, rolling her eyes, "because it's Anna, after the requisite year she throws a you-saved-my-life dinner party, and they, like the rest of you here today, also became her best friends."

Now Helen tells that first story of meeting Anna on the playground and all the wounded animals she mended and named Anna.

After an audible *Awww* bends through the room, Helen imitates Anna's father's growling declaration that it was a fanciful invention, that at best his daughter had a couple stuffed animals that needed sewing, and the room explodes into laughter.

This is what Anna wanted. What she promised. *Don't let it get boring.*

Helen looks over to Ming, Caroline, and Molly. They nod approvingly, impressed that she's holding it together. But Helen sees that the nod means that something else has been discussed between them. An agreement. No! Helen wants to shout. No way, I will not do this ever again. I will not do this for you and for you or for you. I will not tell all our stories. That story of the time in eighth grade when we tried to skip out on the restaurant bill, or all the afternoons riding around in Molly's car, or when Caroline showed us the break in the fence and we climbed through vines and brush to claim the Farm.

I have done this for my mother. And now, here, for Anna. That's enough.

But it doesn't matter. It's not enough. Looking at the faces in the room, she understands that this is what we do. We are here. And then we are not here. For a little while, we are a story.

Helen looks again to Asa. She was wrong. She will do this one more time. And he will do this for her. And knowing that, without knowing when, they will make a life.

Finally Helen nods to the band. They move with simple gravitas to their instruments "Hello, we're the Lost Zeuses," Jarrett says, waiting while a ripple of laughter acknowledges the band's new name. "Here's an original tune by our Anna, who was an original." And the band begins to rock.

■ ■ ■ ■

2015

■ ■ ■ ■

1

Party

"Look, look, Amalie." Reuben hoists the baby up and settles her down in the crook of his arm.

He swivels so the baby will find the flowered cake, its two lit candles — one for good luck. But instead the baby smiles up at Reuben.

The shock of love he feels! That familiar comfort of a baby's weight in his arms.

"Let's blow the candles out, my Amalie." Reuben nuzzles his chin against his granddaughter's feathery curls. "Now let's make your first wish."

2

Art History

Helen stands back from the large canvas. Nothing but trouble all morning. Been going at it hard. Pushing paint till she's pushed the life out of the pigment. Mess upon mess. The color flat. The composition heavy. Fussy. Static and lifeless.

She can't get back to get what she'd seen that night.

But what had she seen? She looks at the wall tacked with preliminary sketches. Something's there. There's fluidity in those drawings, the bodies and the exterior shapes together create containment. Energy that allows for distinct figures. And intimacy. They are intimates.

But on the canvas there's distance. Even alienation.

Helen knows better than to strain like this. Knows walking away is sometimes the most important moment of her workday.

She could go out for a walk.

She could call Asa, beg him to meet her for an early movie. Tell him to meet her home, in their bed.

She puts down the brush, leaves it globbed on the glass palette.

Then she's out the studio door to the stairwell. Runs stairs two at a time. Up. Eight floors. Down to street level. Back up again. She pushes. Repetitions. Then more. Till she's back in front of the studio door, hanging over herself, breathless.

There, by the edge of the barn, Helen sees

she's made a smudge. She'd not paid attention to it before. The mark, distinct, has bulk. Somehow she hasn't painted over it in all her fussing. She squints. She isn't sure what the shape is trying to become. This is how she works. Avoids ever saying it in interviews. Sounds flaky. But she tries to allow the initial marks to declare themselves. She feels first gestures might almost best be done blindfolded — letting memory hold the brush, letting deep memory without the instant judgment of self-observation hold the brush. Keep the censors away. At least for the first. These memory markings. What she hasn't noticed or seems unremarkable at the time often provides surprise. The deep surprise. It is what might be discovered. *Un*covered is more like it.

With her thumb she presses the canvas, presses into the mark and feels a shape, muscular, a delicate muscularity. It's right there next to the geometry of the barn. Had she recorded it in her sketches? No, there's nothing in the sketches, but still Helen feels there's something to this.

She tries to draw back into that night. The last night they were all together. Molly driving. The field on the right, the barn. What they had agreed to do if it became necessary. Quiet chatter in the car. Out the window there was the dark mound of the field and inside Anna next to her. How often in any day she thinks, I've got to tell Anna. Or, without thinking, she finds her fingers dialing. Then the blow. Again. No Anna. The recognition like a full-body smack. There'd been months and months that she was exhausted all the time. Could hardly hold a brush. Like a flu, the grief. Or she'd wake, sweaty and breathless, needing Asa, the heat of him planked above her, to fuck her senselessly alive. Then it shifted, and she was painting again. But still forgetting. Every day. This will keep happening, or then — won't it be worse? — one day it will not happen. Never to think, Let me call Anna.

Anna had been holding her hand.

In the car, yes, Anna's hand between her hands.

She's asked Anna a question. She's asked Anna if she, Anna, is afraid. And waiting for Anna to answer, looking out the window afraid of what Anna will say, Helen sees the horse.

The horse, there.

That's what it is. What she's been trying to see.

In the dark, the moon-colored horse and, there, a paler colt below the horse. The colt's head tilted to nurse. The patient mother standing close to the barn. The baby's neck stretches long, its narrow face turned up into the mother.

She squeezes Anna's hand — *Look, Anna* — but they're already past the barn and the horse and the baby, and the road turns through a stand of spruce.

The brush is in Helen's hand. "Look, Anna." She says it out loud in her studio. Then again — "Look, Anna" — and she presses into the wet paint.

White-throated Sparrow

Each time Ming enters the building, she feels an actual physical tug left toward the bank of elevators up to pediatric neurosurgery. How strange, really, that her doctor's office is in the same hospital where all those years ago Lily had surgery. And now, leaving the hospital, turning through the revolving door, she waves, positive it's still the same squat lady guard.

Ming walks down Second Avenue. She needs time alone before she arrives at Helen and Asa's loft, before jumping into a swirl of conversation. The neighborhood hasn't changed. It still seems less a neighborhood than housing for hospital personnel. Same florist. And, mid-block, there's Lily's Nails. She stops in front of the shop. The women inside bow and wave *Come in.* Ming feels a sob rise up. What had Anna said that day? Only a really small part of the story. Lily is one year from graduating college. Anna is two years dead. The new story. Ming bows and waves back.

"I'm not well," she practices. Too flimsy. "I'm sick." Too dramatic. The others know she's come into the city for an appointment, but she's been cagey over the phone — "Something I set up, since we were getting together anyway." She understands now Anna's vagueness. About doctor appointments. About exhaustion, tightness in her chest. Everything that raised alarm.

Ming already hates the attention she hasn't even asked for. Tonight she wants to give Caroline center stage. This evening, dinner at Helen and Asa's loft, is the *after* that Caroline said she would need.

Christ! Some days that's what it seems it's all come to — who has center stage for grief.

When Helen called last week, Ming was outside on the office porch. Twenty minutes, feet up on the railing. It isn't meditation. But that's what she jokingly calls it when she tells her secretary to take messages. She's listening to birds. She closes her eyes. A lot of days, she can't manage to keep them closed. She's identified distinct birdcalls, but she's never checked them with a book. She doesn't care. Warbler, oriole, chickadee — she assigns names willy-nilly. She likes the texture, a sound density that starts in the tree facing the porch and radiates out. Some days she hears miles of bird sound in her body. She tries to breathe it in, as if sound might fill her. It's not the same as the infusion the doctors are recommending, but she's skeptical enough about medicine to think that breathing bird sound might work. She's even found herself wanting to send a note to Anna's Valley friends. She wants to apologize for her lawyerly dismissiveness when they suggested burning herbs.

For these twenty minutes, Ming makes a point of shutting off her phone. But when she felt a vibration, quick-checked, and saw HELEN, she'd picked up.

"Caroline asked me to call." Helen sounds careful.

"No. What?" Ming hears three short trills of a bird.

"It's what you think but not what you think."

Ming's default is Caroline's sister's suicide. There have certainly been enough practice tries for her to one time botchily succeed.

"I guess that's good."

"It seems the driver lost control. Of his truck. Elise had been doing great. A new job and everything. Caroline doesn't want us for the funeral. But she'll need us after."

Again the three trills. White-throated sparrow.

Ming walks along the gate of Gramercy Park. I've waited to tell them, I can wait longer, she thinks. But from the meeting today, she's not sure what longer means. The doctor was clear — there wasn't a time-line, or even exactly predictable markers.

"It's MS," Ming practices, bonking her fingers along the park's metal fence. A mother and two kids cut quickly in front. The woman smiles as she hurries her children. A slight twitch of the chin and Ming understands that the woman heard her talking out loud.

She's sorry. Mostly she feels sorry for herself, for the changes that are happening, and for suddenly not being able to read one thing about her body. This sturdy, steady body that — up until it didn't — worked perfectly. What Anna once told her was the grand betrayal. There's a change in her walk, numbness on her left side. Not every day. But unsteadiness, the slowing. She's always been sturdy. She can't read her body at all. What's a symptom? She's tired, but is that the tired anyone might feel? Then there's the on-and-off blurry vision, a pressure below her ribs, and that weird electric pain that randomly shoots down her arm. It's as if she has a stethoscope up against her body and she has no idea what anything she hears actually is.

Today the doctor had names for everything, like that was any comfort.

Here's an odd comfort. She feels closer now to Anna than she's felt in the two years since Anna died. Like she's walked into a room Anna lived in that she hadn't been inside before. And now she recognizes and understands what she had not fully noticed. Ming had been so focused on Anna's getting well, on her being back in the midst of everyday life during the remissions. But Anna, Ming understands, was living a double life. That secret life with illness. And, like any clandestine life, it was a full world with its own furniture and wallpaper and doors. Its own private conversations. Every good day, every normal day, was unsteady, unbalanced by the possibility that she'd be sick again. Any random ache a sign that she might already be sick.

These last two years what she's mostly

missed is how *she* felt with Anna. That with Anna she laughed more than with anyone else. Not Sebastian. Not the other friends. With Anna she was her most wayward self. With Anna she was always a teenager, the irresponsible, carefree teenager she'd been. Cautious Ming, practical Ming, with Anna she was always adventurous Ming.

As she approaches the top of Union Square Park, she's wobbling. She won't be able to walk down to Helen's. She'll taxi. But she can't remember the exact address, though she's been plenty of times since Asa and Helen bought the loft. Is this the memory fog the doctor spoke about or just regular getting-old brain?

Ming wanders through Union Square, the tents of farmer stalls. She's half looking for what she'll bring to the loft, but mostly she needs just to slow down, rest. She won't tell the others anything tonight. Tonight is for Caroline. And honestly, Caroline's grief will be a small relief. Ming recognizes a vendor from up the Hudson where she lives. She's never bothered to stop at his farm. But here the variety of greens, the Japanese radishes, the garlic scapes — the very abundance seems amazing, his produce so beautiful. She wants it all. There's a display of locally brewed ciders and, farther down, a stand of

Amish cheeses, each displayed under a mesh cap. She stops at a flower vendor, his mustache waxed into curlicues. "Good afternoon, m'lady." The mustache, the invented accent. Such gorgeous eccentricity, being alive. He has tea roses. Buckets of sweet peas, with their gentle scent. Exorbitantly expensive. Beyond ridiculously expensive. Ming bends to the pink and purple stems of sweet pea and breathes. She stumbles over her legs, and the man braces her from falling. "Excuse me," she says, hating how dependent she's about to become. "No, I'm the lucky one," he says with a bow. She asks for two bunches. He wraps three.

French Doors

Tessa stands in the doorway, holding the last cardboard box. She takes in the open French doors of her bedroom. French doors and a tiny balcony! In Brooklyn! She can't quite believe how awesome her bedroom is, and her awesome roommates and the awesome kitchen with the shelf of mason jars used as cups and the ridiculously awesome internship she's landed. Ridic. She's described to her moms that the other interns are all seniors; one's even out of college. But at the interview they were all over Tessa's programming skills. Tessa's confident she's got the chops for the work.

Life is amazing. Life is so totally, perfectly amazing.

Ridic.

Not to mention that there's a Thai restaurant, a falafel shop, and a café with gluten-free muffins on the block.

On the block where she has an apartment in Brooklyn, New York!

Amazing.

She should probably tell her moms to stop unpacking her duffel. At least keep them from making her bed. They always want to do so much for her. Sometimes, honestly, it's a burden. Hello, I'm not five years old. But they actually look kind of stupid happy stretching the fitted sheet over the mattress. If it makes them this happy to shake the pillows into flowered cases, who is she to argue?

"Aren't you going to be late?"

"I called Helen. They know we'll be late. They've all moved kids in."

Molly takes a picture of Tessa holding the box. Then wiggles her fingers, motioning Tessa and Serena over to the French doors to take another.

"Everyone gets being late as long as I show up with proof."

Tessa puts down the box and wraps her

arms around Serena. They act up for the camera. Tessa's T-shirt rides up, showing her flawless skin.

"You're going to be okay?" Molly asks, though she promised on the drive down that she wouldn't ask stupid questions or choke up. "You're going to take care of yourself?"

But it's not Tessa who's brought on Molly's tears. It's Anna. Who won't be at Helen's to see the photograph. Who won't point to Tessa's loving smile. Who won't tease Molly, Remember your massive panic over Tessa's Magic Marker doom tattoo? Who never needed proof that Tessa would be fine.

"Mom." Tessa good-naturedly stretches out the vowel. Nothing like a little mock annoyance. "Nope, I'm going to starve this summer because I don't know how to feed myself and probably get lost on the subway and maybe join a cult that regularly sacrifices young women and kittens, and oh, yeah, I forgot, my bosses are both meth addicts, and they said it's a job requirement."

Serena kisses Tessa twice on her temple. And Molly clicks that photograph, too.

"We're on our way, honey. Just humor us for five more minutes."

Lilacs

"There's another thing I've been waiting to tell you until we were all together," Caroline says. So far she's only told Danny. "You're under stress, baby," he said when she told him that next morning, and when she barked, "Don't call me baby," it only seemed to prove his point.

She knew what she'd seen. And even Danny admitted he'd woken and heard singing, two voices singing.

"That night I went outside after Danny had gone up to bed. For no reason other than that it was warm enough to sit on the patio, which is really the only thing I'll miss when the house gets sold. The patio when the lilacs are in bloom. Especially at night, the night fragrance, that's what I'll miss. I heard footsteps. I assumed it was Danny coming out to bug me with another million annoying questions about why I wasn't sleeping. I turned, ready to snip at him, but it was Anna. 'I thought I should come by,' Anna said.

"It was so weird," Caroline says. "It was just Anna. Anna wearing her boots, those red cowboy boots. They clipped against the slate, and I realized those boots always made that clippy sound. And her voice. It was exactly Anna's voice, even that gravel thing

344

that rasps at the ends of certain words. I'm not sure I'd ever been specifically conscious of it, but you know what I mean? It was Anna before. Just her in a pair of brown leggings, a T-shirt, and her red cowboy boots.

" 'Oh, Anna,' I said, and started to say how beautiful she looked, but she cut me off.

" 'Can we sing?' " Anna said.

Caroline watches her friends' faces as she describes how the two of them went right into the usual songs, things they'd worked out harmonies for back in high school. "Heart of Gold," "Natural Woman," and, of course, most of Joni's *Blue*.

"Every time I started to ask how this was happening or why, Anna shook her head.

"So I stopped asking. And at some point — pretty early, actually — it seemed completely normal, singing 'Big Yellow Taxi' with Anna. More normal, really, than that she's dead, which never in these two years has seemed normal or possible to me. We sang for a long time. Not just *Blue,* we were like a jukebox of seventies classics. Songs neither of us had sung for years. Loggins and Messina. Crosby, Stills, Nash & Young. We were laughing 'cause we couldn't believe that we could pull up all the lyrics even on 'Suite:

Judy Blue Eyes.' We were having the best time. We sounded pretty awful. We didn't care that we sounded like shit trying to hit those harmonies. We were belting it out, leaning in close like we were on the same mike. And that was another thing. She smelled like that coconut body lotion. Remember when she was into that? Skin Trip. 'Carrie,' she says all of a sudden. You know how she calls me Carrie. None of you do. No one else ever has. 'Carrie, I'll take care of her. She's going to be great.' Then she walks away. Walks down the patio stairs onto the lawn. I didn't know what to do. Follow her? I wanted her to stop. I said, 'Wait, Anna. Who are you talking about?' She was at the edge of our yard, the place where my kids used to hide out in the bushes. She turns and looks at me. With such kindness. Even in the darkness, I saw how she looked at me. Such kindness. 'Oh, Carrie,' she said. 'Here we go.'

"And then, just then, the phone rang inside the house.

"I looked at Anna, a *what's-going-on?* look.

" 'You can believe what they tell you,' Anna said."

The rest of what Caroline describes she's already told all of them on those first days after. Danny shouting for her. Her running inside. What the police said about the accident. Elise's death had been instant. She hadn't suffered, they said.

"I waited to tell all of you when we were together. Anna was with me. She came to be with me, to help me with Elise. So now, go ahead. You can all tell me I'm bonkers. But it's what happened."

"I want that dream." Helen folds her hands over her face. "Please tell it to us again."

3

August, Starfish
Then, of course, the house. It was time for the house. Reuben called, and they'd all shown up. Had he possibly thought otherwise? They'd promised they would. Not just Ming and Molly and Caroline and Helen, but Connie and Layla. Others from the Valley keep walking in the back door.

"We'll make it a party," Helen says when Reuben calls. "We always do."

Now Reuben stands outside on the porch, his hand resting on a stack of labeled plastic containers. Inside, it's noisy. As it had been, that March and April. All the women. All through the house. Rooms alive with conversation. All their conversation. They never stop. News of kids. Who's up to what. The back-and-forth. Questions of people who know what to ask one another. Answers that assume everyone knows the backstories.

It's a good thing, all this talk. He knows it helps.

Still, Reuben is glad to stand outside and listen from the fringes. To take a moment to admire all the damn work he's completed in the last four weeks. The new porch railing is smooth and sturdy as he leans back against it.

A shambles? A hazard? What's worse than a wreck? Whatever it was called, if the house has a chance of ever selling in this terrible market or, as it turns out, even renting, it had to be fixed. Needed work two years ago. Then the house stood empty. Stunning, really, how quickly an unoccupied house breaks down. It's not that he locked the door and left the place to mice for the last two years while he tried to patch up his own life. Managing the heating alone takes time. Not to mention money. Not to mention the February burst pipe, the rotted pipes, the broken refrigerator. Not to mention the roof. Or the March basement flood and the mildew reek through August. That's what the kids don't understand. A museum of childhood, that's what they seem to want. It doesn't matter that they're grown up. Apartments, jobs, romances, tangible forays into adulthood. He's so proud of how they have managed the loss together. And now there's a grandchild in the mix. Exactly, they argue, turning his practicality into sentimentality, we want to be able to come back for holidays with all our children.

But the women agree with Reuben. Turns out all three kids have called Connie and Helen. "I sympathized. Up to a point," Helen told him. "Then I told them to pay the bills on this place for a year and see how long it's all about feelings."

If the kids can't deal with the house, Reuben knows they definitely won't be able to deal with the woman he's begun seeing these last three months. First time anything has felt possible and right. Lovely. That's the word that comes to him when he sees her standing barefoot in his hallway. Lovely. To turn onto his side and watch her waking up. But he can't introduce her to the kids. Not yet. Anyway, it's okay, even a little lovely, to be kind of secretive.

First things first. Let them get used to renting the house.

The renters will be in by September 1 with a negotiated rent-to-buy contract. He can only hope.

Recognize this? Layla's tempted to call out to Helen as she bubble-wraps a piece of driftwood, a beach treasure from Anna and Helen's summer on Nantucket. Layla remembers the exact morning — was it twenty years ago? — on a speed walk, early in their friendship, Anna with her disarming abruptness announced, "Before I had any of my children, when I was still in college, I got pregnant. Reuben and I were together. It was ours. I never told him. Ever. I actually told him that it was Helen who was pregnant and I was taking her to a clinic. And then, after the abortion, I fainted." Anna described waking to Helen's terrified face. "I'd fainted, and Helen had just run into my dad while getting cash at the bank. Later that day, after a car and a bus and God knows what else, we ate fried clams by the Nantucket ferry. Not strip clams but belly clams. With that gooeyness. We called them 'ninth-month clams.' Reuben's never known, and he never will."

Layla had been shocked that Anna was confiding this to her. She remembers the crisp, dry scent of pine on the walk, and she remembers the secret she then shared with Anna.

Now, instead of calling out to Helen, Layla nestles the wrapped piece into a half-filled plastic container labeled LIVING ROOM. She'd be so happy we're all together, Layla thinks. Another party in her house.

She picks up a ceramic bowl. Before wrapping it she holds it to the light, the shell-pink porcelain so thin it's almost see-through.

"Hey, I gave her that. Maybe for a birthday." Caroline points.

"No, sweetheart. You gave it to me. For my thirty-fifth," Molly calls from where she's seated on the floor, boxing books. "She convinced me to give it to her."

Caroline laughs. "That's so typical."

Suddenly everyone chimes in. Everyone has a story. A necklace. Those hand-painted dessert plates Connie's packing belonged first to Ming.

"My best-fitting pair of jeans," Connie says. "She basically stripped me out of them at a restaurant."

"It was almost an accident." It's Layla's voice Reuben hears. He pokes his head through the door to finds her across the open room, at the hutch wrapping plates in newspaper.

"One class. I'd planned to audit just the

351

one. Now I'm in the Ph.D. program. Who could have guessed that one?"

Reuben nods to Layla across the room. He didn't know anything about her starting a Ph.D. But why would he? Except this week's call to tell her that the women were gathering to help him pack up the house for renting, Reuben hasn't spoken or run into Layla in any of the Valley haunts in more than a year. After that week they accidentally wound up in bed together.

"This is all about Anna," Layla announced that evening a year ago, though it sounded a little like a question. She and Reuben had gotten entirely flipped around, their heads propped against the bottom of the sleigh bed. "Knowing Anna, she orchestrated this and is up there watching."

"Believe me, Layla, she was never that generous." Reuben's laugh more whisper than anything robust.

They agreed it probably wasn't unusual, that there was probably even an official name for what happened. But, predictable or not, neither Layla nor Reuben had foreseen that after the afternoon and night they'd spent in Reuben's bed or after he called the following evening — just to check in, to see if Layla was freaking out — he'd wind up over at her house, not even making it all the way upstairs before they were at each other. Again it was a frenzy. Fierce. Unquenchable. Fucking.

"This has got to be in some book about grief."

"The hot-sex-and-grief chapter."

Reuben sat at the raw maple table watching Layla sprint about her kitchen. He drained his glass of wine. They were both starving. Had he ever noticed the small arch in the back of her neck before? To sit in a kitchen and watch a woman move knowingly. A gift. Mincing garlic. Snapping leaves from potted herbs arranged in a window. She stopped to pull her hair from her face, twisting it into a practiced bun, tucking the ends so it stayed fixed without a clasp. She kept turning to look at him. She'd shake her head. Or laugh.

"Stop watching me," she said. He couldn't imagine anything more beautiful than a fifty-six-year-old woman in underwear and a T-shirt moving through her kitchen.

Holding up a fist of dry spaghetti, she pointed it at him — "Reuben, this is a bad idea" — then fanned the spaghetti into the pot.

"It's not like it was exactly an idea."

"I'm not telling anyone. Ever."

"Then we can do this a few more times?"

Reuben chortled.

He wasn't actually certain that he wanted more, but Reuben felt so lighthearted. When was the last time he'd felt such scraped-out lightness? Why wouldn't he want that? Pleasure. The pure endorphin relief? Of course his. But to feel hers. To give pleasure — rough and insistent — instead of that worried and delicate care.

"You've got to admit, Layla, we feel good. It's healing."

"Don't go all Marvin Gaye on me. It's what it was, and that's all."

She tossed the spaghetti and set the bowl on the table between them. She refilled his glass of wine. They ate hungrily from the same bowl, their forks going at the pasta until they were scraping up every last loose thread.

Then last week, after Reuben called Layla to tell her about packing up for the renters, he asked, "You're good?" Layla said she was actually doing very well. And of course she'd already heard about packing from Connie. She'd be over to help.

"I'm looking forward to hanging out. I didn't want to shut down our friendship, Reuben. I just thought a little distance between us was useful."

"I'm good with time, Layla. It all takes time."

"I've seen the pictures of your beautiful granddaughter. And I've heard some other very sweet rumors about you."

"Trusting Valley talk is dangerous." Reuben laughed, denying nothing.

"Well, believe me, I'm happy for all happiness. For your happiness. Any happiness."

Ming rests on the blue love seat, Molly chatting beside her. They've figured out it's the only way they can get Ming to take a break. She's begun using a cane. Though she says it's only for Sebastian's peace of mind. But they know about the falls. She arrived looking exhausted. Still, it's impossible to get her to slow down.

Molly leans her head back. "She loved that stupid chandelier," she says. "I never got it." The two women watch light from the cathedral windows flash against the hundreds of crystals. Dust sparkles through the air like glitter.

"She loved it all so much," Molly says quietly. "And then she was ready to give this up."

"I'm not ready to give up," Ming says. "Just so you know."

■ ■ ■ ■

Someone is crying in the next room. It's to be expected. But still. Get it under control. They'll never get anything done if the day goes weepy. And it could. They calibrate how much to talk about, how much to acknowledge just how completely weird it is not having her here.

Especially when she's everywhere. Each of them holding something of her.

Just look at that trestle table with its array of perfectly arranged things. The cobalt glass bowl filled with starfish. An inlaid bone box. Three pewter frames, in each a grinning child with missing front teeth.

Then there's another sob from somewhere in the house. The mason jar gets wrapped in newspaper. Should the cardinal feathers be saved or put outside? There's so much to be done.

Caroline and Helen pull pictures from the refrigerator. It's slow going, less because the fridge is a dense collage — photographs, birthday cards, postcards layered over one another — than because the two women keep stopping each other. There's so much to look at, to comment on. Every elementary class and soccer team. The three kids, their years of baby curls. Then mullets and shags, all the bad hairstyles. Mouths of braces. Horse jumping, swim meets. Anna and her brothers on top of Mount Washington. Cousins' weddings. The wedding of Anna's eldest son.

"Which summer was that?" And they bend in to look at Anna and Reuben with the three kids in tow parading lobsters.

"Look closer, you'll remember. Come on. It's that Cape rental. The summer the twins both broke their arms."

It's also all the other children, their tribe. Rusty and Lily costumed as Fred and Ginger. Pirate getups from the Halloween-in-July party. A holiday greeting of Caroline's trio equipped in helmets, life jackets, and paddles looking terrified beside a river raft. Tessa and Shana in matching Little Mermaid outfits. Postcard after postcard announcing Helen's openings.

"She was my archivist." Helen laughs.

"You were lucky," Caroline says.

They peel off the photographs. Snip the bits of extra tape. They're careful not to let anything tear. Slip them into a brown envelope.

An archaeology of all their lives. Curated by Anna.

Under a full family picture from a cousin's wedding, there's a Polaroid, that old familiar square shape.

"Look, it's from Fox Road," Caroline says. The bit of the slate path and the first of three cement steps up to the front door of Anna's family's house, the Tudor on Fox Road — it's instantly recognizable.

It's all of them in the small square photograph — Caroline, Molly, Ming, Helen, and Anna — they're out on Anna's front lawn. A sprinkler in the foreground, the arc of water. The girls are upside down, having kicked up into handstands. They're all wearing bathing-suit tops and cutoff jean shorts, like they've planned the outfits.

"Of course we planned." Helen bends close; her finger traces the photograph's white border. "I remember cutting those shorts."

It's the summer of sixth grade. The last days of August before school starts. There's a lot to worry about. Whose homeroom? There's the worry of seventh-grade algebra and the teacher who's a hundred years old and reportedly hasn't given an A in eighty years.

The girls have spent days perfecting handstands. The Old Friends. That's the summer they took on the name.

It's Anna who comes up with handstands. They need to record the moment. All of them need to be able to do it. Anna and Helen take gymnastics, and Ming is on a dive team and does handstands and back-flips. Only Molly and Caroline need to learn, and, Anna says, that will be a cinch. The first plan is to scissor open their legs. They'll balance touching toe to toe like upside-down paper dolls. The cutoffs and bathing-suit tops, their hair cleanly parted and bunched in pigtails, that's also part of the choreography.

By the end of the first afternoon, they've revised the plan and just want everyone upside down holding long enough for Anna's brother to take a picture.

"I'm the most pathetic," Caroline says.

"No, look at —"

Upside down, none of the faces are visible, but Caroline and Helen recognize each of them, their young-girl bodies. There's a wobble to Caroline, all legs and knobby knees. Next to her, Molly's kicked up, cockeyed, the weight unequal between her hands. She can't quite get vertical, her body having begun its curvy changing. Ming's a straight boyish arrow, determined, like she might hold her handstand for hours. There's the deep gymnastic sway of Anna's back, her sharply pointed toes, one foot angled to touch Helen's foot. Helen's foot meets Anna's, the other leg bent in a declared fancy pose.

Helen remembers that she and Anna planned to have their feet touch just as the sprinkler water hit. And they did.

"Anna and I still had the fantasy that we were heading to the Olympics."

"This took two days of solid practice." Caroline leans against Helen. "I felt like a total klutz."

"You were." Helen nuzzles her face against Caroline's. "But look, you did it."

"I did do it." Funny how all these years later, Caroline finally feels proud. Of her young-girl effort, however awkward. But also of all of them. All the things they each might now say to the children they were. The great unworrying spell they might cast backward. Caroline's gawky body no more a betrayal than Molly's abruptly changing one. Same shorts, bathing-suit tops, even their hair braided in matching French braids, and still each girl upside down is her own complete and changing self. And just outside the Polaroid's thick border are the streets of their town and Caroline's sister, Elise, still a happy and eager tenth-grade girl practicing for fall cheerleading.

"We all did."

"Ming. Molly. Get over here."

"We're busy," Molly snarls. She can't quite believe the others have already forgotten that they've sworn to Sebastian not to let Ming overexert. Do they remember it's not just her difficulty walking? Ming's losing vision — a tapered, narrow hallway is the way she describes it.

"No, you both need to see what we found," Helen says.

"What?" Ming's already pushing off the couch, her cane positioned to steady and bear her spastic gait. Molly puts out her hand, not touching, just spotting at the elbow in case Ming stumbles or falls back.

Ming and Molly pick their way, a slow, zigzagged path through the maze of taped-up boxes in Anna's sun-flooded living room toward the open kitchen.

Helen squeezes Caroline's hand, and Caroline squeezes back — Yes, yes, I see. Right now this seems good — bifocaled and progressive-lensed — to be one another's compassionate eyes, one another's witness, it seems very good. Wait long enough and The Old Friends actually become old, Anna could tell them — though that moment, too, has come and gone. But it's not just witnessing the ineluctable decline. Or the aftermath. And who's to say it is not actually Anna just now nudging Helen — Heli, now here's a painting. A house's undone clutter. The summer light stippling the faces of intimate friends clustered and packing. Ming walking regally through the dismantled house with Molly in attendance, the two of them clucking slyly at some joke. The private joke, isn't that the most interesting part? Or how the others straining to hear are lifted, connected by a curl of laughter. Always it was this, the layers of lived life and, still, the unanticipated pleasures. And the afternoon sun dusting gold light over the scuffed floor prevails — if only momentarily — over sadness or worry at watching Ming manage her cane.

"What's so important?" And here's Ming, her free hand out to hold the photograph Helen passes to her.

"It's us. Before everything."

ACKNOWLEDGMENTS

First and always, Nancy Rockland-Miller — who hounded me to write a book celebrating friendship — I hope in some measure this novel lives up to what she believed might be achieved.

This book could not have been imagined without the abundant gifts of friendship that have sustained and shaped so much of my world vision — to that beautiful, motley, sprawling tribe I owe a debt beyond words.

All gratitude and love to Bill Clegg for being a dear friend, sublime reader, and agent extraordinaire over many years. A deep bow to Carole DeSanti for her editorial rigor, generosity, and brilliance. Raucous shouts of thanks to the teams at the Clegg Agency and at Viking Penguin for all efforts on behalf of this novel. I am beholden to my supersmart and precise copy editor, Maureen Sugden, and to Chris Russell, who each saved me from numerous infelicities.

I am all thanks to Fran Antell, Tracey Rogers, Sonya del Peral, Martine Vermeulen, Maria Basescu, Marie Howe, Honor Moore, Dani Shapiro, Melinda Lockman-Fine, and Emma Herdman, who offered attention, wisdom, and enthusiasm to the novel in various incarnations. Dr. Bob Weitzman, Robert Chodo Campbell, and the Zen Center for Contemplative Care helped me more fully understand aspects of medicine and end-of-life care. A shout-out to Suzanne Gardiner, whose cards led me through dark to greater dark and to song. And to the Rocklands and Rockland-Millers, thank you for my place in your family all these years. I am every day blessed by a life as a reader; I thank the poets and writers whose work is both a solace and a beckoning to go further and truer. Always thanks to my family — my father, Claudia, and Jessica — for unwavering belief and true north; my appreciation always and again to the insights (literary and otherwise) of my sons — Jonah and Gabriel — and for the ways they continue to open my heart and shape my attentions. And thanks too to the new brood — Zane, Wynn, and Dara — who, without genetic obligation, put up with me.

Oh, Bruce Van Dusen. Every day. Every

single day I am astonished. And beyond lucky.

I am deeply grateful to the Guggenheim Foundation, Hedgebrook, the Borg, Camp Otterbrook, and Sarah Lawrence College for valuable support, sustenance, and time.

This novel is, finally, a work of imagination, which, of course, has been liberally influenced by a lifetime of places, people, and events. I am grateful for the leniency of everyone who believes they recognize an angle of chin or the echo of something once uttered.

ABOUT THE AUTHOR

Victoria Redel is the critically acclaimed author of four previous works of fiction and three collections of poetry. Her debut novel, *Loverboy,* was named a best book of the year by the *Los Angeles Times* and won the S. Mariela Gable Award from Graywolf Press and the Forward Silver Literary Fiction Prize. She has received fellowships from the Guggenheim Foundation and the National Endowment for the Arts and has contributed to the *New York Times,* the *Los Angeles Times, Elle, O, the Oprah Magazine, Granta, One Story,* and the *Harvard Review.* She received her MFA in poetry from Columbia University and teaches at Sarah Lawrence College.